BARBARA B
WINE OF

C000285486

BARBARA Proctor Beauchamp was born in 1909, and brought up in France and Switzerland. She had a younger brother and sister, twins, who both died in early adulthood.

Before World War Two Barbara Beauchamp was a freelance journalist and the author of three novels. In 1939, living in London, she joined the ATS, and *Wine of Honour* (1945) was her first novel since the outbreak of war.

After the war she continued to live in London, with her partner Norah C. James, a fellow novelist. In later life she shared a house with Millicent Dewar, a renowned psychoanalyst.

Barbara Beauchamp wrote three further novels after *Wine of Honour*, the last published in 1958. She died in London in 1974.

TITLES BY BARBARA BEAUCHAMP

Fiction

Fair Exchange (1939)

Without Comment (1939)

The Paragons (1940)

Wine of Honour (1946)

Ride the Wind (1947)

Virtue in the Sun (1949)

The Girl in the Fog (1958)

Cooking

Greenfingers and the Gourmet (1949)
(co-authored with Norah C. James)

BARBARA BEAUCHAMP

WINE OF HONOUR

With an introduction by
Elizabeth Crawford

DEAN STREET PRESS

A Furrowed Middlebrow Book
FM38

Published by Dean Street Press 2019

First published in 1945 by Macdonald & Co.

Cover by DSP

ISBN 978 1 913054 33 5

www.deanstreetpress.co.uk

To

NORAH C. JAMES

. . . . "ARRIVAL.—N. arrival, advent; landing; de-, disem-barcation; reception, welcome, *vin d'honneur*," . . .

Roget's Thesaurus of English Words and Phrases

INTRODUCTION

As a reviewer explained, '*Wine of Honour* takes its title from the thesaurus listing of synonyms for "arrival", which includes "reception", "welcome" and, finally, "*vin d'honneur*"' (*The Sphere*, 29 June 1946). Set in an English village immediately after the end of the Second World War, Barbara Beauchamp's novel charts the arrival back home of demobilised men and women and the effect their return has on their families and, indeed, on the pre-war social order. This was a subject of which the author was acutely aware, having herself only recently been demobilised from the Auxiliary Territorial Service (ATS).

Barbara Proctor Beauchamp (1909-1974) was born in Surrey, the eldest child of a stockbroker, and brought up and educated in France and Switzerland, where her parents had a chalet at Château d'Oex. Her younger brother and sister, twins, died young; Alice aged 21 in 1934 and Philip killed in Singapore in 1942. Before the war Barbara was a freelance journalist and by 1940 was the author of three novels, two of which were set in Switzerland. She was adventurous and athletic, photographed for *Tatler* (5 February 1936) taking part in a skiing event. However by late 1939, when her photograph appeared in *Bystander* (6 December) and *The Sketch* (20 December), she had joined the Auxiliary Fire Service as a driver. The following year she joined the ATS, becoming a Senior Commander, the equivalent of an Army major, and for a while was in charge of the ATS Publicity Branch. We can be sure that Wine of Honour, her first novel since 1939, draws richly on her service experience.

Barbara Beauchamp assembles her cast in the village of Kirton in the late summer of 1945, after the general election has brought a Labour government to power. This hits the local gentry, the Gurneys, particularly hard as they come to realise that their inherited family wealth has all but disappeared. 'What with the taxes which nobody could afford and the high price of living, the Manor was already run out of capital.' The elder son, Peter, who in pre-war days frittered and gambled away whatever money he made in the City, initially found some significance in his wartime service. He had joined up as an ordinary seaman but was later made an officer and then, as his brother Brian commented, 'started to slip badly once he'd got rings on'. Drink was his solace. Brian has had a long affair during the war with Helen Townsend, the wife of the village GP. As one character comments, 'Faithfulness was unfashionable during the war'. Helen, the novel's central character, was a captain in the ATS and now awaits the return of her husband from service with the Royal Army Military Corps in the Far East, the war having separated them for five years.

As the novel opens Helen is having tea with resolutely middle-class Laura Watson, also recently demobilised from the ATS and once more at the beck and call of her cantankerous father. Unlike Helen, she looks back on service life with longing. As she later explains to a group of former comrades, 'I just know that I loved it and I miss it terribly. It was the companionship and freedom.' They agree that when they were in the ATS 'We were all in it together and working for the same thing', while now 'It's cut-throat competition and every woman out for herself.' This conversation takes place in a London club recently formed for former service women, to which 'only women in the upper income groups could afford to belong.' On entering Laura was relieved to note that the staff 'were very definitely of the ex-orderly category.' She had been worried she would be waited on by a fellow officer. Here, at least, the pre-war order prevailed.

However back in Kirton the Cock and Pheasant, the village's venerable public house, was witnessing what before the war would have been an unnatural mixing of classes. Helen, Laura, and Brian Gurney and his sister were seated with Dick Cobb, the landlord's son, as though he was now an equal and, as his father mused, 'There were others, too, villagers, all of them ex-service.

A queer mix up for the saloon bar at the Cock and Pheasant.'
In fact Dick Cobb is the one character on whom the war has
wrought the most obvious harm, mentally and physically. From
the ranks, to which he was fitted by his station in life, he was
promoted to captain when awarded an MC, subsequently suffering severe head and leg wounds. When Laura Watson was told
that he was regularly pulled up by the police who thought he was
an imposter for wearing his ribbons, she suddenly realised 'Dick
Cobb didn't look like an officer; he looked like the lanky country
lad he was, blunt featured and rough, honest and working class.
Why hadn't she thought of this before? . . . For the first time in
her life Laura sensed the burning indignation of injustice.'

Over the course of the next few months we follow the lives
of these and other characters as they re-adapt to 'civvie street',
both in Kirton and Bloomsbury, where two of the inhabitants
have flats and where 'The blitz scars of Guilford Street were
healed with fresh green weeds.' At the heart of the novel is
Helen's readjustment to married life as she and her husband
rediscover each other. 'It is, of course, a new life. New, that is, in
our reactions to each other. The routine has not changed beyond
the revolution – or evolution – which a war and a peace inevitably bring to the community life of a nation.'

While writing Wine of Honour Barbara Beauchamp was
living not in a bucolic English village but at 9 Cumberland
Gardens, Islington, a quiet enclave close to King's Cross, in the
house she shared with her partner, Norah James, to whom the
novel is dedicated. Norah was also a novelist, notorious as the
author of Sleeveless Errand which, when published in 1929, had
been censored on the grounds of obscenity. In this post-Second
World War period Norah's publisher was Macdonald & Co.,
suggesting it was not a coincidence that the same firm published
Wine of Honour. The two women wrote at least one short play
together, broadcast on the BBC Home Service in 1947, and one
book, Greenfingers and the Gourmet, which combined instruc-
tions for growing a wide range of vegetables with a 'number

of specially good recipes in which these vegetables played an important part'. They had been partners since at least 1939 when Norah dedicated her autobiography, *I Lived in a Democracy*, to Barbara, but by the early 1960s appear to have separated and for the remainder of her life Barbara shared a home with Dr Millicent Dewar, a renowned psychoanalyst. Barbara continued her journalism career after the war, for a time reviewing novels for provincial newspapers and herself publishing three further novels, the last in 1958.

Elizabeth Crawford

PART I

I, Helen Townsend, am going to have tea with Laura Watson.
She and I have little in common and I am always surprised when
the threads of our lives get intertwined. But they do. It might be
said that Laura and I have woven a colourful, if sober, pattern
during the past six years. A strictly austerity pattern, of course.

The Watsons live in an adapted cottage at the end of Pilferer's Lane. As I walk through Kirton High Street, round the Cock
and Pheasant Arms—Lily Cobb is hanging Tommy's smalls on
the line in the yard—and turn into Pilferer's Lane where the
honeysuckle intrudes over the hawthorn hedges, I am conscious
of being much less of a foreigner than I was two months ago.

In my pocket I have a letter from Brian, and in my head I
have the thought of Gyp, who is my husband. The one hurts
whilst the other worries me. I know that I am in a muddle. But
who isn't these days? I am untidy and for the first time for a
great many years I have got to plan for myself instead of merely
trying to carry out the decrees of others.

Laura's father is leaving Vine Cottage as I reach the gate. He
is going to tea with the vicar—that is what Laura said when she
asked me to come round today. It is funny the way some people
always remain true to one's first impressions of them. I remember the first time I saw Mr. Watson. It was, I suppose, about two
years before the war, just after Gyp had bought the practice and
a few months after our marriage when we came to live in Kirton.

There is a sort of pleasure in hating at first sight, the satisfaction of meeting a stranger's glance and being quite sure you will
never like him. I have not changed in my feeling towards Mr.
Watson. He has the mannerisms and physical features I most
dislike in men. He creeps like the ivy on his cottage walls—there
is no vine—and he is acquisitive, materially and emotionally.

I notice again how much the war has changed him.
Outwardly, he is softened; his white hair flutters gently in the

breeze as he raises his hat to me. Mrs. Watson died in 1943—
she'd been ailing since the first time Gyp was called in to see
her before the war. Laura was given two months on the reserve
when her mother died. We were both at the Training Centre
in Nottingham at the time; I had a Company and she was the
Assistant Adjutant. Since then Mr. Watson has grown old. His
eyes are watery and he moves more slowly.

But I know he is just the same. He is still acquisitive and his
claws are on Laura now. Not that Laura needs claws to hold her.

Mr. Watson smiles and says:

"I hear we are soon to have the doctor back, Mrs. Townsend?"

"Yes," I reply and Brian's letter in my pocket screws itself into
a crumpled ball. But it is only my hands playing stupid tricks.

"We shall welcome him back; he is a good doctor," Mr.
Watson continues and I wonder if he glimpses the turmoil his
words arouse in me.

Laura sees me from the window and I am rescued.

The Watsons' drawing-room is busy with satinwood tables,
gilt-framed watercolours, china ornaments and pink chintz.
Laura makes me sit in the wing-backed chair facing the window
while she goes to bring in tea. I am not allowed to help because
Laura is like that. Maybe it is also because, in the A.T.S., I was
always senior in rank and army habits will die hard with her.
It seems rather silly when we are both over thirty and Laura
has been demobilized for several months. The Release Scheme
they called it or Re-allocation of manpower during the Interim
Period. As a married woman I re-allocated myself two months
ago when I knew Gyp was on his way home. Otherwise I think I
should have stayed on.

Laura comes back with the tea and soon we are talking a
great deal. Laura loves talking; nothing is trivial enough for her
to spare words over.

"And so," she says, "we thought we would give her a trial.
She's an ex-W.R.N.S., which Father approves of. He always
wished I'd been one instead of A.T.S. And she can cook, although

she wasn't one in the service. We'll keep Mrs. Boulter on in the mornings for the heavy work until we see what the new girl can manage. She was medically boarded out, you know. Nerves, I believe. It will really be almost like old times to have someone living in again."

"It will give you time to breathe for a change," I say quickly as she pauses to do so.

"What, me?"

I watch her big, capable hands pouring hot water from a silver kettle into the Queen Anne teapot.

"Yes, I suppose I shall have more time to do things," she muses.

"What sort of things?" I ask, because I prefer to keep the conversation on her than, possibly, me.

"Oh, well, the garden, you know, and . . . just things," she finishes doubtfully.

"I thought you wanted to take up relief work abroad? I remember you put your name down for U.N.R.R.A. at one time."

"And then withdrew it. Yes, I would like to but I don't honestly think Father could manage alone without me."

"He did for a number of years," I say, crossly, because we have had this argument before.

"But Helen, it's different now," Laura exclaims, "that was during the war, and everybody had to manage somehow then. Besides, I used to get home very regularly on leave, you remember?"

I do remember. Could I ever forget Laura's leaves, her sleeping out passes, her days off—all arranged to suit Mr. Watson, not Laura or the Unit or the war effort.

"In any case," Laura continues calmly, "he's got used to me being at home again now. I couldn't really go away, not abroad, not for years on end which it might mean."

I help myself to some home-made plum cake—Laura is an excellent cook—and I wonder how many women today are back in their pre-war ruts. For how many was the war merely a temporary disarrangement and for how many others has it meant complete re-adjustment, an entirely new set of circumstances? This is a stupid thought for me to have when, even in my own case, I don't know the answer.

Laura is still talking.

"And anyhow, I don't suppose I'd be any good at relief work. Now you would be, Helen. You'd be so much more able to deal with out of the ordinary happenings, and I'm sure relief work would be full of those. You'd be able to cope; I shouldn't. You remember how I always got in a panic in the A.T.S. when I couldn't find any rules or regulations to cover the situation? You always knew what to do, by instinct or something."

"What nonsense!" I am laughing. Laura is a very capable woman. I look at her rather heavy face. She has remarkable eyes and a lovely smooth skin. She looks placid and full of strength, and I wonder if many people have told her she is beautiful. I think not, because her looks are too static. It's mostly plain women with mobile mouths who get themselves called beautiful.

Laura is looking at me in a speculative way, so I hurry on.

"Do you remember Peggy Travers?" I ask, and realize my mistake at once. Peggy and Laura were my subalterns when I had the company which worked for the Commando Training unit in Scotland. They were there with Brian. But it is too late now. I go on, self-consciously, "I heard from her last week. She's with the Allied Control Commission in Germany."

"How interesting." But I can see that Laura is not interested. Her thoughts are elsewhere. I prattle on, foolishly.

"She says it's pure Alice in Wonderland. They're so enveloped with red tape and barbed wire that at times she finds it difficult to remember whether she's on the outside, looking in, or the inside, looking out."

"She always exaggerated," Laura replies, and switches back to herself. "Helen, I've been thinking that I might get some part-time work at the Government Training Centre at Little Copse. Have you heard about it?"

"Vaguely. Tell me more."

"It's carpentering and cabinet making. They have a large instructional and catering staff. I thought there might be something on the welfare side I could do. Not full time, of course, because of Father."

I feel irritated with Laura, but I am not going to start an argument.

"I think it would be a good idea if they have anything of that sort which is part time," I reply. Laura looks pleased.

"Little Copse is only five miles away. I could bicycle there and back in the summer and Father might let me use the car during the winter."

"Have you talked to him about it yet?" I ask.

"No. I thought I'd discuss it with you first. You do really think it would be a good plan?"

I repeat that I do, and it occurs to me that Angela Worthing works at the Little Copse Training Centre. I mention it.

"You remember her, Laura? Oh, no, you wouldn't. I came across her at Godstone and you weren't there—one of the rare occasions when they didn't post us to the same group."

"Was she an officer?"

"She wasn't in the A.T.S. She was one of the education people's civilian lecturers. She stayed in the mess once or twice. I rather liked her."

"What does she do at Little Copse?"

"I believe she's secretary to the Director, or whatever they call the head man there. And she still does lecturing on outside subjects. I met her in Dimstone about three weeks ago. I'll give you an introduction if you like. She'll certainly be able to tell you what your chances are if you're seriously considering a job."

"Helen, would you? That would be lovely." Laura is so delighted that I feel mean because I am sure her idea will come to nothing. Mr. Watson will see to that. But she continues to enthuse.

"If only you were going there too," she exclaims, "I got so used to us working together during the war, I shall feel quite lost on my own. But of course you don't want a job, do you? I hear Gyp will be home next month?"

I know quite well that she has been wanting to say this since before tea, and I am ready for it.

"Yes," I reply, "he should reach England by the end of September. After that I suppose it will be a little time before he's returned to civilian life."

"But he's coming back to the practice, isn't he? Everyone's awfully pleased about it. They don't really like Doctor Rawlins, you know; he's not sympathetic like Gyp; besides he lives out at Little Copse and they can't get hold of him in the same way. Aren't you getting frightfully excited, Helen?"

"I still can't believe it, it seems unreal, after nearly five years," I answer carefully. Is Laura really as naive as she appears? I know that she knows about Brian. She saw us in Dumfries. I have never spoken to her about it, naturally, but because she is probably the only outside person who does know about us, I am over-sensitive where she is concerned and horribly eager to read her thoughts.

The garden gate makes a noise and Laura looks up.

"Oh dear, it's Lady Gurney, and the tea must be stone cold. Fill up the pot, will you, Helen? No . . . it's all right, I will. No, you do it while I answer the door."

I do as I am told, and compose myself to meet Brian's mother. I see Laura's unguarded glance in my direction as she follows Lady Gurney into the room. Of course Laura knows—not that I ever had any real doubts about it.

"My dears"—Lady Gurney is like an old-fashioned bathing tent in her striped dress—"I didn't mean to intrude and I certainly don't expect a cup of tea at this late hour. Oh, well, perhaps. . . . thank you Laura, dear. What a pretty frock Laura is wearing, isn't she, Helen? But I must tell you my news. You'll never guess. . . . He's home!"

For a moment I feel physically sick. How silly, when Brian's letter is in my pocket. My mind catches up with my racing pulse.

"Not Peter?" I exclaim joyfully and notice the sharp look Laura gives me. Peter is Brian's elder brother.

"Yes, Peter, my dears. All the way from heaven knows where on the other side of the world, and for good!" She sits back, quite deflated after her sensational announcement.

Laura and I chorus together, "How lovely for you! Is he well? What a surprise! He must be thrilled!"

A shadow crosses Lady Gurney's face.

"As a matter of fact, my dears, he isn't."

"Not pleased to be home again?" Laura asks, incredulous.

"Well, in a way of course he is, but he's changed somehow. Mind you, he was very tired when he arrived and the silly boy hadn't eaten anything for twenty-four hours. He'd spent the night in London instead of coming straight down to Kirton; burning his boats or something, he said."

"But he must be glad to be out of uniform," Laura persists. I wonder whether she emphasizes the point because, subconsciously, she feels Peter ought to be glad; that everyone should be glad to be released. I have a feeling that, already, she is nostalgic for her own discarded khaki. Laura is going to live a great deal in the past, I fear.

Again my thoughts turn to Brian. It will be his turn next. We're all back, or on our way back—like Gyp.

"Of course," Lady Gurney is saying, "I think he'd been celebrating. You know what the Navy's like. But he kept on saying he'd lost his home. 'I haven't got a home now, Mother,' he told me. He said it at least ten times."

"No home?" Laura says, puzzled.

"He meant his ship, though I admit we didn't understand at first," Lady Gurney explains, "I must say that after everything his father and I have gone through these years to keep the home going at all, I think it was a little tactless of him," she adds with characteristic candour.

Laura is full of sympathy which is somewhat wasted since Lady Gurney is not seriously perturbed.

"And now, my dears, I must be off. Thank you, Laura, for my excellent tea. It is indeed nice to see things like currants and real eggs reappearing again. And you, Helen, I hear, are expecting Gyp back very soon?"

"Next month," I reply and wonder, with slight hysteria, whether she is associating Gyp with a currant, a real egg or just Peter.

"How lovely for you, my dear, after all these years. Now, where can my gloves be? Ah, here, on my lap. I'm just going round to tell Mrs. Cross about Peter. She was so kind when her Michael was demobilized and I had no boys at home. I think she'd have lent him to me if I'd wanted. Good-bye, Helen dear. Don't bother, Laura, I can see myself out."

Laura accompanies her to the front door and I am left with the strange picture of Michael Cross on loan to Kirton Manor.

*　　*　　*　　*

People were apt to describe Mary Cross as a woman with a man's mind. Less charitable critics even went so far as to suggest that she probably was a man. All of which was, of course, quite untrue for, behind a façade of tweed and tobacco, were the maternal instincts of a tigress and the ultra-feminine personality of 'Aunt Jennifer' of *Women's Chat*, that successful monthly journal for wives and business girls.

'Aunt Jennifer' had been the material expression of the maternal instinct. After only three months of married life—during which time she saw her husband for exactly seven days and seventy-two hours respectively—Mary Cross had found herself a widow, an expectant mother and practically penniless.

After a brief period of apathy, the combination aroused her to an infuriated acceptance of the circumstances and a militant determination to overcome them.

Having given birth to a son whom she worshipped from the moment she first saw him being slapped to life by an over-worked doctor, she proceeded to censor letters for the government until 1918.

In 1919 she was writing copy for advertisements of gas cookers and in 1921 Cookery Notes for the *Sunday Sketch*. This led, almost uneventfully, to her Household Hints in the *Daily News*, and her column on Housewives' Problems in *Home and Hearth* until, some fifteen years ago, she took over, at a generous salary, the considerable activities of 'Aunt Jennifer' on the permanent staff of *Women's Chat*. No domestic contretemps, no lonely heartache, no marital tiff was too trivial for Aunt Jennifer's sympathy and constructive advice. Apart from the published page, Aunt Jennifer had innumerable private correspondents to deal with, and had been instrumental in bridging numerous matrimonial breaches in addition to preventing a great many mésalliances.

The drawbacks to being Aunt Jennifer were that Mary Cross suffered, vicariously, but nevertheless quite sincerely, the misfortunes of her correspondents. Each letter brought to her—although in lesser degree—the mental stress of its writer, so that by the time went to press each month, Mary Cross would require a great many cigarettes and a number of whiskies before she could face up to the batch of new letters which must be dealt with before the next edition.

"But," as she explained to interested friends, "if I didn't feel like that, I should not have a postbag of over two hundred letters a week, nor should I be allowed a staff of two secretaries. In fact, I probably shouldn't have kept my job at all."

All of which had brought bread and butter and substantial helpings of jam for her son, Michael, a comfortable cottage at Kirton and a flat in London.

At the age of twelve, Michael had shown every sign of being spoiled and a mother's darling. This so alarmed Mary Cross that she made up her mind, then and there, to concentrate on developing in herself the characteristics of the father Michael had never known. Against all natural instincts she stopped fussing about his health, spoke sharply to him when he cried and allowed him to be beaten up by the village boys, even in front of her drawing-room window, without rushing out to his assistance.

To foster confidence in herself in this new role of the father which she considered so important to a boy about to go to boarding school for the first time, she discarded the more fanciful garments in her wardrobe and took to shirts, tweed suits and flat-heeled shoes, which were not only much more comfortable for her spreading figure but also an economy—Michael being at the growing stage when new outfits had to be purchased for him at the end of every term. This was, of course, before the days of 'Aunt Jennifer.'

Michael was very fond of his mother. Whether this was due to the efficiency with which she fulfilled the dual role of father and mother or whether it was just because their personalities happened to blend harmoniously would be hard to say. The result, however, was that they found in one another a companionship which neither disparity of age nor the accident of relationship could disturb.

This appeared strange to some people for, outwardly, they were contrasts. Where Mary Cross was gruff, Michael was charming; where he argued, she was placid. In one thing only were they obviously of a single mind and that was in their mutual affection and admiration for each other. Michael respected his mother's judgment on all things; in her eyes, he could do no wrong.

It was not surprising that the war hit Mary Cross hard.

By 1939, the memory of Michael's father had grown even dimmer than the photograph of him in R.F.C. uniform which sat in an old-fashioned frame on the far corner of the piano in the Kirton cottage. Even if she tried, Mary Cross could not visualize Eric clearly; neither could she recall his voice, nor recapture, even for a second, any detail of their life together.

Michael was tall and fair, as his father had been, but there the resemblance ended so far as Mary was concerned. Unlike many widowed mothers, she had never been known to say that her son's smile, or his mannerisms, or his character were like his father's. Maybe she had known her husband so little that she would not have recognized likenesses, even had they existed. As it was, to her, Michael had never been anything but an individual—her son by some strange coincidence about which she remembered practically nothing, but a definite entity with a personality which owed nothing to anyone else, least of all to herself.

But September 1939 had stirred her memory. She remembered what war was like. That first air raid warning revived for her only too acutely the destruction of war. Michael was twenty-four at the time and working in Fleet Street.

All along Mary realized that he would go to war. They had discussed the prospects together so often during the previous year and she knew she wouldn't try to stop him. The first time she saw him in uniform, it seemed as if not only her heart but her whole life had stopped. 'Why, but why the R.A.F.?' she asked herself again and again, but to Michael she only said:

"Well, it will give you invaluable experience if you really intend being a writer after the war."

Michael trained in England—on bombers, as a rear gunner. They said he was too old to be a fighter pilot. During the Battle of Britain Mary wondered, for a brief moment, whether some kindly providence had perhaps guided him to Bomber Command. Later, she realized the irony of that thought.

The staff of *Women's Chat* evacuated to the country. Mary let the flat in London because Michael preferred Kirton for his leaves. This meant a cross-country journey to her office where she would spend three nights a week in an uncomfortable hotel. Gradually the staff were called up or directed to more vital war work and Mary found herself editing the fashion section in addition to Aunt Jennifer's page which became more and more pre-occupied with service women's problems. In her spare moments she cooked and cleaned out the cottage at Kirton—domestic assistance being a thing of the past.

During most of the war, Mary Cross was overworked, but she would willingly have done twice as much again. Anything would have been better than lying awake listening to the R.A.F. going out, night after night, like some vociferous thunder storm, and then, in the early hours of the morning, returning one by one, limping like the uneven patter of summer rain.

However, she never complained. She never even talked about Michael unless she was asked first; but anyone with a son in the forces or a daughter away from home could come to her with their problems and be sure of sympathy and warm friendship.

To many it seemed almost a miracle that Michael Cross got through the war. Once he was missing for three months. Mary lived on the knowledge that his plane had come down over occupied France, and that every day R.A.F. crews were returning from there, via Spain, as Michael did eventually. Once he was wounded slightly. Mary could have wished it more serious. Then came a spell of training in Canada and eventually the Air Ministry.

"I'm too old for ops," he told her, angry with the powers who could decree such nonsense, and Mary began to come alive again. He was demobilized quite soon after the cessation of hostilities with Germany.

Now he was back in Fleet Street, sub-editing and, in his spare time, writing like a maniac. Poems, short stories, a play and his first novel.

Mary gave him the flat in London, but would have been deeply hurt had he not spent week-ends at the cottage. Fortunately, it never occurred to him to do otherwise. Mary commuted to the office three times a week from Kirton.

The arrangements suited them both. Mary felt profound satisfaction that, so quickly, she and Michael had been able to resume the quiet flow of their lives, to seep themselves again in the richness of their companionship. She was aware that other people were less fortunate, that the acid of war had bitten deeply into too many lives. Even as 'Aunt Jennifer,' who now dealt almost exclusively with demobilization and re-settlement queries, she was sometimes startled at the problems confronting her readers. In some she detected a dangerous apathy to existing conditions and in others a too fanatic desire to go on fighting—anything and everything, without seeming reason or purpose.

Sometimes she became depressed because it seemed to her that the world, as she saw it, would never again appreciate the simple things of life. When the thought became too disturbing, she would withdraw into the security of her life with Michael and plant her feet more firmly in the soil of Kirton which was outwardly little changed by the war, being a village of simple tradition and no importance. Even the result of the General Election had not left its mark. The Conservative candidate for Dimstone was quietly elected.

"Besides," she would tell her friends, half jokingly, "I'm getting to be an old woman now and if I prefer to walk backwards rather than in other directions, it's really nobody's concern but mine."

It did, of course, occur to her at times that one day Michael would marry, and she was too cynical to imagine that a third person could enter their lives without unbalancing one of them. She did not welcome the thought. She knew she would no more like Michael's wife than she had liked his girl friends, although she had approved of some.

As she sat, at ease, on the sheltered terrace bordering one side of the cottage, content because today was Friday and Michael would be at home this week-end, she tried to remember whether there was any girl he had gone about with whom she had instinctively liked at first sight. She was quite prepared to admit that her judgment of girls was poor—she'd always preferred boys—but even so she had to maintain that Michael's choice had been on the whole rather appalling.

Luckily he hadn't been very serious about any of them, and usually he let her know to what extent he was involved. Not that she imagined for an instant, that he'd told her about all of them or, for that matter, all about any of them. At a shrewd guess, she'd put her knowledge at about fifty per cent of the truth. It would only be dangerous when he kept ninety per cent to himself. Oh, well, perhaps it wouldn't happen for a while.

The telephone rang and Mary went inside to answer it. It was Michael. She listened and said:

"No, dear, it won't be any bother. I'll expect you both about sevenish."

Putting down the receiver, she thought, 'That serves me right for harbouring uncharitable thoughts about harmless females!' So Michael had run across Angela Worthing again, and now she was working at Little Copse. Mary hoped that he would not find it necessary to spend every week-end in her company, as he had once. She didn't think he would. He'd worked Angela out of his system at least four years before the war started. It had lasted a year.

Mary remembered Angela as one of the girls she had definitely not approved of. For one thing, she was older than Michael, four or five years at least. He'd been in love with her, of course, and Mary could understand why. Angela was a very attractive girl with a lovely figure and waving dark hair which she wore in an untidy halo round her pale, oval face. She had good eyes, too, and a full, generous mouth. It would be interesting to see what the years, and the war, had done to her. Funny she hadn't married.

The thought brought the scene back as if it had been yesterday. It was the one time she'd felt maternal towards Angela. Such an odd trio they'd made. Michael was getting over bronchitis in London at the time, and Angela a constant visitor at the flat. Mrs. Thrush had started it, of course—or rather, Mary had, by overhearing Mrs. Thrush's comments to Mrs. Jones who did for the tenants in the flat above.

"That Miss Angela Worthing, she's no better than she should be," was Mrs. Thrush's opinion, expressed very vocally one morning. Mrs. Thrush was Bloomsbury, with years of experience as daily woman in the neighbourhood.

Maxy was angry. She didn't like hearing things like that said about Michael's friends. Particularly by someone who obviously knew human nature as Mrs. Thrush did. Sitting on one side of Michael's bed, watching him play picquet with Angela, Mary decided it was time someone told that young woman a few home truths for her own benefit.

In spite of the tweeds and tobacco, Mary could be as feline as any other woman. Once, after she'd been ill for a week, Michael said, "I was quite worried about you, Mother—you lost your tongue. It's come back now, so I know you're O.K. again."

So she began, brightly, to discuss marriage. Angela had a number of men friends, but, apparently, no thoughts of marriage. The three of them were in the habit of bantering about the more serious of Angela's admirers. Mary reviewed the current situation like an officer selecting a suitable candidate for promotion. Michael listened to his mother with amusement. Angela looked her most imperturbable.

"But why should I marry any of them unless I want to?" she had asked.

That gave Mary her chance and she sailed in like a frigate in a fair wind.

"Because you're at your very best now. A woman is, at your age. It's the age to marry and have children. It's the age to settle down. You think that because you get admiration from everyone now it will always be like that. But it won't. One day you'll find you're alone. It'll be too late then. I've known a lot of girls like you in my life and I've had a lot of letters from the sort of women they grow into. So much—and then nothing. You're a silly girl, Angela, and I'm beginning to think you're an unintelligent one, too."

Of course it had had no effect on Angela. Mary remembered the swift look she had given Michael at the time, a look which said, 'Isn't she a darling,' and meant 'silly old woman.'

Looking back, Mary realized that she had admired Angela Worthing. Anyone who could live quite so intensely in the present, glancing neither behind nor before, was admirable. Or perhaps she meant enviable. Mary had, for too many years, been forced to live in the future because of her responsibilities towards Michael. Had she been able to have her life over again, she would have liked to have been an Angela Worthing. What she didn't like was Michael's infatuation for the girl. And then, in more objective moments, she would decide that perhaps it was not bad for Michael after all. It was bound to have happened sooner or later and as Angela obviously had no intentions of settling down with anyone, she would give more than she took. Michael was a man, however much Mary still thought of him as a boy.

Once, Mary had said to her:

"Let him down lightly, Angela," and Angela had replied.

"Michael's all right, don't fuss about him."

It had been a curious time with too many conflicting emotions, too much that was known to the three of them, but spoken of by none. It was like being deaf and dumb, but at the same time gifted with mental telepathy. And then quite suddenly Angela Worthing had disappeared from their lives. Mary could not now remember how or when Angela went. She did not know whether Michael had continued to write to her, but for years they had never mentioned her name nor heard news of her. How strange that she should now be working in the next village.

Mary only had time to set an extra place for supper and tidy herself up when old Jake's taxi drove up from the station.

Michael said:

"Mother, you remember Angela?"

"Of course, I do. How nice to see you after all this time, my dear." As Mary moved forward to shake hands she was conscious of two definite impressions. One, that whatever had existed between Michael and Angela would never be revived—for which she offered up a speedy thanks—and, two, that Angela had not grown into the woman Mary had predicted some ten years ago.

She looks, Mary thought, what she must be, a woman who has experienced too many opportunities.

She was lovely still, but in a different way. She no longer ran her hands through negligently dressed hair. Instead, she was soignée, shining hair shaped carefully above her forehead and in the nape of her neck. Luminous eyes, and the bone of her face more obvious beneath the taut pale skin. One thing was quite unchanged and that was the vitality of her personality, the impression of intense absorption and pleasure in everything that was happening at the moment.

Michael said:

"Don't stare at each other. It's rude."

"I met Michael in the Strand, before lunch, and we even remembered each other's names! Wasn't it clever?" Angela said.

"So we lunched and gossiped as only you know how to, Mother."

"And discovered that for the last six months, Mrs. Cross, I've been working almost on your doorstep."

"Don't say you didn't remember we owned a mansion in Kirton, or Mother will never forgive you!" Michael grinned.

"I suppose I should have remembered sooner or later, but you know how one's associations slow down after a long time. Besides, Little Copse isn't Kirton, as the Little Copsians, or whatever they call themselves, are so fond of pointing out!" she laughed.

Mary said:

"And I remember you never would be persuaded to come and be quiet in the country for a week-end, Angela."

"Wouldn't I? How stupid of me. It's lovely here. . . ."

Mary knew again then that Angela had no sentimental memories. She felt a little indignant at the complete dismissal of the past so evident in Angela's voice and manner, and thought, curiously, 'here's the woman who seduced my son—because I'm quite sure she did—and I don't believe she even remembers it now.'

Michael said:

"What about going down to the local for a drink, Mother? There's plenty of time and I know you and Angela are dying for a quick one."

Mary had been looking forward to going to the Cock and Pheasant with Michael, but Angela's presence would minimize the pleasure of a drink with him.

The whole idea now became rather boring. She said:

"I don't think I will, thanks. Mrs. Baker's gone off to see her sister in hospital so I'll be getting supper while you two are out. Or you could have drinks here if you prefer," she added, "I managed to get some whisky from Jackson's today."

"Oh, I think we'll go along to the Cock and Pheasant. You don't mind, do you, Mother?"

"Good gracious, no. Supper'll be ready by eight, so don't stay too late." She still wished Michael and she were going to the pub together, but it didn't matter really. Suddenly, she wanted them to be gone, so that she might get on with the supper. There was a restless indecision about Michael since he'd been out of the R.A.F.—an urge to be on the move and a lethargy which rooted him, physically, to where he stood. She could see the conflict in him at this moment. If only he would learn to relax.

Angela said:

"Won't it be a bother if I stay to supper, Mrs. Cross, as you're on your own?"

"My dear girl, of course you must stay. It makes no difference being three. Michael's always bringing unexpected friends home at all hours of the day and night. I'd hate it if he didn't."

"I'm sure you would—you haven't changed a bit, Mrs. Cross, and it's simply lovely to see you again." Angela linked her arm affectionately through Mary's, but Michael caught hold of her on the other side.

"Come on, Angela. You and Mother can chitter-chatter all you want at supper, but Mr. Cobb's spirit quota will have run out if we delay much longer."

When they had gone, Mary thought, 'I don't dislike her a bit now,' and then, as she began to lay the dining-room table, 'I wonder what they'll talk about at the Cock and Pheasant.'

She poured herself out a sensible drink of whisky and carried it into the kitchen.

*   *   *   *

The Cock and Pheasant was more than just a public house. Built over a hundred and fifty years ago, no one had made the mistake of trying to modernize it. It was gracious and well proportioned, with open log fires in winter and cool recesses to sit back in when the road outside lay deep in dust and the sun parched the cobblestones in the yard at the side.

Kirton had other public houses; even, at the outskirts on the London Road, a modern road-house with petrol pumps, an American bar and a dance floor. But these establishments were constantly changing hands and war had seen the disintegration of the road-house which remained bereft of paint, petrol and an owner.

The Cock and Pheasant had an atmosphere of continuity. Wars might be fought and won and the world go mad, but the Cock and Pheasant still served cool beer and good sherry, and opened and closed its doors with hospitable rhythm and an eye to the law. Darts were played in both bars, a snooker table stood in the back parlour and there was a piano for special occasions. Pin tables were barred, beer was always served in tankards, and although Mr. Cobb could mix a perfectly good cocktail, his wife feigned ignorance of such matters and would pass on the order with a slightly reproving look in her bright blue eyes.

Maggie Cobb had been in the trade all her life. Her grandfather and father had ruled over the Cock and Pheasant and it had been a deep disappointment to the latter when he was left a widower with no son to carry on after him. Maggie was a sensible enough girl and she knew the business, but it wasn't the same as a boy. Besides she might marry a farmer and then what would happen to the house?

Maggie didn't marry a farmer. Instead, she married a Londoner. John Cobb was a Cockney from Islington who had never lived in the country before his marriage to Maggie. The villagers said no good could come of the marriage. The governor at the Cock and Pheasant had always been a Kirton man for as long as they remembered. Even Maggie's father was not optimistic. But John Cobb's people were in the trade, so the lad had good background. Not that a house in Islington could compare with the Cock and Pheasant at Kirton.

The marriage was a success. John Cobb settled in Kirton as though he'd been born in Little Copse and Maggie's father was able to die content in the knowledge that Maggie's two sons and a daughter were there to carry on the next generation.

The Cock and Pheasant was the centre of Kirton life. The vicar played snooker in the parlour every Wednesday night. Sir James and Lady Gurney would accompany their young people down for a sherry before lunch on Sundays. The village darts club originated in the public bar and had a keen opposing team amongst the saloon bar customers. Nobody ever stayed in Kirton without being brought to the Cock and Pheasant at least once during their visit.

Maggie Cobb surveyed the bars with a thoughtful glance. Things were getting back to normal again, although stocks still remained restricted. It was strange to see the same faces again as regulars, and not in uniform. Maggie tried to remember them as they'd been in 1939, but she could only visualize those who had not come back. Then there were those who would not come back or who had perhaps come back only to go away again. Like her Arthur. She and John would take a long time to get over Arthur marrying that Canadian girl and going off like that. Not that she wasn't a nice girl and looked lovely in her C.W.A.A.C uniform, but Maggie would never feel that Betty was a real daughter-in-law, as she'd imagined Arthur's wife would be.

It was funny, Maggie thought, how you planned for your children and then along came a war and everything went quite differently. Not that she should complain—John's brother and his wife had lost their only son, and John's sister who'd married Percy from the Finsbury Brewery had been bombed out three times and Percy would never be the same again.

No, she and John had plenty to be thankful about, she supposed. It was just Arthur being the eldest, and trained up to the Cock and Pheasant, that had made his departure so difficult to understand. Arthur had always been an easy child and a good boy. The army had changed him, it was true, but he'd been happy enough to come home on leave. Until he met Betty. She fixed it so that her people arranged a job for him in Canada when he was demobbed. Maggie put it down to Betty and that Army Education plan that Arthur used to tell them about. Still, she supposed it was all right so long as Arthur was happy. Betty was a good girl. Not what she and John would have chosen for Arthur, of course. A bit too high flying, but you couldn't always place people when they came from a foreign country, even if it was a Dominion. Maggie didn't approve of mixing nationalities any more than she approved of associating out of your own class.

At the thought, her glance wandered from the public bar across to the saloon where it focused on her younger son, Dick. Her expression softened, but there were still furrows of worry between her eyes. It never seemed natural, somehow, that her Dick had been an officer in the army. A captain like young Brian Gurney who had come home last week.

The war had done queer things to people, Maggie decided, and drew her breath in sharply as if something were hurting her. It had done queer things to Dick, sending him to strange lands, making an officer of him and giving him a Military Cross; finally, half murdering him so that he came home with a plate in his head and a leg which would never walk properly again.

Now that the war was over Mary felt things ought to go back to being what they used to be. But they weren't. The people who'd come back looked much the same—a bit older, of course, but the same. It wasn't obvious things like Dick's limp which were different, but an indefinable something she couldn't put her mind to, like Dick talking to the Gurney boys. He wouldn't have talked like that before the war. Perhaps being an officer had done it, or perhaps it was his head wound. The doctors said it would take a while to get over that.

Maybe she oughtn't to worry about Dick, but it was difficult not to. She knew that Elsie worried too. Dick had been a good boy and Elsie was a good wife to him, but she didn't like it when he started his talking any more than Maggie did. It had been awful when he first got his ticket. He'd just sit about the house, still wearing his uniform with his Sam Browne all polished up and his ribbons looking ever so bright on his chest. That was before they gave him coupons for his civvies.

Then there was the day he'd gone to London to get his pension fixed up. Someone had pulled him up in the street and asked to see his papers because they didn't believe he was a real officer. Maggie had never known who the 'someone' had been because he wouldn't talk about it afterwards, but he'd been ever so bitter, and Elsie had cried a lot.

Things were better once they had the baby. Dick had been on a training course, and, after that, he got the Government job teaching the ex-service lads carpentry at Little Copse. Maggie was pleased because he'd been a carpenter before he was called up. He was back in his own trade now, which was how things should be.

John Cobb came across from the public bar. He was a little man with grey hair and a trim moustache. Neither the years nor life in the country had erased the brightness of the Cockney from his personality. His clothes still had the nattiness of a Londoner's.

"Lil says your tea's ready, Mum, and she'll be down in a moment to take over."

"I wonder, John . . ." Maggie began and then broke off.

He smiled at her, used to her deliberate thought and speech.

"Well, don't let it put you off your feed, whatever it is, Maggie."

She looked back at him with affection.

"I'm always wondering, aren't I?" she asked.

"Better wondering than worrying, I should say."

"You always were right, John. Who's the lady who's come in with Mr. Cross tonight? We haven't seen her before, have we?"

"A Miss Angela Worthing. According to Dick, she works over at Little Copse with him. Trust Dick to know all the nobs." He spoke with pride, but Maggie noticed the quick darkening of his eyes which meant that he, too, was not yet happy about Dick. She didn't want him to think about it so she said:

"Mrs. Townsend doesn't look well. It's time the doctor were home to look after her. They say he'll be back very soon now."

John Cobb looked over at the party in the corner. It seemed strange to him, too, that his son could sit talking there with the doctor's wife, the two young Gurneys and their sister from the Manor, Miss Watson, of Vine Cottage, and Mr. Cross with that Miss Worthing. There were others too, villagers, all of them ex-service. A queer mix up for the saloon bar at the Cock and Pheasant. Maybe if he were young again he'd like it too. As it was, from what he'd heard them chatter about, it didn't make sense. If he were Dick, he'd rather have a game of darts with the regulars in the public bar.

Lily Cobb came into the bar.

"It's dished up for you, Mum," she said.

"Is Tommy asleep?" Maggie asked.

"Yes. He went off a treat tonight, thank goodness." The girl looked listless, drained of vitality. Maggie gave her a quick glance as she went out.

The bars were comparatively quiet. John and his daughter leaned against the counter without speaking. These two seldom needed words—they understood one another too well. Lily began to wash and polish empty tankards by the sink beneath the smooth, thick counter. Presently there was a call for fresh orders and she slipped across to attend to them.

John watched his daughter's neat movements, the trim set of her figure and the youthfulness of her neck and arms. A sudden feeling of love and impotence surged through him, stinging his eyes, bitter in his throat, so that he went across and drew himself a pint of mild.

Because he had always wanted a daughter—someone like Maggie only smaller and more dependent—Lil was his favourite child. He remembered her as she used to be; the quick smile and softness of her mouth, her delight in the things he enjoyed, like crowds on the green when Giles' Fair came to Kirton and the glow of a log fire lighting up the brasses on the mantel. She loved movement and light and laughter, and for him, she had personified these things. That was before the war. Now, he could only see her that way when she was playing with little Tommy. In company, in the bars, she was quiet and dim, all shut up in her small, taut body.

Lil was a corporal in the W.A.A.F., on a bomber station in Norfolk, and had been engaged to Charlie for six months by the time he was due to come off Ops. He got killed on his last mission. Lil wrote and told them and then she wrote again and said she was getting her ticket because she was going to have a child. She said she could manage all right, her officer would put her in touch with an institution if she wanted.

Maggie took on ever so when they got Lil's second letter— John didn't ever remember seeing her that way before, but they wrote off next day telling Lil to come home straight away. They got a letter from Lil's officer after that, saying she was so pleased they were taking Lil back and what a good corporal she'd always been, and how she and Charlie had planned to get married on their next leave. As if John and Maggie hadn't known that.

Tommy looked like Dick had when he was a baby, blue eyes and a lot of yellow curls. John sometimes saw Lil looking at him as if she were searching for something, and he would stop playing and stare back at her, solemn like a little old man, and then he'd suddenly chuckle and screw his eyes up all funny in the sun.

When he did that Lil would laugh back at him and gather him up in her arms with a quick, sure movement, and shake her own dark hair from eyes bright with pleasure. John would think, 'That's how she used to look, and that's how I want her to be all the time.'

Lil came back to her father's side and leaned her elbows on the counter again. It felt good to have her near him like that. She said, suddenly:

"It seems odd to see Miss Daphne in at this time, doesn't it, Dad?"

John looked across again at the party in the corner. The Gurneys' daughter wasn't 'Miss Daphne' any more, but because they had always called her that, the name would stick. She'd married a foreigner with a difficult name. A Pole, they said, in the R.A.F., who'd got killed a month after the baby was born.

John felt, once more, the bitterness in his throat. Daphne Gurney's bloke had married her. She'd come back from the factory where she worked and had a slap-up do in London. But it seemed mighty soon she was home again to have the baby. Well, he supposed, it all depended on your luck, and, come to that, Lil's Tommy was a smashing kid and looked a deal healthier than Miss Daphne's dark-skinned little fellow up at the Manor.

John looked at the girl by his side to see if she was thinking like he was. She often seemed to pick up his thoughts uncannily, but this time he could read nothing in her pale, set face. The voice of his son, Dick, floated across to the counter. Arguing the point, no doubt, like he always did these days. John thought, 'It's a rum world; things might have been the other way about.'

Round the table in the corner they were reminiscencing the war and arguing the peace, for what it was worth, content because they were together and the drink was good.

To Angela Worthing they were strangers and she wondered what it was that made her feel the companionship of the group so strongly. And then, as their characters began to develop more clearly through the things they said, she knew what it was that linked them together: they were all ex-service. All, that was, except herself and the girl called Daphne. Angela quickly dismissed Daphne; the girl was good-looking, but she lacked warmth and personality; she was affected without being an individual.

The boy, Dick, she had seen at Little Copse. He was an instructor in carpentry, but she had not actually spoken to him before. He had wide eyes and a nervous habit of thrusting one hand inside the top of his open shirt and rubbing the palm against his flesh. She noticed the scar running from his left temple into his crisply curling fair hair. She noticed, too, the way Brian Gurney would stop talking to listen to what Dick had to say, as though this attention would give the boy confidence.

Peter Gurney was drunk, but he got drunk so often and so nicely that no one seemed to mind. Angela had an impression that the confusion of his drunken moments and the inconsequence of his sober ones might be indistinguishable. But she thought, 'he and Brian have all the charm that the sister, Daphne, lacks.'

The bar began to crowd up and tobacco smoke floated, friendly and blue, above their heads. Angela felt rested and alive. She thought, suddenly, how well people can size one another up in a pub. It was something in the atmosphere that made everyone more affable so that their defences were lowered and you could glimpse characters and emotions in a way that was impossible at other times. The voices all around were soothing like a caress. She heard the tail end of Peter's voice saying: "And so I probably know as much about them as any of you. I've seen them in the docks and aboard ship. I've talked to them in pubs and cafés, all over the world. I've lived with them and fought with them. All they want is to be home again, in the home as it used to be. Back to their old jobs and a bit of quiet. They don't want to change anything." He spoke in soft, uneven sentences.

"You're wrong there, Commander." Dick Cobb rubbed his chest nervously. "Maybe that's what they thought they wanted when they were a long way away, but they've changed their ideas pretty quick since they've been back and found out what's been going on all this time."

"Not all of them, surely?" Laura Watson interrupted quickly, "Not the ones with wives and children."

Angela thought, "She's typical—the war's taken such important years out of her life that she wants to build them back into everyone else's."

"Wives and children?" Dick snorted. "Take Bill here"—Bill was a dark man with hot eyes, wearing a Sid Field overcoat in spite of the mild evening—"what did he come back and find after five years overseas? That he hadn't got a wife he could call his own, but he'd got a new toddler some two years old! Didn't you, Bill?"

Bill agreed, with simplicity, and added:

"Some overpaid dodger what could have had the pick of the skirts in this country, but he had to go and take my wife."

Angela noticed the quick contraction of Helen Townsend's hands and thought how unwell she looked. Thin and strained and singularly helpless. It was strange how getting out of uniform altered women, particularly if you'd only known them in uniform.

Dick was talking again:

"And what about me? I know I got my ticket back in '44 on account of my leg and all, but what happened when I went job hunting? And I'm not the only one, mind you. I've heard the same tale from others since."

"Tell them what happened, Dick," Brian said gently. Dick looked round the table and the strain in his eyes made them appear wider than ever. He went on:

"I went to three firms back in '44, when they was calling for a quarter of a million more men for the army and talking about conscripting women to go overseas, when they should have been pleased to get a man who'd got his ticket and wasn't on the run. They said, 'Have you got a pension?' So I said, 'Yes—80 per cent, but I'm fit to do a job. The doctors have said I'm okie-doke.' So they say, 'Oh, we're not worrying about that, but if you've got a pension we can't offer you employment. We keep our jobs for non-pensioned men.'" Dick stopped suddenly on a high note, as though listening for something.

"I know that's true," Brian said, quietly.

"But you know what it really was?" Dick asked, vehemently again. "They'd got chaps in those firms who'd been having a cushy time dodging the column for years, and when the ex-servicemen came back—lads who'd been on the pay-roll before they were called up and who thought they'd get their jobs back—what happened? They got their jobs back all right, for a few months, till things were made so uncomfortable for them that it was a case of leaving or getting the sack. They saw it coming all right. And the dodgers who'd been having a cushy holiday on their savings all went back to the jobs again. Re-instatement, they call it. Trouble is nobody's made it clear yet whose re-instatement they mean. But we know, don't we, Bill."

"That's right, Dick. We know."

Peter said:

"I gave all the chaps on my ship my address and told them to get in touch with me if they couldn't get a job. I can give them all the introductions they want."

Angela thought, 'You pathetic fool, your introductions won't help anyone, least of all yourself; life isn't going to be like that again.'

Brian said:

"What about starting with me, Peter? Greater love hath no man than this. . . ." But he was looking at Helen. Dick interrupted:

"Not you, Captain. You're with us. With Bill and me and all the chaps sweating over at Little Copse learning to be carpenters and cabinet makers. Poor suckers like us. By the time the Government's finished training a few thousand cabinet makers you'll find it's also bought all the cabinets it needs from the Yanks or someone. And the poor muggers'll be right back where they started from—only they'll have spent their dough by then. Smashing planning, ain't it?"

"Well, what are you going to do about it?" Michael Cross asked, softly.

"Do about it?" Dick's glance held theirs defiantly, and then, quite suddenly, he seemed to crumple; his whisper was bitter and helpless, "Do about it? I wish to God there was someone to tell us."

Silence held them, isolated, like a vacuum, draining them of power. Then Brian laughed, mockingly.

"I tell you what we'll do, old chap," he said. "You and I are going to start a fund for Duped Servicemen. We'll register it as an official peace charity and wrap it in blue prints. There are plenty of ways of collecting money for it. I'll go round with a little tin and Mary's dog, Belinda, who has puppies on the slightest provocation—that always appeals to the family man. I'll sit outside the War Office before lunch and when the Chief of Staff comes out I'll say, 'Spare a copper for the Duped Soldiers, sir, spare a—'"

"Don't be a fool, Brian," Helen said, fiercely, but he ignored her as he went on.

"And when the Secretary of State hurries home at four p.m. I'll waggle my little tin in front of his nose and Belinda will waggle her tail and we'll ask him for a contribution for all the ex-servicemen who've been duped by white papers, duped by post-war promises, duped by the Treasury and duped by their women at home."

Angela saw Helen go white in the face, and, in a flash, she understood the bitterness behind Brian's fooling. Those two were in love—or had been. He was hurt, painfully angry about something.

Michael Cross said:

"Let me know when all this is going to happen, Brian. I'd like the exclusive story for my paper!"

"There's going to be nothing exclusive about this, is there Dick?"

But Dick was not listening. He sat twisting an empty tankard between his hands, and his face looked smoothed out and young again, as though someone else being vehement on his behalf was all he asked.

Laura said:

"Dick, Mrs. Cobb is trying to make signs at you from the other side of the counter."

Dick looked up.

"That'll be Elsie come to fetch me away," he said. "Come on, Bill. Can't keep a lady waiting, you know."

"Good night, all. See you tomorrow?" He was pathetically eager that they should say yes.

Michael spoke for them.

"Sure thing. Same time. Cheero."

They watched him limp across the room. Angela asked:

"Where did he get that?"

Brian said:

"Italy. They'd just made him an officer. His head wound's more serious. He got his captaincy and an M.C. at the same time. It's all very confused to him now and he's sore as hell because he can't remember. He doesn't remember going to O.C.T.U. or anything. That's why he's got such an inferiority complex; he feels he's never been a real officer and yet he's as proud as a peacock when you introduce him as captain. Poor devil."

Daphne said:

"Brian, dear, we ought to be getting home. I promised to say good night to Ian before supper."

Brian laughed:

"All right, fuss-budget, we're quite aware that your promises to your son transcend all else."

"Well, they do," she agreed, simply. "Can you make Peter move, he's half asleep." She prodded her elder brother, gently.

"What's that?" Peter asked, jerkily.

"Your sister," Brian explained, "is the lucky one of our family. Her future career is assured. She has full time employment as a mother, guaranteed for at least sixteen years to come. Which is more than we can say, old fellow. Come on." His glance went back to Helen. "Shall I see you home, Helen?"

To Angela it sounded like a plea.

"No, it's all right, Brian. I'll walk back with Laura. We go the same way."

"Oh well, good night then. It's been nice seeing you again." His hurt was thinly disguised.

*   *   *   *

I asked Brian not to come, but he has.

I am afraid when I see him walk into the room. Not of him, but of Emily who has just opened the door for him, of Lady Gurney who will have asked him where he was going, of Laura whose cottage he has passed on the way here. And of all the eyes and ears in the village waiting to transmit to avid tongues everything they see and hear.

This isn't like the army. In the army to put on a uniform was to put a barrier between your personal life and the world. You can find more privacy in a uniformed crowd than anywhere else.

In Kirton, in my own home, I am naked. I am Dr. Townsend's wife and, next week, my husband will be home. Everybody knows that and everybody, every busybody, is rejoicing on my behalf.

Brian is near me and I am caught up by his presence. I can't help it. It has been like that for two years now.

"Why did you have to come back here?" I ask, stupidly.

He laughs.

"Darling, where else can a bloke come back to if not to his own home?"

"Unfortunately it's my home too."

"Yes," he says, very gently, "your home and my home. But not our home. Helen, we've got to talk about this. We've got to decide something. We've so little time left."

Outside the sun is going down, irrevocably. Because its rays are level with the window, shining on the mullioned panes, I cannot see the garden outside, with its blaze of dahlias. Instead I see Brian outlined sharply against a golden haze and I derive intense physical pleasure from the sight. With equal intensity, I despise myself.

"Brian, there's nothing to talk about," I say. "I wrote to you."

"Your letter, darling?" He is smiling as we stand facing each other. "Your letter was the silliest I have ever read. It didn't make sense."

I hadn't thought it would when I wrote it. That's the drawback of arguing something you don't altogether believe in. Brian is right. We've got to talk this over.

"I wish you'd sit down," I say.

"I don't want to, thanks."

"Then I will. There is a chair I have always liked. It is wing-backed and when you sit in it you can feel it fitting safely all round you."

"You look very small out of uniform," Brian says casually.

"I feel rather small. The cigarettes are in that box on the mantelpiece."

"Thanks." But he doesn't take one.

"I'm sorry I can't offer you a drink. There's absolutely nothing in the house."

"What a place." And now he is fingering his own cigarette case, opening and shutting it by sliding it and letting the spring force back his relaxed fingers before he snaps it shut again. He repeats this with great concentration and the stillness of the room is punctuated by metallic clicks. I think I am going to scream. Instead I say:

"I'd like a cigarette, please."

He lights two cigarettes and hands me one. Then he goes on snapping the case.

"Please, Brian, don't do that!"

"Sorry." He walks up and down in front of the window. I can't help watching him and I feel awful because, inside me, is the restless tingle of pleasure that his proximity arouses. I like the way he holds himself and the outline of his figure against the light. My senses respond to the clearness of his skin and the tautness of his body. It is no good pretending to myself that I am not attracted. I may be stupid, but I do know myself. I understand my feelings only too well.

"Helen"—he pauses with his back towards me—"Helen, you've got to come away before Gyp gets back."

"I won't. You know I can't. I've told you why already."

"But you don't love him." It is the beginning and end of all our arguments. "You love me."

"Brian, I don't know . . ." What an admission—and yet it's true. To be so conscious of attraction and so uncertain of love. I must see Gyp again, here in our old home, before I can know. I am quite certain of that, and quite sane about it. To be in love with one man and to love another is nonsensical and muddle-hearted; it's wanton and unethical; but it's not madness. After everything which has happened since 1939, it's almost inevitable. Of course I want to make excuses now. I know that. Not to Brian or Gyp but to myself. And I want to be fair. I don't think it would be right to go away before Gyp comes back. He knows nothing about Brian. If he is to know, I want to tell him myself. I owe that to Gyp—and to Brian. If I were to go away now with Brian I should never be comfortable again. Besides, I want to see Gyp.

"You'll make yourself ill." He is looking at me and I feel a moment of panic that he has read my thoughts.

"You don't make it any easier," I say.

"Easier? I suppose you think it's awfully easy for me to come back here and find you installed in Gyp's house, waiting to welcome him back, playing at being the faithful wife, building up an atmosphere of home and sanctity. And I suppose you think it will be easy for Gyp to find you again as he's always pictured you, only to discover that you don't love him after all."

When I get angry I get a lump in my throat and my eyes fill with tears. It is happening now and I can't stop it.

"But I do love him." The words sound muffled and childish.

"I'm sorry, Helen." He is near me and he has put an arm round my shoulders. What disturbing comfort that gives.

"I shouldn't have said that. I don't really think you're playing at anything. You're just being you, I suppose. You can't help it any more than I can stop myself saying stupid things." He gives my shoulder a reassuring squeeze.

I am staring straight into the browny tweed of the jacket he is wearing, somewhere below the lapel, and the furry surface of the material is magnified and blurred. The lump in my throat is not from anger now.

"For God's sake blow your nose," he says. I comply with the most sensible suggestion he has yet made, .and suddenly we are smiling at each other. It's always that way with Brian. Maybe that's why we like each other so much. We have always laughed at the same things. Until I came out of the A.T.S. we never thought about anything seriously for long. We smiled, ridiculed, and were gay, secure in the laughter of our love. We are laughing now.

"Darling, now we're being sensible again." He lights us another cigarette each, and then stands looking down at me. If only we hadn't got to talk any more. But he goes on: "I accept your decision, even though I think you're mad. You shall stay here and Gyp will come back and you will then make up your mind what you're going to do. That's what you want, isn't it?"

"Yes." If only it were as simple as that, but of course it isn't.

"I don't like it—that's obvious and we needn't go into the reasons again. I don't think Gyp would like it if he knew the truth. He doesn't, so we can't argue that point. But you're not even going to like it yourself, Helen, so why do it?"

"There's nothing else I can do."

"Don't be silly. I've told you what to do. Get away from here before it's too late. I don't mean with me, but alone, somewhere where you won't see me or Gyp. Write and tell him what's happened. Tell him the whole thing and see what he wants to do about it. It's the only fair thing for all of us. Can't you see that?"

But I can't. It's all very well for Brian to say go away before it's too late. Can't he see that it is already too late? I should have written to Gyp two years ago, when there seemed no end to the war, when he was thousands of miles and thousands of years away from me. I can't do it now when time and miles are dwindling to nothing before our meeting again. Besides I want to see him. I tell this to Brian and he doesn't understand. If you haven't been married yourself—happily married—I suppose you can't understand.

Brian is walking about again. I want him to be near enough for me to force him to listen. If I could hold him, I could explain better. But he will keep moving.

"At least," he says, "we can thrash it out now, while we've still got time."

"It won't make any difference, Brian. I thought we'd agreed on that?"

"We'd agreed?" he laughs. "You mean you wrote me that idiotic letter telling me what you intended doing, and expected me to say, yes and God bless you, and then do a nice vanishing act until somebody had come to their senses. You couldn't really have thought it feasible after all that's happened."

"But nothing's happened so far as Gyp's concerned, that's the point."

"Oh, all right, all right. I won't bring it up if you don't want me to. I'm not going to harp on the fact that we fell in love, that we've lived together for two years and that we both go crazy when we can't fake up an excuse to meet each other on every possible occasion."

"That's just what you are doing. That's why I knew it was silly of us to meet here in Kirton. We always said we wouldn't and we never have before."

"Listen, Helen. Listen, darling"—he is very close to me now—"no, I'm not going to make love to you. Don't get scared. I don't feel that way at the moment. But I'd like to tell you something. Can I?"

He is holding my hand, in a detached, impersonal way. I can feel my face flushing because he is just that much more impersonal than I can ever be. Who suggested that women were cool and men impatient? I say:

"Yes, tell me. What?"

"It's a story. A true story, so far as I'm concerned. I think you ought to hear it, from my point of view. D'you mind?"

"Go on."

Up and down the room he paces. I can count the number of steps he will take before he turns each time. Oh, Brian, why can't you be still?

"I met a girl once. She was very lovely. Sub-consciously I suppose I realized it the first time I saw her." He has stopped walking and, for a moment, I have stopped breathing. Physical jealousy does that to me. I hate it and despise it and it catches me unawares, like missing a step in one's dreams.

"This was all a long time ago." Brian flings the butt of his cigarette out of the window and lights another. "A very long time ago. Another existence. Before the war. And she was lovely. Everyone agreed on that but, as I said, I wasn't consciously aware of it at the time. I played tennis with her; I went on the same picnics as she did; I even danced with her on several occasions. But it wasn't until I'd seen her quite twenty times that I suddenly realized what was wrong with her."

"What was it?" I prink my face into an expression of interest. I don't care what was wrong with this girl of Brian's, whoever she may have been. I hate her. Why have I got to listen to this story now? I could kill Brian for hurting me at this moment.

"She was married." He sounds quite cheerful about it. "Not that there was anything wrong in that. It was just the way marriage had affected her. I suppose she was about twenty-five when I first met her and she'd been married a couple of years. Her husband was all right too. They were very fond of each other. I don't believe they really noticed anything outside themselves. That's what was wrong. You can't at twenty-five ignore the world, but that's what she was doing. My God, she might have been married for twenty years, not two. Settled, in a rut, devoid of curiosity at the age of twenty-five. D'you know what I mean?"

Of course I know what he means now. But I wasn't like that. I wasn't like that in the very least.

"Go on," I say, while the numbness falls from my mind and limbs.

"It seemed to me that this girl had never really experienced anything deeply. She was happy, but it was a superficial happiness. Not because she was a superficial person, but simply because nothing had stirred her emotions or intellect sufficiently to bring her real happiness—or real sorrow, for that matter."

How wrong you are, Brian, how very wrong. I was tremendously happy with Gyp. That is what I want to say, but I don't.

Brian has only been right about one thing so far: Gyp and I used not to notice much outside ourselves. Why should we? We were self-sufficient, we were complete. Everything we did and saw was exciting because we were together. We weren't in a rut; we travelled on air. Then the war happened.

As though I had spoken aloud, Brian says:

"And then came the war. I was sent to the other end of England and her husband went into the R.A.M.C. I didn't hear of her again until someone told me she was joining one of the women's services. A pity, I thought, because I dislike women in uniform. Someone said he'd gone overseas. The usual snatches of news one gets from home. I thought no more about either of them."

I thought, how easily he can dismiss those snatches of home news but how enormously eventful they were for me. Gyp's embarkation leave, with both of us trying to hide from the other the depths of our unhappiness; the long-drawn-out pain of those swiftly passing days and nights. I can't recapture it now, but the memory is still inside me, twisted and miserable. And then the sheer discomfort of being a recruit in the A.T.S., memorable chiefly for aching feet and a surfeit of starch at every meal.

"No, I can't say I really ever thought of her again." Brian lights two more cigarettes and passes me one, casually. I take it and remember that he had many things to think about then. Dunkirk amongst others.

"Until she suddenly walked into the mess," he continues. "That must have been nearly three years later. I couldn't think where I'd seen her before. Then I remembered. But she'd changed, and it wasn't just the uniform and the three pips on her shoulder. She seemed more vital. She was interested in the outside world, and people and everything that went on around her. I was delighted to see her again. You know how it is when you meet someone from the same place as yourself. At least it was like that in the army—particularly in that damn awful hole in Scotland where the mist lifted once a year, and that was when you were away on leave. Oh, it was good to have a link with the south and the past and those strange years when one knew there must be war and was busy getting the most out of life before the balloon went up. I think she got a kick out of it too. We were Livingstone and Stanley in an uncouth land of rain, shrouded hills and unintelligible voices. Of course we got together. It was obvious, wasn't it?"

I am silent. It was true. I'd thanked God for Brian during those months in Scotland. And we did, as he said, get together.

We were gay and forgot the rain and the snow and the desolation of winter. We forgot loneliness too.

We neither of us speak for a while and the room is filled with memories in the autumn sunset.

"We fell in love," he goes on, slowly, "and I don't mean that it was another case of propinquity and all the rest. It wasn't. I'd left the unit by then. I'd gone travelling, not only south but over the water and back again—missions as the Yanks called them—to Norway and other spots. An exciting life, so long as it lasted. Luckily it did for me and we next met on leave in London. That's when we realized we were in love."

I remember it, of course. The gladness of spring and the unendingness of war. War-time London with the Yanks pouring into the city, overflowing the taxis, and a new generation of gum-chewing floosies in the streets. We isolated ourselves, foreigners almost in our own capital. Yes, I was in love, and there was madness in London in the spring of '43. An inconsequential madness because time had ceased to count and weariness had not yet reached its climax. I was happy—happier than I'd been since 1940 when Gyp went away.

"I know," Brian said, "that she was happy. Oh, we'd both been in love before, naturally. But this time it was different. I know it was. I know it as definitely as I know I'm still alive."

For the first time he is vehement and, to my mind, uncertain of his story. I ought to say, 'You are right, but not quite right.' I don't because I am weak. Every day now I realize how weak I am. If I were to tell Brian that although I fell in love with him it hadn't been comparable with the emotion I'd felt for Gyp, he would crumple and I would feel despicable. More than that I would probably start acting like a fool and undo the small barrier I have built up as a defence for Gyp's return. I'm not strong enough to hurt deliberately, however necessary the hurt may be.

Brian is waiting for me to say something. I can feel him looking at me.

"Why was it different?" I ask, foolishly.

"Because we loved with complete abandon and there were no ties to our love. We were subject, of course, to the etiquette of khaki. She more than I, because it was like that with the A.T.S. Those temporary soldiers were more conscious of their military careers than any regular soldiers I've ever met. But with the majority, thank God, it was superficial. She was a good officer—I saw that from my time in Scotland—but she was essentially a woman. The only masculine trait she possessed was that of being able to keep her private life severed from her official one. And her private life, at that time, had no shackles. She was free to go her own way whenever she wanted to. Just as I was. That's why our love was great. We loved because we wanted to and not because we had involved ourselves in some conventional formula of faithfulness."

"So you think marriage is unnecessary?"

"Until you want to have children—yes."

"Brian, you've got it all wrong." I feel constricted and the room is suddenly sultry.

"No I haven't. She would have married me and I would have married her. Then the war ended."

"It was bound to, some time."

"Damn it all, having got to the stage we had, what difference could that make?"

"Her husband." I must answer back now.

"That doesn't matter. She and I had built up something sure and, I think, lasting. Sounds silly, but we'd got something we'd never known before and could never get again. She'd come to life, she'd become a real person. Before that she was just pretty and conventional. Now she'd got character and personality. Like coming up from your first dive into the deep end of the pool and knowing you can swim."

"I hate swimming; maybe she did too."

"No. She was a good swimmer. Oh, Helen, don't you see the madness of your ideas? You're changed. For God's sake be honest and own up to it. Life's ahead of you. Take it as it takes you. Don't go building little sand castles which false emotions must wash away. Face up to the impossibility of what you're planning. You're good and honest and you don't want to let Gyp down. Don't you see that staying here to receive him home will be a let down for him in the long run?"

"Brian, I'm not doing it for him, but for myself. Can't you understand that?"

"I think you're falling in with the popular fantasy of the returning hero." He sounds bitter.

"There are plenty of heroes in this country, thank you."

"Thank you!"

The bitterness has gone from his voice but I must go on now, or not at all. "Brian, will you listen while I say something that I really mean and that you won't like?"

"Go on, say your piece if you must." He has sat down at last, sprawled on the sofa with his hands deep in his pockets and his head flung back on a cushion. It's a mean, defenceless attitude and I won't look at him. Instead I fix my glance on the room I know so well with the silly things Gyp and I bought for it before the war. "Well, go on," Brian urges.

"All right, I will. Brian, I don't know whether I love Gyp or you, and that's the truth."

He doesn't speak. He doesn't move, and I can't look at him.

"Brian, it's true. I wish it wasn't. I wish it were as you have depicted it. Only it isn't. I can't do anything about it."

Still he won't speak.

"Brian, please say something."

He gets up then and his tallness has crumpled into a slouch.

"For God's sake let's go and have a drink at the Cock and Pheasant." His voice is as tired as I feel.

PART II

IT WAS GOING to be a hard winter—or so the villagers foretold. October had blazed, but since then grey clouds and gusty winds held the skies. Too soon red berries were traditionally profuse. In all probability it was going to be a long winter, with the coal situation no better than it had been during the war.

"We might just as well make up our minds to shut up the drawing-room and the library again after Xmas," Lady Gurney remarked to her family at lunch time.

"Oh, must we? With all of us at home we'll be falling over one another in the morning room." Daphne Zarek stopped attending to her son, Ian, whose high chair was pushed up to the mahogany dining-table next to her own place.

"Well, your father always uses his study during the day." Lady Gurney decided that her daughter was becoming just a trifle difficult and then dismissed the thought as uncharitable. Poor Daphne, she'd been home more than two years now and, since Ian's birth she'd been mother, nursemaid and general factotum to the child. And she had not really got over Kurt's death. Or had she? Watching the placid, almost sullen, expression of her daughter's face, she thought, for the hundredth time, how little she really knew about her children's thoughts and emotions.

"That still leaves the evenings to fight for the only comfortable chairs!" Daphne laughed, but there was no gaiety in the sound.

Sir James Gurney looked across at his daughter. Their faces were strangely similar: straight, dark brows above the grey eyes, full mouths and tapering chins. He said:

"You have your room upstairs, Daphne, and Ian's nurseries. At the rate the government re-housing scheme is progressing, you're about five years ahead of schedule in space per body. It's a deplorable state of affairs." It was reproof administered in the gentlest voice, and even his wife could not decide whether Daphne or the Government were to blame most.

At this point Ian created a diversion by flinging a spoonful of rice pudding into Peter's lap. Peter said:

"Oh God, what a filthy feeder he is," and began to mop up the results with his dinner napkin.

"A few more spots won't be noticed on your suit," Daphne replied sharply to her brother.

Lady Gurney thought, I wish they wouldn't bicker. Her mind, receptive to confused impressions, registered the fact that Daphne had been quite right about Peter's suit. It was dirty. All his suits were dirty and most of them had cigarette burns too. He ought to have a new suit, but men's clothes were so expensive. James wouldn't agree to spend more on Peter and the boy had no money of his own. If only he'd settle down to a job again.

All the time she was seeing a picture of Peter as a small boy, in long grey flannels and a white open shirt. He'd just hit Daphne who was ten years his junior. Not hard, but enough to make her open her mouth wide and screw up her eyes in the way she did when she was going to yell. There would be a time lag of several seconds between the grimace and the yell. She saw Peter rush across to his sister and clumsily clap one hand over her mouth whilst the other hugged her tightly as he made soothing noises to prevent the yell. Daphne did not cry, but, when she had regained her breath, she slapped him back with all the strength of her tiny fist.

They had always fought: Peter, the adored eldest son, and Daphne, the daughter she had so longed for, the pretty child who could be dressed up in frilly frocks and depended upon to smile at visitors.

Lady Gurney suddenly wished that Brian were still at home. She had never really got on with her second son, but unconsciously she recognized a strength in him which she could not discern in her other children. It was easier when he was at home. But he had not stayed for long. It seemed that he was only just back from the army when he went away again.

It was all very different from what she had planned. During the war, those interminable years when she and Sir James had somehow carried on at the Manor with evacuees and billeted officers and then evacuees again during the Flying Bomb months, Lady Gurney had always pictured the children returning from the war. It was a lovely picture which bore no relationship to reality, but it had helped her through those years as nothing else could have done.

All the time she was making do and mending, digging for victory, and fighting on the kitchen front with marrow jam and carrot marmalade, Lady Gurney was planning the children's homecoming. It never occurred to her that Peter in the navy or Brian, first a commando and then in the airborne forces, would not come home. Any more than it occurred to her that Daphne would marry a Pole, be widowed and give birth to a son all within a few months. She was as shocked by the latter as she would have been if the War Office or the Admiralty had announced the death of her sons.

She expected her children to return to her as they had left her. Peter from the navy, Brian from the army and Daphne from the factory to which she'd been directed after she gave up her job as a land girl on old Blaker's farm.

Moreover she had visualized this return as a combined operation with herself and her husband meeting the afternoon train from London and the children hanging out of a first-class carriage window, eager to be the first to see them on the platform. It was a lovely picture, misted with her tears and rosy with the port Sir James would bring up from the cellar and decant for the first family gathering round the dining-room table. There would be flowers and a huge joint and, somewhere, in a hazy background, flags. There must be flags to welcome them home. Ever since Lady Gurney had seen Mrs. Murphy's cottage bedecked with the standards of the Allies and displaying a bold, hand-painted notice 'Welcome to Maurice' above the door, she had secretly planned flags for the children's return.

And the children themselves would step out of their uniforms and overalls and put on the nice clothes they always wore before the war and everything would be just as it always had been, carefree and gay.

But nothing happened as Lady Gurney planned. Daphne came back after 'D' day to have her baby, and Kurt—the stranger with the dark eyes and foreign accent who had so suddenly become a member of the family—was killed. More than a year later, Peter turned up, unannounced and a little drunk, saying he'd lost his home; and then Brian arrived, but only to go away again almost at once.

At the back of her mind she still saw three children playing on a green lawn, while the voices of Mary and Peter argued above the head of a small, strange child with dark eyes who splashed rice pudding. She felt a little breathless and very old.

After lunch, in her husband's study, Lady Gurney pottered. She had so much she wanted to discuss, but somehow her tangled thoughts would not be translated into the right words.

She knew that she was irritating him. She could tell it from the way he hunched himself into his chair and dodged her glance behind the *Financial Times*. Sometimes, she thought, it was a pity James had neither profession nor career, which the boys could have gone into. Something for Peter to do now instead of lolling about the house. She supposed it was because she and her husband had too much money when they married. There had been no reason for him to work, they'd been rich then. Now they were poor—however much he juggled with the *Financial Times*.

They were very poor, almost uncomfortably so. Sir James had moved their capital about, like an amateur chess player, experimenting with the possibilities of his Knight, popping it into new ventures and far-away countries. The ventures had turned out to be misses and the countries either changed their names, ceased to exist, or were invaded by other countries which Sir James had overlooked.

It didn't really matter for Sir James and Lady Gurney, because their lives were nearly over, but there'd be no inheritances for the children. What with taxes which nobody could afford and the high price of living, the Manor was already run out of capital. Then there would be death duties and so on, until there'd be practically nothing for the children to live on after she and her husband were dead.

Daphne would have what little remained because of Ian. Kurt had left her nothing. It was all very unsatisfactory.

Lady Gurney sighed. Thank goodness the children had at least been well educated. They'd been to the most expensive schools and Peter and Brian had both got their 'blues' at Cambridge. That was worth something—or it used to be.

She knew in her heart that she wasn't worrying about Brian. It was Peter, with his vagueness and lack of energy, who kept her awake at nights trying to think of some nice job he could go into, or some kind friend who would give him the right sort of introductions. Sir James didn't appear to know anyone who was important now and Peter himself, once so popular with his well-off friends, seemed to be disinterested and incapable of making any efforts for himself.

She sighed again, more loudly this time.

Sir James Gurney stirred uncomfortably behind his paper. He didn't want to listen to whatever his wife wished to talk about. Not because he wasn't fond of her but because she had a maddening habit of asking him questions he didn't know the answers to. He felt weary and longed to be left alone, warm and quiet in front of the log fire. His wife always worried. It never did any good—life went on just the same whether you worried or not. But because he was soft-hearted, because he loved her and hated to sense her distress, he said:

"What's the matter, old girl?" in his most off-hand voice.

"Oh, James, it's Peter. What shall we do about him?"

He rose from the arm-chair and went to fill his pipe from the tobacco jar on the mantelpiece. He stood, round-shouldered, pressing the tobacco into the bowl of his pipe with a long, white thumb. Very careful, very conscientious, with legs apart and his head bent so that only the baldness on top showed, not the loose, wrinkled skin of his neck nor the Adam's apple bobbing above his too wide, soft collar.

"Why have we got to do anything, Agnes? He's all right. After all, he did nearly six years in the Navy. Not bad for a chap who was thirty-five when he joined up. He's earned his spell of rest."

Lady Gurney, who was much shorter than her husband, put her head on one side and blinked up at him, rather like a budgerigar, in her yellow knitted suit.

"But, James, it was you who said you must talk to him about getting back to a job again."

"Well, so I will, so I will. All in good time," he replaced the lid on the tobacco jar and began to scratch at a box of matches. "He can always go back to the city, you know, my dear," he continued between puffing and sucking at his pipe.

"But he can't," she twittered. "He sold up his Stock Exchange membership, and he'd have to start all over again."

"Nonsense, my dear, we'll find something for him to do. Don't you worry yourself about him. We've got to give him a chance to look round and find his feet again. Something'll turn up all right. It always does." He straightened his shoulders and let his glance wander above her head and out of the window.

He didn't want to go on talking about Peter. He didn't want to think about his eldest son. There were some things which made him feel awkward and one was having a middle-aged son living at home. Last night, for instance, when the boy had come in drunk. It wasn't pleasant. Thank goodness his mother had already gone to bed. She wouldn't have understood that Peter hadn't really meant all he'd said about unsuccessful parents, blaming them for not providing security for their children. Just a lot of alcoholic twaddle, but hurtful because it came from Peter. Besides, it was in bad taste.

His wife seemed to have forgotten what they were talking about. She was staring at the photographs above the mantelpiece. He followed her glance and felt comforted. There was something very secure about the group of young fellows sitting, stiffly upright, behind a foreground of silver cup perched precariously on a spindle legged table. A faded and yellow print, but a fine set of whiskers and muscle. Those were the days.

"I'm glad," said Lady Gurney, cheerfully, "that you got rid of that moustache, James." And she went up and straightened the old photograph affectionately. "And I'm glad," she went on, inconsistently, "that we've had this little conference about Peter. I feel much better now that I know you are going to do something about him."

She went across to her husband and he kissed her, absent-mindedly on the head.

"Now you run along, old dear, and stop bothering your head about a lot of silly nonsense." He picked up the *Financial Times* and settled himself in front of the fire again.

She said:

"We're having tea early because May's going to Dimstone to the pictures this evening, but I'll come and tell you when it's ready." Straightening a cushion here and a chair there, she made her way from the room.

Back in the drawing-room, Daphne Zarek was staring out of the long french windows. She heard her mother come into the room but made no attempt to acknowledge her presence.

"Hello, darling. Not taking Ian out this afternoon?" Lady Gurney used the voice her daughter had learned to hate. It meant 'Aren't you failing in your duty as a mother.' She replied, dully,

"It's pouring with rain."

"Then we might," suggested Lady Gurney brightly, "get on with those chair covers. I'll get the sewing machine out."

"Oh, God!"

"Darling, what's the matter?"

"I'm bored, bored, bored!" Daphne turned desperately from the window. "I shall scream if nothing goes on happening in this damn awful place."

"Daphne, my pet . . ." Lady Gurney felt unable to cope with this outburst. It was so unlike Daphne not to be calm and silent about everything. Coming on top of Peter's lethargy, it was almost more than she could bear.

"It's no good staring at me like that, Mother. I am bored. Sometimes I feel I can't breathe in this house. If only I could get away for a week—for a day even."

"But there's Ian and—"

"I know. Oh, God, I know. Don't tell me it's a lovely home for him. Don't remind me that he's got a beautiful nursery and a safe garden to play in and good country air. I know it all, and I know it's true and that I'm lucky and he's lucky and everything's for the best in the best of all possible worlds. But that doesn't stop me wanting to go away sometimes."

"Well, you could go to Aunt Isabel for a change, darling, I'd look after Ian while you had a holiday," Lady Gurney said placatingly.

"But I don't want to go to Aunt Isabel. I want to live. I'm twenty-nine and I still want to live. I love Ian, better than anything else in the world, but that doesn't stop me wanting life as well."

There was a silence between them. Daphne, glowing and fretful, her mother hurt, but not defeated.

"And what, Daphne, are you proposing to do about it?" It was mean, it was the sort of question Lady Gurney would have hated to have been asked. She knew, as she said the words, that Daphne would go sulky. She watched the features on the young face set into well-known lines. She wanted to put her arms round her daughter and tell her not to worry, to go out and have a good time, to do what she wanted to do. But she didn't. It wasn't like before the war when it was so easy to give in to the children, to let them indulge in the things they enjoyed. Nowadays everything was difficult. It wasn't just the question of money, but war had brought restrictions and responsibilities which could somehow not be got rid of easily. War had brought Ian to Daphne.

Ten years ago, Lady Gurney would have said to her daughter, "Go abroad for a holiday, go for a cruise, go where you want," and she would have engaged a nurse for Ian and all would have been well. Those sort of things were no longer possible. Instead she looked at her daughter and said again:

"Well, what about it?"

Daphne shrugged her shoulders.

"Nothing. I'm all right, really. It's just this eternal house, with Peter slopping ash all over the place and May looking daggers whenever Ian upsets anything or crawls over something she's cleaned. And having no money and being completely untrained to get a job of any sort. Oh, just everything. At least during the war, we had the peace to look forward to. Now there's damn all to look forward to. I suppose I'd better settle down to living in the past like Laura Watson. To hear her talk you'd think there'd never been a better life than the army." She laughed in a mocking way.

Lady Gurney said:

"Peter will be getting a job soon, and May's just overtired like a lot of other people are after the war, and Laura Watson's very happy to be home again with her father, so let's get on with those covers, shall we?"

Her daughter laughed, this time without bitterness.

"All right, Mother; thank goodness you at least haven't changed. Where's that damned sewing machine?"

And as they cut and tacked and machined the new covers for the drawing-room chairs, Daphne seemed satisfied to talk about Ian and how wonderful he was, but all the time, Lady Gurney was thinking, 'I never thought the children being home was going to be as difficult as this. It isn't a bit as I'd planned it.'

*   *   *   *

For years Laura Watson had fought for freedom without ever having experienced it, either emotionally or by upbringing. But now she was, in effect, going to enjoy a week of it.

To be asked by the station-master on Kirton platform where she was going, for how long and whether she would stay with friends or at an hotel was something Laura was used to since the days she first went to boarding school. To a lesser extent, and subject to the station-master's acute sense of security, it had happened when she was in khaki and departed from leave. That it was a violation of her privacy and an infringement of her independence never occurred to her, for she had been brought up to disclose to those in authority her everyday actions. In his own way, the station-master represented authority to Laura: he wore a uniform and had the power to question the validity of her railway ticket.

So she answered his questions as politely as she had answered them a hundred times before.

"Going no further than London, Miss Watson?" He swayed a little on his heels with the toes of his well-polished black shoes overlapping the edge of the platform.

"Not this time, Mr. Brent." Laura wished he would not stand on the edge like that. It made her nervous, reminding her of her own childhood and her mother's voice gloating on the awful fate which would befall anyone who overbalanced before an incoming train.

"Now let me see," said Mr. Brent, shuffling his feet even further over until it seemed impossible that he should still remain standing on the platform, "this must be your first journey since you came out of the army?"

"Yes, it'll be my first visit to London as a civilian," Laura replied and watched, fascinated, as Mr. Brent performed an acrobatic volte face which brought his heels, this time, to rest on nothing, some two feet above the railway lines.

"You're not leaving us for long, I hope, miss?"

"Only a week. D'you think the train's going to be crowded?"

"Can't tell these days. Depends whether there's a draft of troops disembarked up North." Even now, with the war a thing of the past, Mr. Brent could never bring himself to mention a port by name. He continued in a low voice, "As you probably know, Miss, they send all the lads to the dispersal centres nearest their homes to be demobbed. That's why we get a full train to London when there's a draft in." He rocked precariously on his feet and Laura wondered, in a moment of panic, whether he had forgotten just how near the edge he was. But she kept silent. You didn't point things out to people in authority.

"Going to stay with your relatives, I suppose?" Mr. Brent rubbed the slight stubble on his chin with a bent forefinger and surveyed, sourly, the efforts of a small boy to molest an empty chocolate machine at the far end of the platform.

"No. I'm going to spend a week at my club to do some shopping and see a few shows, I hope."

The train was rounding the bend beneath the bridge and, to Laura's intense relief, Mr. Brent stepped briskly forward and picked up her suitcases.

"I'll see you're fixed up with a seat, Miss Watson. Mustn't neglect our old customers!" He laughed inordinately at his own wit and Laura followed him along the platform as the train drew up. It seemed suddenly that a great number of people were getting on at Kirton—probably they were from the Training Centre at Little Copse. Laura thought she saw Angela Worthing at the far end of the platform with a man who looked like Peter Gurney. The train was crowded, but Mr. Brent managed to find her a seat in a third-class carriage. He was so apologetic about this that she got the impression he must think she had a first-class ticket; she hadn't, but somehow she couldn't make up her mind to tell him this now. She went through an acute moment of embarrassment wondering whether she should tip him for helping her with her luggage; she only had a sixpenny bit and a ten-shilling note on her. Neither would have been justified and, just in time, she discovered that what she had thought was a florin in her pocket was really only a button off her coat. In a flurry, she couldn't remember whether her father tipped the station-master or not. How stupid of her to forget a thing like that. Luckily Mr. Brent ended her discomfiture by touching his cap, wishing her a good journey and disappearing from the corridor in a combined operation worthy of a more appreciative audience.

Seated between a man in a neat blue suit and a harassed-looking mother with a baby and a small girl sprawling about her, Laura began to assimilate the other occupants of the carriage from behind the barrier of self-consciousness which always encompassed her in the presence of strangers. In the corner opposite was a W.A.A.F. in an incredibly faded and spotted uniform, her bleached hair carefully bunched above her forehead and straggling into untidy curls round her clean starched collar. She looked a baby behind a façade of lipstick and mascara and was identical with thousands of other girls of her generation, a monstrous regiment of maidens who had marched through six years of war: good girls, bad girls, clever girls and stupid girls, who remembered little before the reign of Bevin.

Laura sighed. She would have liked to have been the W.A.A.F. and to have begun the peace in her early twenties.

In the other corner was an elderly man in a city suit with an appliance for the deaf festooned between his waistcoat pocket and his right ear. Between him and the W.A.A.F. were two soldiers in battle-dress. They had sunburned faces and shrewd eyes. Healthy men with powerful limbs, they exuded an atmosphere of aggressive cheerfulness.

The man in the blue suit leaned forward and offered a cigarette to the W.A.A.F. She accepted with a smile that made Laura forget the affectation of the bleached hair and scarlet lips. The man pointed out of the window and said:

"I used to be on a gun site here back in 1942. You can still see the Nissen huts; proper little country cottages now—I don't think."

The W.A.A.F. gazed out of the window and the two soldiers flicked their glances over the young man, observing everything about him from the hat on the rack above his head to his serviceable socks and new-looking shoes.

"Had your ticket long, mate?" The elder of the soldiers asked.

"Couple of weeks."

"Got a soft number?"

"Not yet. But it's early days still."

"Um." The younger soldier brought out a fingered packet of gold flake and stuck one in his mouth. As an afterthought, he stretched an arm across to Laura: "Cigarette, Ma'am?"

"Oh, . . . thank you . . . yes, I will. Thank you." Laura was brought back from her contemplation of the man in the blue suit. Of course that was why there was something familiar about him: the blue suit, the serviceable socks and new shoes, the striped shirt and collar and too bright tie: a demob. outfit, value twelve pounds ten. You saw them everywhere, good clothes but with a sameness which made the wearer as obvious as had his discarded uniform.

The soldier who had given her the cigarette continued:

"Going far, Ma'am?" She warmed again to the use of the word, 'Ma'am,' recalling the hundreds of times she had been called that, or had uttered it to her superior officers during the past years. But probably the soldier had picked it up from his American friends.

"No, only to London," she replied.

"That's where I live too. No place like it. Know the Angel?"

"I don't think so," she answered cautiously, wondering whether she should explain that her home was not in London. The baby on the lap of the woman next her created a diversion by beginning to cry, at first intermittently and then in a long yell of angry discomfort.

"Steady, little 'un," said the soldier while his companion pulled a comic face to distract the child.

The attention of the carriage was now focused on the mother and children.

"He's tired, poor sweet," said the W.A.A.F.

"He's wet," said the mother in a weary voice. "I'll have to change him." She glanced at the suitcase thrust beneath the feet of the other child.

The older of the two soldiers said:

"Here, I'll hold him while you get the necessary." He stretched out lean, strong hands, broad and tanned, but with remarkably clean finger nails. The mother let him have the baby and turned to the suitcase on the floor. While she was opening it and searching for a clean nappy, the soldier deftly stripped off the wet one, letting the baby lie across his knees whilst with one hand he held its tiny feet in the air. His gentleness was amazing and the child stopped crying.

"Mopping-up operations," said the soldier, grinning at the carriage. The mother looked up to see what was happening:

"Coo," she said, "you know how to do it. Got one of your own at home?"

"Had," said the soldier, and his face hardened suddenly, "but a V.2 got him and the wife."

"That's bad," said the woman and continued wearily: "my husband's in a sanatorium. Got his ticket two years ago, but he didn't get no better and they sent him away last week. T.B. they said it was. I'm taking the kids to live with his mum, so's to cut down on the overheads."

"That's tough," said the soldier, "but you've got his pension, no doubt?"

"The government won't give him one. They say it wasn't anything to do with the army." She took the baby back and quickly pinned on the clean nappy.

"Not attributable?"

"That's right. You see, there's always been T.B. in his family." She rocked the baby softly in her arms and already it was dozing off.

Laura, listening and watching, felt a sudden panic at the appalling ignorance which allowed people with tuberculosis to procreate without thought. And it would be worse now. War had increased tuberculosis just as it had increased venereal diseases. What chance had science against the complacency of the ignorant?

With both children asleep against her, the woman talked softly to the soldiers:

"Got your tickets at last?" she asked.

They were silent and then they looked at each other and laughed.

"Not yet," the elder of the two replied.

"Spot of leave, I suppose," the woman went on.

The younger soldier laughed again.

"Well, some might put it that way," he said.

The man in the demob. suit leant forward confidentially:

"On the run, pal?"

"Certainly not," replied the young soldier.

"It was just a case of whether we'd go to Germany again or stay at home," his companion added.

"So we thought it about time we started trying a bit of that 'private enterprise' you keep reading about in the papers."

"So there we are." The soldier lighted another cigarette.

"I know," said the woman, "my Bert did it once but they came and fetched him away."

The W.A.A.F.'s eyes were wide.

"I'd never dare," she said, and her voice was envious.

Laura felt shocked. It was somehow wrong that two soldiers— two nice soldiers like these—should be defaulters. During the war, going absent without leave was something to be ashamed of, something that the fighting soldier didn't do. Or if he did, he came back of his own accord and took his punishment in good humour. There had of course been cases of youths who'd managed to stay on the run for years, real deserters, but they hadn't been the sort of men these soldiers in the carriage were.

At least Laura didn't imagine they had. Now that the fighting was over she supposed that there were lots of decent men who just walked out of the Forces. Perhaps it didn't really matter. But she still felt shocked: desertion wasn't a soldierly act.

The train was rushing forward now, swaying its occupants gently as it sped along. Inside the carriage there was silence. The air was thick with breath and smoke. It was warm and soporific. Laura found herself drowsing. Her eyes closed and her thoughts juggled with the noise of the train, beating disconnected sentences through her mind. On the run . . . on the run . . . on the run . . . said the train and Laura thought: 'Aunt Bessie's come to stay for a week; that's an achievement.'

Got a soft number . . . got a soft number . . . jogged the wheels and Laura was conscious of well-being because her father had suggested that she should—if she wanted—go up to town for a week. That was nothing short of a miracle.

T.B. they said . . . T.B. they said . . . I'd never dare . . . I'd never dare . . . rumbled the train and Laura slept.

She did not awake until they arrived at King's Cross. One of the soldiers offered to carry her suitcase, but she said she could manage. He went off with his friend who was helping the woman with the children. The W.A.A.F. and the man in the demob. suit had already vanished. The deaf man had a porter.

Laura found a taxi. The situation had improved since she was last in town. Women porters and taxi queues were becoming things of the past. She gave the address of the Reunion Club for ex-service women which was in Seymour Street and sat back to enjoy the drive through London.

The city still looked drab in the late afternoon drizzle, and one was chiefly conscious of the enormous amount of scaffolding there was about the place. London was re-building, but what were the newspapers saying? That if rebuilding progressed at ten times the pace it was, there would still be ten times too few houses. It must be terrible to have no house to make a home in. Laura felt depressed.

She felt better as the taxi passed through Portland Place. The B.B.C. had discarded its blast walls. Funny how one had never really noticed that it had been camouflaged. So much of London had gone unintentionally grey during the war.

Once at the club, her exhilaration returned. She had a tiny room at the top of the building and she began to unpack her belongings with a sense of excitement. It reminded her suddenly of the feeling she had experienced when the black-out was finally lifted. A daredevil feeling because you could leave your windows uncurtained for all the world to look in. You were safe from V. weapons and at the same time protected because other people could keep an eye on you.

She washed, made up her face carefully and went downstairs.

The Reunion Club was run for ex-service women by ex-service women. Laura had joined as a founder member, but had not yet had an opportunity to use it. It might, she thought as she went downstairs, be rather awkward. For all she knew, she could find herself waited on by a fellow officer and taking coffee with a past batwoman. At least that is how the circular announcing the inauguration of the club had read. It sounded very democratic.

Actually it wasn't a bit like that. The overheads were sufficiently high to warrant a substantial membership fee. Only women in the upper income groups could afford to belong. Almost at once, Laura realized that the staff were very definitely of the ex-orderly category and that the members weren't. She was relieved and at the same time perturbed because her mind reflected the picture of the soldiers in the train, the woman with the children, the W.A.A.F. and, strangely, Dick Cobb at the Cock and Pheasant with his group of friends from the Training Centre at Little Copse.

It was much too late for afternoon tea. Laura noticed a hatch in the wall through which a waitress was receiving drinks on a small tray. She caught the girl's glance in passing and ordered a sherry. There was no sherry. Gin, Marsala or Dubonnet were available. Laura chose Marsala and sat back to survey the room. It was newly painted and rather bare. Framed and signed photographs of various members of the Royal family, disguised as members of the various women's services, adorned three walls. Her Majesty the Queen—not in uniform—held the position of honour over the fireplace as commandant-in-chief of all three services.

There was a green baize notice board by the door, a letter rack, a table with periodicals on it, and a number of arm-chairs, cushions and sundry furnishings reminiscent of those provided in war time by the Duchess of Northumberland's A.T.S. Comforts Fund.

The room was crowded, and its occupants seemed to know one another well. Laura thought: 'There isn't a face I can recognize; how much simpler it would be if we were still in uniform.'

And then someone spoke to her:

"Hello, Watson. It is Watson, isn't it?" The speaker was an elderly woman with short grey hair, wearing a neat tweed suit.

Laura said:

"Why it's Senior Commander Hall. How nice to see you again." With difficulty she prevented herself from adding the prefix 'Ma'am.' Geraldine Hall had been a group commander in Scotland when Laura was at the commando training centre. She said:

"I saw your name on the members list, but I don't remember seeing you in the club before."

"No. This is my first visit," Laura replied, and remembered that Miss Hall had been the nicest sort of senior officer. She did something very well too. . . . What was it? Of course, she played the piano; not classic but swing and dance music. At the time it seemed a little out of keeping with an A.T.S. officer of senior rank.

"You remember Prudence Wain?" the elder woman continued, looking towards a table in the corner.

"Why, of course. And there are Jill Fearnley and Mary Summers who were at Nottingham with me, and that girl who used to be the R.S.M. there before she went to O.C.T.U.," Laura exclaimed.

And quite suddenly the room which had been filled with strange females in strange attire broke into well-known faces with familiar voices and personalities remembered against a background of regimental life.

Geraldine Hall took Laura over to the far table. There were greetings and expressions of surprise and the surreptitious glances which women flicker at each other's clothes when they are no longer dressed alike.

Mary Summers was now secretary to a nerve specialist; Prudence Wain had a job in an advertising agency. The girl who used to be a regimental sergeant-major had taken up teaching and Jill Fearnley wrote scenarios for a film company. They said:

"What are you doing, Laura?"

"Living at home and keeping house for my father." Laura felt as she had in the old days when people asked her what her army job was and she said: 'General Duties,' whilst other women had exciting jobs like tactical control officers on gun sites, or technical ordnance officers.

Geraldine Hall said:

"Like me you've gone back to your old life. Mine's playing in small clubs of dubious character!"

The others laughed.

"Gerry plays at the New Merlin's Cave in Chelsea. She's a riot. And she doesn't do too badly in radio either."

Laura asked:

"What happened to Pooks Barber?"

"Married. Got her ticket, as they say, in Group 1. You remember the man? That rather wishy-washy little doctor who was M.O. when old Johnson was Commandant."

Jill Fearnley looked up from her nails which were long and red and received a great deal of attention. She had wide grey eyes and an impudent pale face:

"You don't by any chance mean Mildred Johnson?" she asked.

Mary Summers, who had a dark subdued beauty calculated to calm the most neurotic of her employer's patients, said:

"That's the one. She came to the Training Centre from the Scottish Group you took over, Gerry."

"I remember the take-over," Geraldine Hall said dryly, and the other girls laughed.

Laura said:

"Chief Commander Johnson? She was very efficient."

Jill pulled a face and snorted.

"But she was," Laura emphasized.

Jill Fearnley folded long, nervous hands together and put her head on one side.

"If ever there were a bitch," she said, "Mildred Johnson was the Queen Bitch. Oh, I know, she ended up a Queen A.T., too, but promotion always did come to those who could no longer be supported on a human level."

Laura remembered vividly the woman they were talking about. A tall, thwarted creature who suffered from a bad skin. Unloved and unlovely, but not inefficient. She said:

"The troops liked her, and they always knew best."

"The troops?" Jill's voice was scornful. "The troops she dealt with in Nottingham knew her for precisely three weeks. They were recruits and only heard her speech of welcome and her speech of farewell. Then they went to their units. It was we officers who had to bear with her month in and month out. I shall never forgive her for the way she made our life hell in the mess."

Mary Summers cut in:

"Jill's right. We can say it now. She treated her officers like convicts. We were never off parade. I put in for a posting in the end."

"And tell them what happened," Jill urged.

"Well," Mary's lovely, calm face, looked a little wry, "I wasn't well. The M.O. said I should have a rest from training. I got a certificate and sent it in with my application for a posting. I'm afraid I was a little malicious then." She paused and smiled.

"Go on," said Jill.

"I put in my application that, in any case, sarcasm and constant nagging were not conducive to good health or good work. I asked for this to be passed to higher authority."

"What happened?" They were all curious now.

"She tore it up. I saw it burned in front of my eyes."

Even Laura was shocked. Gerry Hall said:

"What did you do, Mary?"

Mary's face grew wryer:

"I was weak," she admitted. "I should have sent a copy on myself, but I didn't. I simply said I'd like a job at the War Office. I got it too, on Johnson's high recommendation. Pure blackmail, I know," she laughed softly.

Laura said:

"I can't believe it."

"It was true."

"Of course it was true," Jill added vehemently. "She was a bully with all the cowardice of a bully when it came to a show-down. God, how I hated them all."

"But they weren't like that. The A.T.S. wasn't like that a bit." Laura's voice sounded almost desperate.

"Of course it wasn't, my dear," Geraldine Hall spoke softly. "It was a fine organization. I was in it all through, both in the ranks and as an officer. It was big and vital and had magnificent people in it. You'll always find some individuals who don't come up to standard, just as you'll always find some who can't adapt themselves to community life. Like Jill," she twinkled across at the impudent face opposite. "But I am quite convinced that not one of us sitting round this table did not benefit in one way or another from having been in the A.T.S. We gained as much as we gave—in some cases more."

They looked at her solemnly for a moment and then Jill said:

"All right, Jerry. Have it your own way if you like. I'll admit that even I gained something: the capacity to wait for hours without getting impatient. Does that satisfy you?"

"It wouldn't satisfy me, but maybe it does you," Geraldine replied, dryly.

"I think," Mary Summers said, "that I probably learned more about how to deal with all sorts of people and situations during my three years' service than I would have in a hundred years otherwise."

"And I know that I got self-confidence," Prudence Wain put in. "I can never be grateful enough for that now that I'm back in civvy street, particularly in my madhouse of an advertising agency. What about you, Laura?"

"I don't know really," Laura frowned. "I just know that I loved it and I miss it terribly. It was the companionship and the freedom . . ."

"Freedom?" Jill broke in incredulously.

"Yes, freedom. From trivial upsets and fear of the future. I don't know how to put it really. It was just being one of a lot of people all with a job to do but finding time to enjoy life as well. Not having to worry. Not having to be on one's guard all the time."

"Well, that's the strangest description of the pleasures of army life that I've heard yet," Jill replied.

The girl who had been an R.S.M. and was now a teacher said:

"I know what she means. I feel it too. We were all in it together and working for the same thing. We may have had our personal likes and dislikes but it would never have occurred to us to do one another down. Quite the reverse, in fact. We built up a sort of collective friendliness. I think that feeling was perhaps stronger among soldiers than A.T.S., but we had it all the same. Once you're a civilian again you realize the difference. It's cut-throat competition and every woman out for herself. I am conscious of it all the time, even in my profession. It's a pity, but I suppose it can't be helped."

Prudence said:

"My brother said exactly the same thing—only less politely!"

"So did Helen Townsend's husband," Laura mused.

"Helen Townsend?" Geraldine asked. "Have you seen her lately?"

"Yes, we live in the same village."

"She was at the War Office with me for a short while," Mary Summers said. "What's she doing now?"

"Her husband's back from the Far East. He's our local doctor."

"She had a handsome Commando boy friend in Scotland, if I remember rightly," Prudence Wain said laughingly.

"Faithfulness was unfashionable during the war," Jill added, maliciously.

Laura said hastily:

"He was an old friend of the Townsends. His family live in the village too. Helen's terribly happy now Gyp is home." She wondered why she bothered to defend Helen. These other women did not know her well and would probably never see her again, so no harm could come of their casual chatter. She remembered again seeing Brian and Helen at that hotel in Dumfries. Helen was supposed to have been on leave in Oxford at the time. She hadn't seen Laura who was having tea in the back lounge. Or had she? Laura was never quite sure about that. And had Helen and Brian been lovers? They must have been, but you could never be certain. It wasn't like Helen. And yet why should she have been in Dumfries when she'd left an Oxford leave address with the unit?

The others were still chattering.

"Do you remember Jane Belmont? She's married now."

"Peggy had her baby last November."

"Doreen took a scholarship for Oxford."

"Old Mother Gardiner stood for Parliament and damn nearly got in."

"Ma'am Fellowes married her Yank and has opened another branch of her business in New York."

It went on and on and, quite suddenly, Laura felt desperately tired. Everybody but herself was married or doing something interesting. Only she was left out and lonely. She could have wept for the years snatched from her life. Years of hard work and happiness with the promise of something exciting just ahead. A lovely phase of her life which peace had cut short, leaving her instead just those number of years older.

Did any of the others have the regrets she had? Perhaps Helen Townsend did. But then Helen had compensations: her home and Gyp.

*   *   *   *

There's nothing nicer than one's own home on a wet winter day. I have always felt that, but I am particularly conscious of it today.

I love this room because I have helped to make it. There is nothing spectacular or expensive about it; the chair covers are old and the carpets well worn and the furniture squats unobtrusively in familiar corners.

I never get a feeling of frustration when I visit other people's homes because I prefer my own. I prefer the colour and the shape of my room, and the way the fire draws and the set of the curtains against the rain-drenched windows. There is a great deal of rain today, but here I am warm and secure.

Gyp may be back for tea—he generally is—and I shall be glad to see him. Even this room is not a good place to be alone in for very long, it is too full of thoughts. I am always thinking when I should be feeling and feeling when I should be thinking.

It was strange when Gyp came back. He looked almost as I'd known he would except that his hair had begun to thin above his brow and was a little grey on each side; and his skin looked burned up and yellow. It still does. He was thin and taut and, mentally, a little out of focus. I remember we went to London to buy him civilian clothes and on the buses he would pull out a handful of silver and coppers and say to the conductor, "Take what you want, I don't understand these coins."

People in the hotel would talk to him about the election and housing and education, and he would answer, quite politely, with a faintly puzzled look in his eyes, as if he didn't really know what they were trying to say. He told me at the time that he'd forgotten the jargon, and then he apologized. I asked him what jargon and he said:

"Civilized talk. It doesn't mean a damn really. I've been talking and thinking in a different language for too long. Never mind, I'm adaptable."

I think he still feels like that at times—a foreigner in his own country. I was like that, to a lesser extent, when I left the army. How much more must he have felt lost after those years in the East. I try to remember that all the time. Gyp seemed too brittle a person to endure great hardship, and yet that is what he has done and it hasn't broken him. But he is different.

No doubt we are both changed. Perhaps it is as obvious to him as it is to me. I can't help wondering what he really feels and yet I can't ask him. It is something he must tell me first—in case the change is in me only. Perhaps it is because of Brian that I am sensitive for both of us.

I don't think of Brian these days. I have neither seen nor heard of him since that night at the Cock and Pheasant. It is strange the way life can parcel itself up so that past vividness becomes a dimness that is barely recognizable.

I am with Gyp and we are happy in our fashion, glad to be together again and bound by things like this room and his job here and the circumstances of the moment. Gyp has come back to me and his presence has ceased to be a surprise. He is the same Gyp and, now that he has been home for a while, he is almost indistinguishable from the man who went away in 1940. He is companionable and secure; but I am married to a stranger.

I can explain that to no one, but it is true. I am a little dazed, for to have such intimacy with a stranger makes me feel rather abandoned. I have never been promiscuous, but if I had I think I should have felt this way. I am in love with nothing and with no one. I feel and I think, but at no time do the two processes blend to produce that state of fulfilment which must exist for true happiness.

I hear the front door opening and the sound of voices. Gyp has brought someone back to tea. I ring the bell which will tell Jenny that the doctor is home. Jenny is the ex-Wren who used to work for the Watsons until she could bear Mr. Watson no longer. Laura does not begrudge me her services now, because domestic workers are becoming plentiful again, but Mr. Watson will never forgive me for taking Jenny over. Gyp can't believe that anyone could seriously be called Jenny and have been in the W.R.N.S., but that is her name: Jenny Cookson. Gyp always calls her Jenny Wren—never Jenny.

He comes into the room and Michael Cross is with him. Gyp likes Michael. They seem to have a lot to talk about. That is something new about Gyp, he is always happy talking to people like Michael and Peter Gurney and Dick Cobb and even Laura Watson—ex-service people. Before the war he wasn't fond of talk; he was almost unsociable, irritated when visitors to the house didn't leave punctually, jealous of our solitude. Now the house is always full, neighbours can come in at any time of the day or night and Gyp is pleased to see them. I don't mind and sometimes I feel closer to Gyp when there are other people round us.

Gyp says:

"Hello, darling. Where is Jenny Wren and the tea, or are we early?"

"You are early, but I've rung and there are muffins."

I turn to Michael: "Michael, I am full of guilt, I promised your mother a recipe for baked rabbit in cider and I've completely forgotten to take it round."

Michael laughs easily:

"Don't worry, Helen, I'm sure she's forgotten too. She's up to her ears in a new series of articles on the resettlement of the resettled or some such post-post-war scheme. An entirely new venture!"

I like Michael Cross because even when he is being facetious he is kind. You can see his kindness behind his deep set eyes and slightly crooked mouth. He has a strange face that you can see through, a brittle expression. You have the feeling that you would know at once if he were hurt or pleased, and that it would be quite easy to do either.

Gyp is fussing about the tea which Jenny has brought in and soon we are smearing our fingers with margarine from the muffins. It will be nice when, one day, peace brings us enough butter.

It is Gyp's day off from evening surgery, so that we do not hurry. It is wonderful what a good log fire and a sense of leisure can do to people. Leisure is still a novelty and neither Gyp nor I have quite got used to it yet. There is all the difference in the world between off duty time in war and spare time in peace.

We have finished tea and pulled chairs nearer the fire. Gyp sits on a pouffe closest to the fire. I don't believe he has really been warm since he came back from the East. He leans back against the inglenook and stretches long legs across the hearthrug. He is thin, like an underfed horse, and the firelight flickers in the hollows of his cheeks and eyes. But he looks wiry and tough and in many ways stronger than Michael whose rounded face is pale and still has the uncertainty of youth in its lines.

"Tell me," Gyp says, drawing up his knees and leaning towards Michael, "tell me . . ."

I wonder yet again at his hungry curiosity. Ever since he has been home he has been acquisitive of facts and figures that happened whilst he was away. His lust for knowledge of what he has missed devours him. It is as if he'd been put to sleep for five years against his will and now he must catch up, replenish that part of his mind which stores important impressions. But he has not been asleep. He has lived those five years just as I have. I know little of medicine and less of the tropics. When he talks about the fighting and disease of the Far East I am fascinated. But he mentions them very seldom. His real interest seems to be in what has happened in England.

However, it is Michael's book he is talking about now, not the war in England. Michael says, self-consciously:

"All this must be terribly boring for Helen."

"Is it, darling?" Gyp takes one of my hands in his.

"You know it isn't; both of you." I smile at them.

"Helen has brought the knack of not being bored to a fine art since I've been home," Gyp laughs and continues, "actually she's one of those rare women you haven't got to bother about boring because she's too intelligent." He squeezes my hand and hunches himself into a more compact shape on the pouffe.

He is between me and the fire. Because I love him, I wonder why he must always be the screen between me and warmth. And I suddenly see Brian there by the fire, too. But he is standing up leaning back against the mantelpiece and firelight is playing over my face and body, warm and caressing.

Gyp has moved to the chair pulled up for him between Michael's and mine.

"You looked cold," he says in answer to my unspoken thought, and I wonder whether he is just very intuitive or what?

Michael's voice is light and quick, but Gyp's unemphatic tones seem to punctuate the conversation with an urgency that is unnecessary in the peaceful setting of this room. The rhythm of their voices beats on my unreceptive mind. But I am interested—I will be interested—in what they say.

Michael is writing a book. It is eating him up a little. Gyp is interested because it is a book about ex-service men and women. As a newspaper man, Michael is sick of the glib reporting novels which sold so well during the war. His novel is to be different. It must be fictional, imaginative, and yet at the same time an accurate representation of the post-war set-up. The reporter in Michael is adamant on that point and the artist in him is distracted. It is his first novel and very important to him.

Gyp is interested in an entirely different way. He believes that there are two groups of people in England: those who fought and those who did not. He sees sharp division and almost active dislike between the soldier and the civilian. Michael doesn't agree. He says that the average service man was only a civilian in fancy dress which he discarded with as little thought as an old pair of shoes. Gyp argues that the ex-service man has a justifiable grudge against the civilian and is not getting the deal suggested to him by the education wallahs and the ABCA pamphlets.

"Neither is the civilian, for that matter," Michael protests, "it's as chaotic today in civvy street as it ever was during the war. Security from bombs and V-weapons isn't everything. They're all in it together now, civilians and ex-service blokes; same hopes, same scares, same struggle. There's no animosity between them. In any case your soldier knows quite well that his pal in the factory had the war at his front door for a good many years."

"I agree, but you've forgotten the big difference: your civilian had his front door—blitzed and blasted as it may have been— but your soldier was hundreds of miles away from his. You'll never convince me that the soldier's going to forget that. I saw too much of what separation can do. The nervous strain of not getting news from home—or getting the wrong sort, distorted by well-meaning busybodies, no doubt. Most chaps could put up with discomfort, dirt and danger. What got them down was uncertainty, and the appalling feeling of impotence. You can't pop back a thousand miles on your off-duty day just to see how they're getting on at home. All you can do is sit down and write a letter which you know isn't going to get anywhere for a hell of a time and, by then, you may be dead—or feeling much better!"

Gyp stops speaking and gives me one of his funny, sideways smiles. Is he talking about himself? Did he feel like that or is he describing what other men told him? I have a sudden longing to put my arms round him and hold his head close against me until he relaxes and can speak naturally. My heart sings with hypocrisy at the thought.

Michael says:

"You're off target, Gyp. I'm trying to get the picture now, not as it was during the war. I'll admit you're right about the soldier overseas, and the airman too; and you could feel pretty far away in a bomber over Berlin even though you might be home for eggs and bacon in the morning. But today, now they're out of it, the men are civilians again, citizens, whatever you like to call them. They're not a little race unto themselves as you're trying to make out."

"I think they still are," Gyp is rocking himself backwards and forwards in his chair. "I think they have a strong urge to band themselves into something worthwhile again. A soldier is toughened and perhaps coarsened by war, but he is purified in battle. I can't describe it exactly, but there is a sort of exaltation and selflessness about a chap who's just missed death and maybe seen his pals killed. And that spirit—if you care to call it that—pervades the whole business of being a soldier."

"But it doesn't make a man a soldier for the rest of his life."

"I'm not so sure." Gyp says slowly. Michael twists the signet ring on his left hand.

"But, Gyp, you're trying to make out that the experience of war, from the fighting soldier's point of view, so affects him that he might as well go into a monastery or a lunatic asylum or anything else that segregates him physically and mentally from the rest of humanity. I just don't believe it."

"No, I'm not. I'm only saying that having experienced the unselfishness of battle, he's noticing the difference now—and disliking it. He's reacting against the competitive, self-seeking everyday existence which is civvy street. He's bitter about it and on the defensive, and he wants to surround himself with fellows who feel the same way. He doesn't put it into words but what he means is that having come up against real greatness, he's got a taste for it. He wants to sun himself again in the brightness of impersonal endeavour; the shoddy and second rate don't satisfy him. That's why he and all his pals are searching for something that's going to bring that brightness back."

"You mean a leader?"

"Or an ideal."

"It smacks too much of dictatorship for me." Michael stretches himself and goes to look out of the window. "What do you think, Helen?"

I watch the firelight making strange patterns on Gyp's face and the reflection in his eyes, and I know that Michael has not understood him.

"Yes, what do you think, Helen?" Gyp repeats and it is his familiar, teasing voice again.

I feel inadequate. What can I, who sat in England, know of the men who spent years abroad? My war was drab with rules and restrictions, broken by intervals of escapism on leave. I was not conscious of real greatness. And yet, when I listen to Gyp, I feel response vibrating within me.

"I think," I begin hesitatingly, "I think that you're both right in a way."

They laugh softly and Michael says:

"Oh, Helen, what an admission of weakness!"

"But I do," I repeat more strongly. "I know what Gyp means and there's nothing fascist about it. But I believe very few people felt like that. Those who did can't forget, and to them life must be disillusionment now. But they're the minority, the few individuals who were different, more receptive than the rest."

"The mystics of the army?" Michael raises an eyebrow.

"No. Just the real people, the truly sensitive."

"And the rest?" Gyp asks.

"The rest are like me, civilians in fancy dress who never disassociated themselves from the families and friends they left at home. I think, at times, we got near to the spirit Gyp was talking about, but not near enough. And we have forgotten so quickly. We have picked up our lives where we left them. The interim period of war has already become something rather difficult to remember clearly."

They look at me as if I were something they hadn't seen before, but their eyes are not unkind, only disbelieving.

"I don't suppose," Gyp says, "that women ever react the same way as men. Perhaps it's just as well. Let's have a drink." He goes to the cocktail cupboard and mixes a shaker of dry martini. "Well, here's to the book anyhow, Michael. When's it going to be finished?"

"Another month, I hope. Thanks."

I have switched on the light and we are no longer three voices but three compact bodies who enjoy the comfort of leisure and the dry tang of an iced drink. I have a sudden feeling that we are very consciously civilized.

Gyp builds up the fire and Michael says:

"Oh lord, I must go. I promised mother to be back before six-thirty. See you at the Cock and Pheasant tomorrow?"

"I shouldn't be surprised." Gyp shows him out and I am left to draw the curtains. The room is so friendly, I want it to be like this all the time.

Gyp comes back and we refill our glasses.

"I like Michael," he says.

"So do I."

"It would do him good to get away from mother all the same."

"But she's awfully nice, Gyp. Not a bit possessive like old man Watson is with Laura."

"Hum . . . I wonder."

We drift into one of those silences which are becoming noticeable when we are alone now. Is it that we have nothing more to say to one another or that we have too much which cannot be spoken of? These are moments of unease when they should be ones of understanding.

"Tell me—" Gyp begins and stops suddenly.

"What, darling?"

"Nothing."

From the wing-backed chair I watch him frowning down at the fire. I wish he would relax.

He turns and looks at me.

"Helen. . . . It's no good pretending, is it?"

All this is something which has happened to me before. The words and the setting are a repetition: Gyp by the mantelpiece with one hand in his coat pocket and the other twiddling a cocktail glass; firelight splaying across the hearthrug and the picture opposite not quite straight above the writing desk. I know what we are going to say and the words we shall use.

"Pretending what, Gyp?"

"That things are the same. I know you don't love me—at least not as before. Don't try to hide it up too much."

He can smile as he speaks whilst I feel nothing but panic in my mind.

"Gyp, it isn't true. I do love you. You know that."

"Put it another way, if you like," he talks calmly as if I were one of his patients, "we're—I mean you're not in love with me any more. You used to be and now it's over. You're not, are you?"

I can't lie to Gyp.

"No, I'm not in love with you, Gyp. But I love you."

He turns suddenly away from me, leaning his elbows on the mantelpiece and cupping his face with his hands.

"You remind me of something," he says.

"What?"

"You remember I broke my return journey in Egypt. I came back from there on a boat carrying several thousand chaps from the Middle East. 'Python' men returning at the end of their overseas tour. There was the strangest atmosphere on board; none of the rejoicing at getting home again which had been evident on the Far East repatriation ship I'd done the first half of my journey on. Instead there was a feeling of unease, a dulled acceptance of the inevitable. I found out why. Most of the men had left a heart in the Middle East, and here they were on the way back to the heart they'd left at home. Tricky work, you know."

There is nothing I can find to say.

"Helen," Gyp continues softly, "have you left a heart somewhere. I'd rather know, you know. Have you?"

Again I cannot lie and I need not lie. I know now that Brian never had my heart.

"No, Gyp. I haven't."

"Then why, why in God's name, must you be so bloody kind to me?" He turns on me and his face is distorted with emotion. I am too startled to answer and we can only stare at each other in misery.

There is the sound of the front door being opened and the voices of Angela Worthing and Peter Gurney asking for us.

"Gyp, Gyp . . ." I whisper, but he has gained control again.

"Put out more glasses," he declaims as Jenny opens the door for them, "we'll soon be rivalling the Cock and Pheasant for customers!"

* * * *

Behind and above the taproom at the Cock and Pheasant sprawled the Cobb home. The windows were small, the ceilings low and there were few modern amenities. Maggie Cobb cooked, and the family ate, in the long kitchen downstairs, above the cellars and next to the public bar. Upstairs there were bedrooms, the parlour and the room that used to be Maggie's mother's and had now become a general living room with John Cobb's big desk at one end where he kept the books. This room had dark curtains and was overburdened with pictures in heavy, black frames: pink hunting scenes with hounds, an interior with two red-faced men toasting an old fashioned, lacy barmaid and a reproduction of 'Bubbles.' Above the mantel was an enlarged photograph of Maggie and John on their wedding day. Above that again, dangling from a kitchen airer fixed to the ceiling, Tommy's smalls.

Lily Cobb and her sister-in-law sat in wicker armchairs on either side of the fireplace. It was Lil's night off from the bars.

"In the W.A.A.F. they made us sew bits of coloured stuff on the black-out curtains," she said, tacking a tiny patch on to a pair of diminutive pants.

"Whatever for?" Elsie asked looking up from her knitting.

"To make the barrack rooms look more like home." They laughed together at this and Elsie, in whom the discomfort of pregnancy was again beginning to make itself felt, shifted her weight slightly and the wicker chair squeaked and rustled at the movement.

"Drat this chair," Elsie said, "it's like the one in my kitchen; looks all right till you try sitting in it."

"In the last mess I was in we had a little dumpy chair they called the Nursing Mother. It was ever so comfortable; supported you right up your back. Nobody ever knew how we came by it. They scrounged it for the officers' mess in the end."

"You still miss it, don't you Lil?"

"What, the Nursing Mother?" Lily smiled across at her sister-in-law.

"No, silly. The W.A.A.F. and being with the R.A.F."

"Not really, but I think about it a lot. More now than I did at first. I keep remembering all the little things like being on night shift and dishing up early breakfasts for the chaps coming in. And what a toffee nose the sergeant was till she was busted. Getting pegged for wearing silk stockings. Oh, all the sort of unimportant things that went on every day. I'd like to have stayed on after Charlie was killed; I'd like to have gone overseas, India or some place; but I was expecting by then."

Elsie looked curiously at the thin young face opposite her. She and Lil had only become friends quite recently. Before that, they hadn't really known one another. Lil had been away in the services when Elsie married Dick and when Stevie was born. It was only since she'd been pregnant again that Elsie had taken to coming round of an evening to talk to Lil and Lil had got into the way of running across to Elsie's and Dick's cottage when she wasn't working.

Elsie said:

"They didn't keep you in after the third month, did they?"

"Not supposed to, but we had a girl who had her baby in her sleeping quarters. Nobody knew nothing about it until the Flight Officer went round on inspection at about half past eleven that morning and there was the A.C.W.1 and the baby both crying."

"You'd have thought they'd have noticed, wouldn't you?"

"She was a big girl and always looked a bundle in her uniform. Besides it wasn't difficult to dodge medical inspection. I was five months before I told them."

"Were you frightened, Lil?"

"No, I wasn't frightened 'cos Charlie and I were getting married anyhow and then, when he didn't come back, I wasn't frightened 'cos I wanted to have the baby. I was just unhappy about Mum and Dad."

"What did Charlie think?"

"Charlie?" Lil looked strangely across at Elsie. "Charlie didn't know, Elsie."

There seemed suddenly a very big gulf between the two girls sitting by the fire and Lil, the younger, appeared somehow to be of greater stature and of infinite maturity.

"You mean you didn't even tell Charlie?" Elsie asked.

"No. I wasn't sure myself for a long time. I'm funny that way. And then he was on ops. and they wouldn't have let him have leave from the station he was on just at that time. He'd only have worried. A pilot has plenty enough to think about as it is. Besides we were getting married next leave. I wish now I hadn't let the Flight Officer persuade me to write to Mum and Dad about it. I'd rather have had Tommy on my own."

"But where?"

"In a home. They tell you all about it in the services if you can't go to your own people. I'd have done better in many ways to have gone to London and then got a job there—something I could have taken Tommy to with me, cooking probably, like I did in the W.A.A.F."

"I don't see why you'd have been better off in London than here, Lil." Elsie shifted her weight again and took a deep breath.

"Too many nosey parkers in the country, Elsie. Kirton's a terrible place for curiosity. You'd be surprised if you knew the questions I got asked. They still think Tommy's father was a Yank. What about a cup of tea?"

"I could do with one if it isn't too early."

"It's never too early for tea. You should have seen the pots we used to brew in the W.A.A.F." She went to a cupboard in the corner and brought out cups, saucers and a teapot. The kettle on the grid by the open fire was bubbling softly. As she made the tea, she said: "D'you remember Mrs. Pilcher, Elsie? No, you wouldn't; she left the village before you and Dick were married. She used to live along the other end of High Street. Well, she came back to stay with her sister, Mrs. Metcalf, last month, and I saw her coming down Pilferer's Lane one afternoon with her eyes popping out of her head for a look at our back yard. So just as she got there, I picked Tommy up in my arms and held him out to her and before she could say anything I said:

"Hello, Mrs. Pilcher, d'you like my baby? That's what I mean about the country, Elsie."

"Oh you shouldn't let it worry you, Lil. It isn't everyone's like that."

"Oh, I don't worry. But Mum don't like it much; it sort of gets under her skin at times. Besides there are other reasons why it would have been better to have had Tommy in London or some big town: Health centres, child clinics, day nurseries and things. You don't get them down here. Not that Dr. Townsend isn't all right and we're on his panel, but in a town you get all the advantages of the best poshed up attention a child can need. I learned all about that in the W.A.A.F. when I took a mothercraft course. You'd have laughed at me, Else."

"Why, Lil?"

"I didn't see it was funny then, but I do now. Me with my corporal's stripes and nearly five months gone, taking a lot of A.C.W.1's to a mothercraft course in the town nearby, being run at one of those Polytechnics. I bet I learned more at that course than any of the other girls. I had reason to."

Elsie laughed, a little self-consciously. She felt very secure in her pregnancy. Lily went on:

"I'd like Tommy to go to school when he's three; you know, nursery school or whatever it is. He ought to mix with a lot of kids 'cos there aren't any others in this house. But what chance do I get here of sending him to school? Oh, the village school's better than it was, I know, but they're still short staffed and the children don't learn nothing. In any case Tommy can't go there till he's five or six. I can tell you, Else, I'm thinking very seriously of packing up here and taking Tommy to London."

"Oh, Lil, you couldn't. What about your mum and dad?"

"That's just it. I couldn't go until they got some help here. But it's not so difficult now to get people. Mind you, I don't think Dad would make the fuss. He's a Londoner himself; he'd understand."

"I don't like to hear you talking like that, Lil. It don't seem right somehow. Besides, what would you do?"

"Same trade as this. It's easy in London and the pay's good." Lily put aside her mending and leaned forward in her chair, her face cupped between her hands, staring into the fire. Against the worn green chair cover and the sombre papered wall she appeared almost luminous. The firelight flowed over her face, softening the curves until she looked like a kid of ten with untidy dark curls falling over her fingers. Or so Elsie thought, watching the changing expressions on her sister-in-law's face.

"And where would you live in London?" Elsie asked firmly, bringing Lily's ideas back to the practicalities of life.

Lily got up and went to the door where her overcoat was hanging. She felt in the pocket and came back to the fire with a letter in her hands.

"You wouldn't tell anybody, would you, Else?"

"Not if you didn't want me to," Elsie replied and her full blue eyes were round with curiosity.

"Not even Dick?" Lily asked.

"Not if it's anything crazy. He's got enough silly ideas in his head as it is." Elsie spoke with feeling.

"Dick got silly ideas? What sort?" Lily was for a second deflected from her own interests. Dick had always been her favourite brother.

"Well you know what he is, Lil. All them politics and things. He's gone and joined the Dimstone branch of the Communist Party."

"Why, that's ten miles away."

"Maybe, but he cycles there just the same. There isn't a C.P. branch any nearer. Mind you, I'm not sure he isn't right in some ways. I've always been Labour myself, but Dick says the C.P. will get more done."

Lily dismissed the subject with a quick smile.

"Well, what I'm going to show you hasn't anything to do with politics. It's a letter from Charlie's sister."

"I didn't know you kept up with his family," Elsie said.

"I don't. Not with his parents. But Joan and I always got along all right; she's married and on her own in London. I wrote to her about six weeks ago and I heard from her yesterday. You can read it if you like." She handed the letter across to Elsie who held it sideways so that the light from the centre of the room fell across the pencilled lines. She read:

'Dear Lil,

Well dear it was nice to hear from you again dear. Jim and I were only talking about you the other day and wondering how you and little Tommy were getting on. Well dear it's funny to think of you with a baby and the photograph was lovely. Jim and I have been here for nearly a year now. The Vigilantes put us here first and it is very nice. A bit difficult to clean but it is very nice. So dear if you and Tommy come to London there is a room you can have. Well dear so long and keep your chin up. Jim sends his love to you dear and Tommy. Lots of love from

Joan.

x x x x x These are for Tommy.'

Elsie handed the letter back to Lil.

"So what?" she asked, trying not to feel jealous that Lil had kept her plans so secret.

"It wouldn't be difficult," Lily said pensively, poking at the fire and adding a log from the wicker basket near her chair. "I could put Tommy in a day nursery for a bob a day while I went out to work."

"Not if you were in your dad's trade, Lil. The hours wouldn't fit."

"Well maybe I'd work in a shop instead. What's it matter? There'd be a job somewhere and Tommy could have the best there is to give him, right on his doorstep so to speak. London— think of it Else—London with all it could give us and no curious eyes, no busybodies wondering every day what you're going to do next." Lily got up quickly and went to stare out of the window. Then she drew the curtains and switched on the light. She turned with her back against the door and her arms pressed back to her sides. "Think what it means to me, Else. London, and safety from nosey parkers. Wouldn't you do it?"

"Me?" Elsie twisted heavily in her chair. "Fat chance I have to do anything." She spoke bitterly and Lily stopped half-way across the room.

"Why, what's the matter, Else?" she asked.

"Matter? Well I'm not a country girl am I? Maybe I wasn't born in London but Nottingham's a town, isn't it?"

"But Elsie, you don't want to leave Kirton do you?" Lily looked in amazement at her sister-in-law.

"I never said I did, did I?" Elsie spoke fiercely.

"I don't understand, Else. . . ."

"Understand what?"

"What you're getting so worked up about then; sort of angry about."

"I'm not getting worked up or sort of angry. I'm just thinking. See?" Quite suddenly the tears were in her eyes, and her shoulders shook.

Lily was on her knees beside Elsie's chair. "Don't, please don't. What's the matter, Else? What's wrong?"

"Nothing." Elsie found a handkerchief and blew her nose self-consciously.

"But it must be something. You can tell me, Else. I won't say anything. Was it something I said?"

Elsie looked at her sister-in-law silently. Then the tears flowed again and this time she was unable to check her sobs. After a moment she whispered:

"It's the war, Lil, that's done it to us. What can I do with one baby and another on the way and a husband that's all knocked to pieces? Even if I wanted something I couldn't get it. That's what the war's done, Lil. I'm all turned up and I don't suppose it'll ever be the same again." She was blowing her nose once more, finding a dry corner to the twisted handkerchief.

Lily said:

"But Else, you're married and you've got Dick and little Stevie, and soon you'll have another baby. You're safe."

"Safe?" Elsie snorted into the handkerchief.

"Well, you're married and you love Dick, don't you?"

Elsie had got herself under control again.

"Oh yes, I love Dick all right. There's nothing phoney about that. And I love Stevie and the baby that's coming, but that doesn't mean safety, Lil."

"It would to me," Lily said simply.

"Oh no it wouldn't. Not with Dick like he is. For two pennies he'd chuck up the Training Centre and cart us all off to London to starve whilst he tub-thumped somewhere."

"You couldn't," said Lil, logically, "starve on his captain's pension."

"Couldn't we? You don't know what it costs to live in a town, Lil. What with babies and everything, you need a packet."

"Well, you haven't got to have more babies after this one."

"But we love them, Lil. I wouldn't mind six, nor would Dick. You don't understand. It's all such a muddle. Dick can't help being the way he is; that's what the war's done to him. It's made him all jumpy so he doesn't know half the time what it is he really wants, and I don't know either. I never feel settled these days. Still it's no good worrying. I don't as a rule, but being pregnant and all that makes me act silly sometimes like tonight. I could do with a cigarette, Lil; have you got one?"

Lily fetched a packet from her coat pocket and lit one for Elsie. All the time she was thinking that perhaps having Tommy wasn't anything like so complicated as Elsie's life. She felt beautifully compact with just herself and Tommy, wrapped into one neat parcel that could be posted off anywhere at any time—and arrive safely—whereas Elsie had all the business of Dick's health and another confinement and getting coal for the cottage and never knowing really when Dick's job would come to an end at Little Copse. Maybe being married was like that, but somehow she didn't think it would have been with Charlie. But Charlie had been killed, not wounded like Dick. She sighed, and in the silence of the room it sounded like a shout.

Elsie said:

"Aren't I silly, Lil? Snivelling away about nothing. I didn't mean I wanted to leave Kirton; I don't. Perhaps some day we'll have to, and that's what gets me down. Still I don't believe in meeting troubles half way, and the doctor says it's bad to worry when you're carrying. You wouldn't tell Dick I'd been silly, would you, Lil?"

"You know I wouldn't, Else. Listen! Was that Tommy crying?"

Elsie said:

"No it's someone coming upstairs. How those stairs squeak."

There was a knock at the door and Jenny Cookson from the doctor's house came in. It was her evening off and she said:

"Hello Lil; hello, Elsie. Mrs. Cobb said she didn't think you'd gone to bed yet." Her eyes were hollowed in darkness and she looked a little vacantly round the room.

Lily said:

"Come and sit down. Where've you been, to the pictures?"

"No. There's only a soppy film this week, something about the Yanks in the Pacific. I've been downstairs with a couple of lads from Little Copse. They got a bit lit up so I thought I'd come and see you. How's Tommy, Lil?"

"Asleep, I hope. You look tired, Jenny. Here, have a chair."

Jenny sat down and said:

"It's my gastric again. I've been having a bit of the old trouble."

"Then you shouldn't be drinking beer," Elsie said firmly.

"I wasn't having anything but a shandy."

Lily asked:

"What's Doctor Townsend say?"

"Just that I must be careful about my eats. And he says I shouldn't ever have been conscripted and I ought to have had a pension for aggravation." She looked a little proud of this.

"Can't he do anything for you now?" Elsie asked.

"He says he'll try but it's ever so difficult me having been passed A1 at my calling-up board and coming out for nerves and not gastrics. He says it would have been easier if I'd been in the A.T.S."

"Why the A.T.S., Jenny?" Lily asked.

"Because of being part of the Army proper. He says they got better attention like."

"So did the W.A.A.F."

"Well, maybe. Anyhow he said it was all something to do with military law and getting certain rights to appeal. I forgot everything he said, but he made out the W.R.N.S. dicing have a fair chance."

"Camp followers, we used to call them," Lily put in. "What made you choose the W.R.N.S.?" Elsie asked. "Choose? I didn't choose. I told them at the exchange I wanted munitions but they put me in the services. Mind you, I'm not saying I minded much. After all it made a change from domestic service. There's nothing like a change for making you glad to get back to the old life."

"Didn't you like the W.R.N.S.?" Lily asked.

"Well I didn't mind it. Being a conscript made it more awkward like. Still there was several of us and we had a bit of a laugh on our own. Most of them was ever so stuck up. They always went with the naval officers. Ever so posh they thought they were, but we didn't mind much, we had our chaps too, and we got more perks than they did in the long run; the galley blokes always saw us right—unless they was W.R.N.S.—and we had some smashing parties the toffee noses wouldn't come to."

"It wasn't like that in the W.A.A.F., not on an ops station. We were sort of a team every night the lads went over. It didn't matter whether you had any stripes on your arms or shoulders. Mind you, it wasn't the same in training establishments."

Jenny said:

"Mrs. Townsend said it was all right in the A.T.S. so long as you were in the ranks, but as soon as you got a pip up you faced a fate worse than death. I don't know what she meant but it sounded awful. At any rate as a conscript in the W.R.N.S. you never had to worry about being made an officer."

Lily said:

"In the W.A.A.F. it didn't make any difference whether you were a conscript or a volunteer, it just depended what trade you were in; you had to be made an officer for some things and you could never be one in others."

"I don't think I would have liked being in the services," Elsie put in.

"Why not?" the other two asked.

"Too chancy. Seems to me that people in the services always found themselves above what they'd been or below and, either

way, it's unsettling. It must have been terribly disheartening to
have been below, but even worse to be above."

"Why?" Lily asked curiously.

"Well, it gives a man ideas and afterwards it's a hurt to his
pride when things are different. Stands to reason, doesn't it?"

Lily didn't answer, but she knew they were both thinking of
Dick. It was funny the way Elsie could put a finger on things at
times. It seemed that way with Dick; but then you couldn't judge
him like others. There he was, ever so proud of being Captain
Richard Cobb, M.C., but he didn't remember a thing about how
he became an officer or what it was like being one: his wound
had cut a great chunk out of his memory. All he knew was that
he had an officer's uniform and a wad of papers which said that
War Substantive Lieutenant, Temporary Captain R. Cobb, M.C.,
had been discharged, medical category E; and another wad of
paper which entitled the same nebulous officer of His Majesty's Forces to draw an 80 per cent disability pension due to war
service. Perhaps, if all that war service were still clear in his
mind, he would be different today. As it was he was touchy as a
land mine on an open beach.

Jenny said:

"Oh lord, what's the time?"

"Half past," Lily looked at her watch but her mind was still
on Dick and Elsie. Jenny gave a squeak:

"Ooh, I must be going. They're ever so strict about time.
Mrs. Townsend is worse than the doctor, but even he looks
angry when I'm after half-past ten. Now Miss Watson and her
father didn't give a hoot when I came in. Funny, isn't it? Still
it's better in most ways at the doctor's; at least I get my own
butter." Elsie said:

"You won't get that if you stand here gassing after half-past
ten." For some reason Jenny Cookson annoyed her. There was
a simplicity about the girl that bordered on half-wittedness: the
way she stayed up drinking when she suffered from gastrics was
proof enough.

There was a noise of someone coming up the stairs and Dick Cobb came in. Jenny said:

"Oh, hello Dick; I was just leaving."

"Then mind the stairs, the light's gone or something." He shut the door when she had gone and looked at Elsie.

"Why aren't you at home?" he asked.

"Why, I was, till I came over to see Lil."

"And what d'you suppose is happening to Stevie while you're out?" He looked angry and Lily noticed the way he thrust a hand inside his open shirt and rubbed it against his chest.

"Stevie's all right. He was sound asleep when I came over an hour ago," Elsie said soothingly.

"The R.S.P.C.C. can get you for leaving a child of that age alone in a house," he went on provocatively.

Elsie flushed and clasped her hands nervously across her distorted figure.

"If you feel like that, Dick, you might come in earlier of a night yourself."

He scowled at her and said:

"Doc. Townsend told you to get to bed early."

"So what?" she said and this time Dick's face coloured up.

Lily spoke quickly:

"Well, it's time we all got a move on. Mum and Dad will be up in a moment. Did you have a good meeting, Dick?"

"How the hell did you know where I'd been?" he turned on her suddenly. She was embarrassed.

"I thought you'd been out at Dimstone. . . ."

"And what if I have?"

"Crack down on it, clever boy." She gave him a look. He suddenly grinned back at her.

"O.K., Corporal. Come on, Else, get skates on." Elsie rose heavily from her chair and went over to her husband. He gave her a friendly pat on the behind and linked an arm through hers. She said:

"Did you remember to post that letter to Mum?" His face crinkled like a puppy's and he rubbed uncomfortably at his chest.

"Sorry, Else. I sort of forgot." But her arm was firmly in his and on her face was the indescribable light of motherhood.

Lily felt a little overpowered by them as she said goodnight. Maybe everybody had their own way of fighting and making peace.

PART III

ANGELA WORTHING could not remember at what point she had begun to be attracted by Peter Gurney. She decided that she must have reached the unsafe age when it became difficult to discern between attraction and being flattered.

Peter had somehow established himself in her life and she was not displeased. She remembered her first encounter with him at the Cock and Pheasant, her impressions of the slightly tipsy and dissipated man who had aroused her pity. Why she had gone on seeing him, she did not know. Another case of circumstances and environment, no doubt: the pleasant hospitality of the Cock and Pheasant combined with Lady Gurney's mania for tea parties had resulted in constant meetings. Added to which Angela's instinctive sympathy for the weak made her respond more freely to Peter's admiration—that was when he was sober enough to indulge in co-ordinated admiration.

Angela was no prude, neither had she any illusions about herself. She finished signing the letters on her desk, dropped them into her clerk's room and prepared to close the office for the week end. A smile lit her eyes and curled her mouth ironically as she pulled on her hat in front of the mirror propped on the filing cabinet.

"What you need, my woman, is a man," she told her reflection and laughed at the memories the words evoked. How many times had she said them about other women? It was refreshing—if rather alarming—to voice the opinion on herself.

She was to meet Peter at the Cock and Pheasant at one o'clock and they were taking the afternoon train to London.

He was late, as usual, but this was better than if he'd been waiting for her since opening time. She ordered a beer for herself and a plate of sandwiches. Mrs. Cobb brought the sandwiches over to the table.

"Thank you, they look lovely." Angela noted the worry in the older woman's face, little lines of anxiety creasing the finely drawn skin. "How's the family, Mrs. Cobb?"

Mary Cobb smiled and eased herself into a chair.

"Mustn't grumble, I suppose. But the world's a strange place these days. My John gets quite put off his breakfast by the headlines in his *Daily Express*. Seems somehow as if we'd won the war only to go on fighting each other with speeches."

"Not fighting," Angela replied, "just stating facts. And surely it's better for all the nations to speak out frankly at a conference table than to bottle things up until there's got to be an explosion?"

Mary Cobb frowned and then leaned across the table.

"Is my Dick doing all right at Little Copse, Miss Worthing?" She spoke in a low, soft voice.

"Why, yes, Mrs. Cobb. He knows his job and I think he likes it. And he's popular with his colleagues."

"He doesn't talk too much politics then?"

Angela laughed.

"Not more than the rest! They all do, you know, and it's right that they should. You've got to remember that all the men there gave their services during the war years, and it's only natural they want a share in making the peace. They don't put it like that. They call it 'having a jaw' or 'watching the big shots.' It means they take an interest in what's happening in their country today, and in the rest of the world. I think it's excellent that they should do so, and a credit to them."

But Mary Cobb still looked unhappy.

"So long as Dick can't be victimized for what he says," she said.

"Of course he won't. Everyone's got a right to their own opinion."

"And the training centre won't be closing down yet awhile or anything?"

"Not so far as I know. Why?"

"Well, it seems to be all right for him there from what you've been saying; it wouldn't be easy for him to get another job like that, where we can keep an eye on him and all. He still gets those fainting fits, you know."

"Has he seen the doctor lately?"

"Yes. Dr. Townsend's ever so good to Dick; has him up for tea and talks to him like he was one of his own sort. Seems like being in the army's given him a real feeling for boys like Dick . . ." her voice trailed off uncertainly.

"What does he say about the fainting?" Angela asked.

"He says it'll be years before Dick gets over his head wound and that the fainting's all part of it. He says not to worry myself; but I do, you know. You can't help it when it's one of your own."

"Of course you can't. But Gyp Townsend does know what he's talking about. He wouldn't say things were natural if there was anything seriously wrong."

"Maybe. But it all makes it more important that Dick should be kept on where he is, so as his dad and I can look after him. We understand him, you see," she concluded simply.

Angela marvelled at the belief of parents—the faith they had in understanding their children. It just wasn't true. Parents and children never understood each other, it was impossible between two generations in close relationship. She said:

"And it's good that Dick seems to like his job. That should help to improve his health too."

"I'm glad to hear you say it, Miss Worthing. You see with Elsie expecting again it would be awful for her and the baby if she had the worry of Dick being unsettled, having to find another job, perhaps a new home somewhere away from us all."

Angela thought how brave these people were. To father children with the shattered manhood of war and to bring them into a world where security was still only an ideal needed courage— or was it faith? Or was it, again, only lack of imagination?

And then she saw Peter come into the bar, blinking a little at the comparative darkness, searching her out in the secluded corner.

Mary Cobb said:

"Good morning, Mr. Peter. What can I get for you?" And she smiled because, in her heart, she felt safe so long as people like the Gurneys existed to give jobs to people like the Cobbs. Angela, watching her face, thought 'you can't change that generation of country people, and they don't want to be changed; it's the Dick Cobbs who must break away, and they will.'

And then she turned her scrutiny to Peter. It was all right, he looked neat and fairly wide awake. He'd had his hair cut—she'd had to remind him about it—and his grey suit looked clean and well pressed in this light. She must remember to take another look outside. Her criticism of his appearance was quite dispassionate and she was not moved to protest at his nicotine stained fingers and bitten thumbnail. She knew he had to be led gently. He looked better today than she'd seen him look yet. That was proof that her methods were having effect.

He raised his glass of beer and said:

"Well, here's to our trip, Angela."

"And to your prospective job," she answered.

He grinned at her.

"Slave driver. Surely we can have a bit of fun, too. I'd like to look in at the Club and go round some of the old haunts."

"After we've seen Jim Cardew I don't mind what we do. Come on, eat up those sandwiches; we've only got about fifteen minutes before the train."

"Oh lord, I don't think I can manage one. Mother poured some filthy malted milk or something down me in the middle of the morning."

"Eat." She pushed the plate towards him. "We shan't get an evening meal till God knows what hour."

He did as he was told and then went to order more beers.

"I like that suit you're wearing," he said as he came back, "is it new?"

"Three years old and you've seen it at least six times!"

"Funny. I don't remember. D'you think Mrs. C. would cash me a cheque? Father did a vanishing act this morning and the bank was closed by the time I got out."

"No, we haven't time now. I can lend you some."

In the train she thought, again, how fortunate it was that she never had to worry about money. Not that she minded for herself—she would rather work than not work—but it was useful when she wanted to arrange things for other people. It meant, for instance, that she had the flat in London where Peter could stay tonight, which made things much easier than having to give him money for the hotel bills.

They went to the flat first, to leave their suitcases. Peter had not been there before and he wandered aimlessly around, peering at the books, while Angela made tea for them. Presently he found an album of photographs and sat studying them and gnawing at his thumbnail.

"Who's that?" he asked as she came back into the room. She put the tray down and went to look over his shoulder.

"Michael Cross. Don't you recognize him?"

"I thought it looked familiar. I didn't know you knew him before the war."

"Oh it was taken years ago." She dismissed Michael with ease.

"And this?" he had turned a page.

"A French naval officer I knew in St. Tropez."

He flicked over more pages while she poured out tea.

"You seem to have had a lot of boy friends," he smiled across at her and helped himself to sugar.

"I graduated in the 30's!" she replied easily.

"You're right—those were the days," he agreed. "God, I'd give a lot to go back to them."

"We can't, so why worry? I have no regrets for what's past."

He stared at her in silence. She noticed the deep lines between his nose and mouth and the puffiness beneath his eyes. In spite of it all he was still good looking. There was bone to his face and vitality in the crisp hair greying at the sides. There was more than that, she decided—a very definite charm which even dissipation could not erase. He could be a real person again, but he needed something or someone to shock him back to reality.

He took a cigarette from a crumpled packet and handed her one.

"I can't think why you've never married, Angela."

"I could say the same about you."

"Me? Oh, I'd never have made a go of it."

"How can you tell unless you've tried a thing?"

"I know myself too well. Lord, I'd have been a rotten husband. Even in the old days when a chap could make a packet on the Stock Exchange—and I did at times—I knew it would be no good. I couldn't ask a girl to marry me. I might be broke a few months later. It was always the same. I wouldn't want my wife to go through that."

She thought, he knows his weakness. If only he could be brought to believe that no human being is entirely composed of negative qualities. He must be built up before it was too late. Then she noticed the time and said:

"Heavens, we must go. Carry the tray back to the kitchen, will you, while I titivate."

They were able to get a taxi. Peter said:

"What about calling in at the Club for a quick one on the way?"

"No, Peter. We'll get drinks at Jim's. I know I'd never drag you from your Club once you got there and this other appointment's important."

He replied, cheerfully enough:

"In other words you mean I've got to stay sober until after the interview?"

"That was the idea," she laughed lightly.

He took her hand and held it between his.

"You're awfully kind to me, Angela."

"I hate that word." She tried to move her hand away.

"No, don't. . . . Darling, I wish we hadn't got to go and see your silly Jim Cardew. I wish we could go straight back to the flat."

"Even without a drink?" she teased.

"Um. . . . God, yes. . . ."

She heard the intensity in his voice and while she responded to his embrace her mind considered, dispassionately, the almost invariable effect that taxis had on men.

Jim Cardew was elderly and rich and somewhat parvenu. He lived in the sort of flat successful business men refer to as a 'pied-à-terre' and anyone else calls a luxury establishment. As they were going up in the lift, Angela felt the first spasm of nervousness about the whole thing. She had not seen Jim since the early years of the war—not, in fact, since the Cardew episode had terminated amicably on both sides. She wondered if Molly Cardew would be there, and hoped not. Molly was considerably younger than Jim and not the sort of woman to foster a business atmosphere which is what Angela hoped to create.

She glanced at Peter standing beside her and mentally drew up a balance-sheet of his assets and liabilities. He was presentable—at the moment—and had been to the same public school the Cardew boy was at. Jim was a snob and would label Peter a gentleman. Peter had done over five years in the navy. Jim had lived by and from the Black Market for almost the same number of years and was now atoning by advertising that he only liked to employ ex-service men in his many businesses.

So far, all right. But against that Angela had to admit that Peter showed no great enthusiasm for work, looked half asleep most of the time, could be childishly insulting about people who had made money during the war and, in general, was incapable of carrying on a coherent conversation after a few drinks. Well, she'd have to use all her tact if they got on to dangerous topics.

Actually everything went much more smoothly than she anticipated. Molly was away in the country. There were champagne cocktails. Jim was pleased to see Angela again and anxious to help any friend of hers. Peter woke up after the second cocktail, uncurling himself like a cat in the sun amidst the luxurious comfort of his surroundings, and was at his most charming.

He can pull it off, she thought, and let herself relax in the corner of the sofa she was on. At the back of her mind memories stirred. She remembered Peter at the Cock and Pheasant and his voice saying, "I gave all the chaps on my ship my address. . . . I can give them all the introductions they want." And her own reaction . . . life isn't going to be like that again.

But life was like that. Influence, favouritism, string-pulling—it was happening here in this room at this moment. The difference being that Peter was no longer in the traditional role. The Gurneys, born and bred to dispense favours on the less fortunate, were now the marionettes who must dance to the string-pulling of others. In this instance, thought Angela, dispassionately observing Jim Cardew's increased waistline and remembering the past, Peter was dependent on a scarlet thread.

She let her glass be refilled and bubbles of champagne and cynicism gurgitated within her. Maybe the war had been won for this, for the same impresarios to stage the same productions, with only the actors reshuffled, re-cast with startling possibilities.

Yes, Jim's waistline had increased, just as everything else in this flat had increased: the size of the glasses, the quality of the drink, the gilded mirrors on the walls and the hydrangeas potted indiscreetly about the room. Angela noted a new Dunlop and an Ivon Hitchens from this year's Academy and remembered Molly's patronage of the arts.

Jim Cardew was successful. His chief interests were in cement and building. War or peace, demolition or reconstruction, V-weapons or V-days—it was all the same to him, cement and building, building and cement.

As a side line he had now bought up a number of derelict boarding houses in London and on the south coast. Once they were restored to an outward semblance of spit and polish he staffed them with managers, accountants, cooks, maids, messengers and boot boys. 'All ex-service,' was his boast and 'A soft number for soldiers' his slogan. The company was called Victory Hotels Limited. But there was no end to the money to be made out of it.

He had a job in mind at the moment for a man to co-ordinate the administration of these establishments, someone who would investigate complaints, check up on the buying of market produce and the hiring of labour. Someone who could standardize the everyday running of the Victory Hotels until each was working at a minimum cost and maximum profit.

"Of course," Jim Cardew explained to Peter, "you'll have to start in the London offices. Say three months to learn the works and then you can get cracking. Jump on 'em, that's the idea. None of your prepared inspections. Just an unexpected call for lunch or dinner and a glance at the books after coffee. Catch 'em as they really are."

Peter said:

"It sounds a pretty good proposition to me."

Angela was glad that he seemed interested. And then she thought 'he fought the Nazis at Dunkirk and on the *Hood*.' But it was stupid to have associations like that. After all, a job was always a job.

As they left the flat she felt confident and filled with the satisfaction of having accomplished something definite. It was pleasant to be successful, even in quite small undertakings. But this wasn't small. It was big and important because it could mean the making of a human life.

They went to Peter's Club in Pall Mall where the atmosphere of defunct respectability wound itself like a shroud around Angela's good humour. Peter explained that none of his friends seemed to go there any more, which didn't surprise her. They found another taxi and proceeded to Soho. Peter was jubilant and amorous and she let him take control of the evening.

In the Soho pub there was warm humanity and the friendly smell of beer, tobacco and cheap scent. Peter elbowed Angela towards the counter and she felt happy and young again. The clack of voices almost drowned the metallic clang of a piano played by a young man in a corduroy suit.

"Two Scotch," Peter attracted the attention of a barmaid.

"No Scotch, sir."

"Couple of gins then."

"No gin. Only rum."

"D'you want a rum, Angela?"

"No. Try sherry."

They drank sherry at an exorbitant price. A man with a Lancashire voice told them:

"Got to make your number here before you can get the Ginger Wine."

"What's the dope?" Peter asked.

"Ginger Wine and a Buster. Vanilla Sandwich if you want a packet of fags, but they're on the counter tonight so you don't have to cut the job up."

Peter glanced at the empty glass in the man's hand and then waited for the barman to approach.

"Three Busters and a ginger ale," he ordered and, miraculously three gins appeared. He split the ginger ale between them and they drank silently.

Angela watched a girl in the corner being kissed by a sailor. There was something very satisfying about the performance. She imagined that it must be rather interesting to be about eighteen years old and to have matured during the most devastating war in history. The girl was dewy with youth and the sailor had a beautiful phallic neck, rising like sculptured marble from a surround of blue and white.

And then Angela saw Brian pushing his way towards the bar. He was shepherding a girl, carving a way through the crowd for her with his broad shoulders and a forceful elbow. She was tiny, not more than five foot two with red-gold hair framing the most perfectly proportioned face Angela had ever seen. 'Good God,' she thought. 'In what nursery do they find them?' The sailor's girl and now this child of Brian's. They had reached the counter and Brian saw Angela and Peter for the first time.

"Hello, strangers," he said, and Angela knew he was not too pleased to find them here.

Peter said:

"Hello, Brian. What's it to be?"

"No. I'm in the chair. This is Serena, Miss Hughes, I should say. This is my brother, Peter, and Angela Worthing. What d'you want, Serena?"

"I'd like a shandy, please, Brian." She had a cool little voice and Angela realized that here was a child from no ordinary nursery. Her mind swept back some twenty years to her finishing school in Paris and the débutantes of the twenties. They'd looked tougher and more tailored then, but they didn't come to pubs like the Golden Fleece.

Brian said:

"You're drinking gin aren't you?" and then ordered a shandy, two Busters and a large Ginger Wine. Peter said:

"So you and Brian know this place, do you, Miss Hughes?" And he smiled inanely down at her because no man could look at anything so young and so lovely without smiling inanely. 'Like the old advertisement for French cheese, *La Vache qui Rit*,' thought Angela, coldly, and then smiled, too, because she was reacting as every other woman must to the beauty of Serena Hughes.

"Yes, we often come here. You see, Brian lives just round the corner," Serena replied. Peter goggled at her, but Angela knew that the simplicity of Serena Hughes was entirely genuine.

They had several more rounds of drinks. Serena went from shandy to gin and lime and then back to shandy again, but her face retained its transparent pallor and her voice remained soft and cool. Peter's eyes took on their accustomed glassy look and he drooped a little over the counter. Angela said:

"We really ought to go and get some food."

Brian, who had suddenly decided to be sociable, suggested they should all go to a club he belonged to where the food was good and they could dance on about two square yards of glass floor if they felt energetic.

"We might," Peter added, "go on to the Music Box afterwards. I used to be a member."

"No," Brian said firmly, "not with Serena," and he tucked his arm through hers as they made their way out of the pub.

"But I might like it," Serena said as they walked along the street.

"I doubt it, and you wouldn't get the attention you merit. You know what a vain little creature you are, peeking into mirrors and rolling your eyes so as not to miss a single admiring glance."

"Oh, Brian, I'm not!"

Angela thought, 'He treats her as if she were his favourite young sister', and wondered exactly how the two had come to this particular relationship.

The Piccolo Club was small and overcrowded, but the food was excellent. Peter said he didn't want anything to eat and Angela could have smacked him as he toyed and thrust aside the hors d'oeuvres on his plate.

Serena said:

"Ooh, steak tonight, and it's not horse, look at the fat. I know it was horse at that funny restaurant the other night, Brian, but I was too hungry to care."

Even Peter enjoyed the steak and as he ate, he became less glassy. When he asked Angela to dance, she knew he was all right. Peter was like that: a few drinks and he appeared to totter with tipsiness; then would come a quite long spell of outward control, during which he managed to consume a great deal without deterioration. After that, it was anyone's guess as to what he might do.

Angela thought, 'it's funny the way Peter can dance; it's probably the one thing about him which hasn't gone blunt,' and she let herself go to the rhythm of the band which consisted of a pianist, a drummer, and a man who alternated between the accordion and the violin. It was, she decided, exactly what a dance band should comprise in a small setting like this.

Peter said:

"Angela, later on, let's talk."

"Yes."

"We will, won't we, when we get back?"

"Yes."

"Just what you want, you know? I'm all right."

"Yes."

They went back to the table and there was coffee. Brian said:

"Serena wants to dance with you, Peter. She says you were the only couple in that crush who looked as if they still had the floor to themselves."

"Oh, I'm no good. I've forgotten all the steps. What about some drink?"

"I'll see to that. You go and exercise the child."

Serena pulled a face at him. Peter said:

"Will you, Serena?"

"If you insist . . ." but she was looking at Brian. He spoke to a waiter.

"A jug of lager and some lemonade. What about you, Angela?"

"Lager, thank you."

"Make it two jugs, George."

When the drink arrived, he said:

"Peter's looking much better. What have you been doing to him, Angela?"

"Nothing."

"I don't believe it. You can tell me, you know." She wondered if he were a little tight.

"Well, I've got him a job," she answered lightly.

"Good God! What in?"

She told him about Jim Cardew and the cocktails in Sloane Street. He said:

"It may work."

"What d'you mean?"

"Angela, let's be frank. You're in love with Peter, aren't you?"

"I haven't the faintest idea. I find him attractive. Why?"

"Oh, don't keep asking questions. Do you really know him?"

"You seem to be the one for asking questions."

He laughed, and poured lager into their glasses. Somewhere in the middle of the tiny floor Peter's dark head was visible, smiling down at Serena.

"Don't worry about Serena," Brian said, "she's not interested in Peter."

"You're quite the cad, aren't you, Brian?" she asked, fingering the glass before her. He looked at her and his voice changed.

"Am I? I don't mean to be, but I spent a long time learning to come to the point quickly. I suppose the niceties got brushed off sometime."

She felt softened then. It was difficult to remember Brian as a soldier, he looked so different now.

"What are you doing, Brian?" she asked.

"Advertising, It's good fun in a way. I can get quite worked up about the merits of somebody's soap and cures for catarrh. Actually, I'm only a contact man. I don't draw pretty pictures or write clever slogans."

"Why should you?" she asked.

"Because I'd like to. I'd like to be that sort of a person. Oh, God, here are the others. Come and dance."

"What about Serena?"

"Serena's all right. I've told her what to do. Come on; let's talk."

Preceding him to the dance floor, she laughed to herself at the thought of the Gurney family. It only needed Lady Gurney to appear with an invitation to tea, for conversational intercourse to be completed. Sir James and Daphne didn't count.

Brian said:

"What are you grinning about?"

"Your family. What do you want to talk about?"

"Let's dance first."

He was not as good a dancer as his brother. Angela was bumped unceremoniously round the room but, physically, Brian was the more stalwart partner: shoulder to shoulder, limb to limb, there was greater security. Twice round the floor and he said:

"Let's go and have a drink at the bar."

It was on the other side of the dance floor from the table they had. He asked:

"Gin or whisky?"

"Gin, please."

He ordered and they stayed silent until the drinks were served. She thought Brian looked thinner and he had lost the deep tan which she remembered most about him. The band was playing a selection of tunes that had been popular in the nineteen-twenties. She found that she knew the words to all of them. Funny the way lyrics of that time stuck in one's memory. It wasn't anything to do with the words or the music, it was just a case of having been at the age when one learned the lyrics of all new tunes. It certainly dated one.

Serena and Peter were dancing again. Brian followed Angela's glance. She said:

"She is a pretty child."

"She's a good kid."

"And very devoted."

His face softened for an instant and then she saw that he had dismissed Serena and the dancing from his thoughts. He asked:

"Are you going to marry Peter?"

"I shouldn't think so. Why?" She did not mind his question because it was put with no unpleasant curiosity.

"I'd hoped you would. It would be the best thing that could happen to him. But perhaps it's unfair on you. After all why should you? You might mess up the rest of your life for nothing. In fact, I think you probably would. There's no great catch in being sacrificed for something worthless."

"Brian, Peter is not worthless."

"Isn't he? I hope you're right."

"It's people like you always thinking that he is, and looking at him as if he were, who will end by making him so if you're not careful." She felt she owed that to Peter.

"Oh, no, Angela; not me. You've got it wrong. I happen to be very fond of Peter."

"But you wouldn't think of doing anything to help him."

"No, I don't think I would. I believe that he's got to help himself. That's why I was stupid when I said I hoped you'd marry him. That isn't the solution at all."

"Thank you," she said dryly, but he only ordered more drinks and then went on:

"We used to be terrific friends, you know. At school, I pretty well worshipped him. It was strange because he was so much better than me at everything—games, lessons, popularity. I should have loathed him. Instead I basked in his achievements and muscled in on his fame. I tried to imitate him in all things. He was brilliant, you know, and he did everything without effort. He never listened in class, and always came out top; he never went into training for any game, and was always in the first elevens and fifteens. The parents doted on him: nothing was too good for him. I don't believe they even knew they'd got a second son. I came to regard it as a privilege to be related to the great P. L. F. Gurney. And I enjoyed it. County cricket, ski-ing at

Murren—it was always the same story, P. L. F. G. was the man. And he was doing pretty well in the City too; ran a flat in Mayfair and a non-stop cocktail party in it. That's what it seemed like anyhow. Am I boring you?"

"No. Go on."

"It was like that until about nineteen-thirty-seven and then, God knows why, the tables turned. He gambled a lot—you probably know that—cards and horses—and it seems that was where most of the money was coming from. Anyhow when his luck broke it broke thoroughly. Away with the flat and the friends who had sponged. Friends! Fancy followers, I'd call them, and when there were no more parties to follow they fancied themselves off.

"Father helped, as he has done since. It struck him almost as hard as it struck Peter. Only Mother was pleased: it was nice to have Peter at home more. Bless her. He'd sold up his Stock Exchange membership to pay some of the debts. I rallied round but wasn't much good. In any case I couldn't afford to keep him besides he was bitter as vinegar. I couldn't cope with that. After all, apart from money and gambling and all the rest, there's bound to be a moment when a chap can't run so fast or bowl so well or win every race on skis. It's only natural, but he didn't see things that way. He was for ever blaming his pals or the government or something.

"Then he took up with a queer set—he's always had a strong homosexual streak, you know—and I went my way. We hardly saw one another for a year or more. We met over Munich—he still worked in the City but I believe there were times when he didn't turn up for days on end. The firm allowed him to stay—he was no asset to them, but on the other hand he wasn't harming anyone, except himself. Then the war came and he joined up as an ordinary seaman. Put his age down five years to do so. It's a funny thing, you know—oh, have another drink, you look thirsty."

"No thanks. Go on, what was funny?"

"The way Peter pulled himself together when the war started. All the time he was on the lower deck, he was grand. He looked well and he was cheerful and seemed on top of the world again. Then some fool of a commanding officer recommended him for a commission. That did it. He started to slip badly once he'd got rings up. Back to the old days. I never saw him sober when he was on leave. Odd the way he couldn't take it. He went right back to the bitterness and recriminations of before the war. Funny, wasn't it?"

"No, it wasn't funny. Why are you telling me all this?"

"I don't know." He was silent, fingering his cigarette case, opening and shutting it by sliding it and letting the spring force back his relaxed fingers before he snapped it shut again. Memory stirred in her mind. Where had she seen this before? Of course—in the Cock and Pheasant, and she saw again Helen's pale face and her expression of desperation—almost irritation— at this mechanical snapping.

"You don't know," she repeated, "but I do. It's because you feel responsible for him. Perhaps not you, personally, but your parents, your family, the way he was brought up. Isn't it?"

"I wouldn't say that. Maybe he was spoiled too much."

"It isn't a case of being spoiled. At least I don't think so. It's deeper than that. It's being born and bred in an atmosphere that's either stagnant or progressive, of being reactionary or pressing forward with the times. I don't mean just politically, but in every way: art, science, even sport if you like. A lot of things died before 1939 and the war buried them, quietly, without fuss or headlines—almost decently. Which is much better and less painful than having a lot of skeletons lying around. You, Brian, have progressed fairly logically out of one war and through another. It's no particular credit to you that you have, because people ought to be able to adapt themselves to the rhythm of their times. It isn't as if we had to live for hundreds of years. But you get people like your parents who for one reason or another dug their toes in about the beginning of this century and have never looked forward since." She paused to light a cigarette.

"How does that account for Peter?"

"It doesn't really, except that you'll always find human hang-overs from one generation to another. They want the best of both worlds, but usually their sense of values isn't too bright and they can't discern which are the good things. But they're not hopeless or worthless. It's just that they need from other people that much more of human intelligence and understanding to bring them up to normality. You know that, and with your tidy mind, you want to shelve Peter on to someone else for a change. You either can't or won't make the extra effort that's needed. You've picked on me as a suitable mentor. God knows why."

"He's in love with you."

"Oh, what's the use. . . . Come on, we must go back and join them."

"No," he put a hand on her arm, "Angela, tell me . . . how's Helen?"

So that was it, she thought. All this long talk away from Peter and Serena so that he could ask about Helen. Why the hell couldn't he have come to the point sooner? She could see Peter leaning on the table at the other end of the room and she knew, even from this distance, that he'd had enough to drink.

"Helen's all right," she replied. "I haven't seen a great deal of her."

"Does she seem happy?" He was so pathetically eager for news that she hadn't the heart to leave him then.

"It's difficult to tell that about anyone," she answered. "But she seems perfectly cheerful."

"And Gyp?"

"Looking much better than when he first got back." What else could she say? It was all quite true.

"All right," he rose from the bar and they began to make their way round the room. He sounded dejected. "I know you know how I feel," he spoke from close behind her. "You didn't mind my asking, did you? I'll have to see her soon; I must."

But Angela felt uncomfortable. Why couldn't he ask his brother about Helen? Peter knew her much better than she did.

They arrived at the table and Brian's voice was confident and teasing again.

"Hello children. Been good? Sorry we were away so long, but Angela and I had a lot to talk about. Has Serena been entertaining you properly, Peter?"

"Serena's quite the most enchanting girl you know, Brian." Peter replied, but his glance was on Angela's face. Brian said:

"Well, I suppose we ought to think about moving. I've got to walk Serena back to Sloane Square."

"Walk? Not on your life." She slipped a hand unself-consciously into his. "Taxi, please Brian. Or at least the underground. I've danced my feet through my Utilities."

She seemed quite unperturbed at Brian's lack of attention. Angela thought, cynically, 'Maybe he's thinking of marrying her; he's certainly trained her well.'

Outside they parted in the half-lit street. Angela and Peter needed only a few minutes to walk to her flat. He put his arm through hers and she felt his weight, warm and a little unsteady against her side as they walked. She found his hand and twined cool, reassuring fingers in his.

"What the hell did Brian want to jaw about?" he asked.

"Oh, nothing in particular. Come on, darling, we'll never get there if you drag like this."

"Yes, let's hurry." He made an effort to walk more quickly and lurched against a lamp post. "Oh God, I'm stinking. But I shan't be in a minute. Damned hot in that club."

"Did you drink all that beer?"

"Lord no. I got the waiter to get me some whisky. Here, where do we go now?" They were on the edge of the pavement.

"Left. Cornering badly, I'm afraid." She pulled him round and wondered, idly, what Brian had thought when he got his bill. He'd been so careful to leave only beer on the table, but he hadn't said anything about Peter's whisky afterwards.

In the flat, she drew the curtains quickly and then folded the counterpane back from the bed in Peter's room. He stood watching her, smiling sleepily.

"Don't go. You promised we could talk." He ruffled his hair with a hand and leaned back on the dressing-table.

"Don't you think you'd better get to bed?" He looked like a rather guilty schoolboy with his hair disarranged like that.

"Sure. But you come back then. You promised, you know."

She stood, silently. He continued, ruffling his hair again and smiling at her.

"No funny business, you know. Nothing you don't want. Just quiet. Please. . . . Angela?"

"All right. But don't just stand there. You know where the bath room is?"

"Yes. But you will come back? Promise?"

She went up to him and kissed him casually on the mouth.

"Yes, I promise."

In her room she undressed slowly. She could hear him go to the bathroom and then return uncertainly to his room. She went to wash and noticed his belongings about the place, shaving things, a squeezed out tube of toothpaste, a rumpled towel thrust untidily back on the rail. She suddenly felt light-hearted, tingling with vitality, glad to be alive.

Back in her room, she brushed her hair until it stood out like a dark halo from her head and fell shinily to her shoulders. She thought: 'Thank goodness that even at my great age I've still got the sort of face that looks all right without make-up,' and the feeling of well-being that had begun in the bathroom grew until it seemed to envelop her whole body with sharp pleasure.

She uncovered her bed and lit the reading lamp near it. Then she turned the light off in her room and went across the passage to Peter's.

He had taken off his coat and collar and tie, but had forgotten to remove his shoes before lying down. He sprawled across the bed, fast asleep, his trousers rucked up showing sock suspenders and the fine hairs on his legs. He would not wake for many hours.

Angela removed his shoes and drew an eiderdown across him. Then she opened the windows, turned off the light and went back to her own room. Sitting on the edge of her bed she laughed until the tears filled her eyes.

Quite suddenly, it wasn't a bit funny.

* * * *

I am re-discovering that life with Gyp can be fun. It is, of course, a new life. New, that is, in our reactions to each other. The routine has not changed beyond the revolution—or evolution—which a war and a peace inevitably bring to the community life of a nation.

Outwardly, little is altered. The country is there and the village with its houses and cottages; the measles and 'flu and the familiar rhythm of telephone calls in the middle of the night; Gyp in his old clothes on Sunday, prodding at the garden. His old clothes are khaki shirts now, but even they are beginning to look as shapeless and grey as his old shirts always did.

The change is in ourselves. We have come to a strange adjustment of ourselves. It has not happened easily. We always seem to be leaping, like mountain goats, from one emotional pinnacle to another. At least, Gyp leaps; I follow and, having a poor head for heights, I sometimes miss my footing. But for Gyp, God knows what precipices I mightn't have fallen into by now. The fact that he has always been there, firm-footed, has meant that I have survived.

And yet Gyp keeps saying I'm the sanest person he knows. He says that if I hadn't been such a fuss-pot about re-registering in good time for the new rationing period, such a stickler for the nine o'clock news and such an ogre about Jenny being late on her evenings off, he would probably have had to go and get himself rehabilitated by the army before tackling civilian life again.

I don't regard this as a compliment. When you have imagined yourself as something rather feminine and appealing for a husband to come back to, it isn't flattering to be told that your other qualities are the ones he admires. How can I help being practical after nearly six years of war—five of them spent in the A.T.S.?

We are, to all intents and purposes, man and wife. Among the villagers I believe we are cited as paragons of married life. Jenny tells me about this. She says that Mr. and Mrs. Cobb say it does their hearts good to see the way the doctor's come home and settled down. She says that Dick Cobb and his wife aren't hitting it off any more. She says that Daphne Gurney, that was, fights with her mother and that Sir James tells his wife that if their daughter had married a decent Englishman like Dr. Townsend, instead of a foreigner, she would be in a much better position today. Jenny also tells me, with innocent glee, that it's well known Daphne Gurney was four months gone when she went to the altar.

Sometimes I am almost tempted to tell Jenny exactly what sort of a life I led during the last years. I want to shout it aloud to the world and to those pathetic fools who look upon me and Gyp as models of family existence. Sometimes I feel so ashamed that I would like to paint my face up and let my hair down and slink round the pubs in Dimstone like the girls who used to be in the munition works there.

I want to tear down the smug mask the village has made for me. I want to exhibit myself and let them understand that no one is alone in the problems—the intimate and sometimes debasing problems—which war has bequeathed to those who come back.

They would be horrified, no doubt, to know that when Gyp returned I lay in his arms and thought about a man who wasn't my husband. They would be shocked that I had compared two men and found one wanting—and that it was my husband. Five years separation can do that to a woman.

Gyp and I have been through a lot these last few months. Like actors in a repertory company, we seem to have played a great many parts whilst always rehearsing for more. I look back on it all now and find it rather embarrassing: the over-rehearsed scene of our reunion and the domestic comedy of the first month—with neither of us word perfect. Then the melodrama of my being too kind to Gyp which ended with him moving into the spare bedroom. An acute spell of cold weather coupled with a lack of coal brought him back to our room and it seemed that we had reached the climax of bedroom farce.

I think we both got tired of play-acting. In any case, things changed. For no apparent reason we are ourselves again. Not our pre-war selves, but nevertheless adult individuals. We are able to talk and discuss things together again, and every moment of the day seems to bring a new topic which must be argued about. Not that we argue in the sense of fighting. It is rather that we have so many ideas in common that we race each other to say them first. We might be strangers meeting for the first time, getting together and experiencing the pleasures of mutual attraction. Except that this time, it is our minds that are courting.

But I am not happy about us. I do not believe in personalities subdivided into emotional, physical and mental facets—at least, not if the personalities concerned are husband and wife. There should be an effortless blending of all three aspects if one is to avoid the disconcerting sensation of suddenly smacking a sensitive limb against an invisible boulder.

Gyp and I are not blending naturally. Perhaps we never did. Maybe, in the first years of our marriage, I mistook the freshness of our pleasure in one another as something more profound than it was. It is impossible to know now what our present relationship would have been without the interruption of war. Perhaps we shall never develop in the way I feel is necessary for lasting companionship. It may be stupid to want that sort of perfection. But I do and, as things are, I seem to be running round the brink of a void.

I have just come in from having tea at the Watsons. The weekly invitation from Laura has become a rite which I am too weak to break with. Every month of peace seems to lessen the interests and to widen the gulf between Laura and myself; but across the tea table we fling a bridge of reminiscence. Laura's memory of A.T.S. life grows more detailed with time, whereas mine becomes dimmer and much less enthusiastic; but I find a sort of fascination in her anecdotes: I cannot believe that we lived and talked and behaved in the fantastic and adolescent way Laura depicts. It would be laughable were it not for the almost religious fervour with which she speaks of those years.

I take off my rain coat and leave it in the hall. As soon as I reach the sitting room, I feel soothed. There is a well tended fire and the curtains are drawn. All around me familiar objects welcome me with well worn faces. The irritating goodness of Laura and the pettiness of Mr. Watson are things of the past.

Upstairs, I can hear Gyp moving about between our room and the bathroom. He always has a bath after evening surgery. As I listen, it seems to me that I am suddenly back in the pre-war years and that there has been no five-year gap in our existence. At the thought, I am conscious of the immediate differences. At one time the thought of Gyp in his bath was exciting and tender; now I only wonder whether he has mussed up the soap or the bath mat. I don't care if he has, but I wish I didn't wonder about it.

In a few minutes he will come downstairs and I shall hear him calling to Jenny:

"What's cooking, Jenny Wren?"

She will tell him what there is for supper and after that he will mix cocktails for us and we will warm our backsides against the fire while we drink. I feel stimulated and a little uneasy— almost as I used to when I left school and was going to a party where I wanted to shine.

Jenny has left the afternoon's post on the mantelpiece. It's funny the way she insists on propping it up there instead of in the hall. I've told her that the hideous wedding-present salver on the hall table is for letters and cards but she still goes her own merry way. Maybe in the W.R.N.S. their Lordships decreed that letters should be propped on mantelpieces or whatever the equivalent naval furnishing was.

I pick them up and there are the usual obvious bills and payments, two O.H.M.S. ones for Gyp and one, addressed in very blue ink, for me. Why do I know that writing?

Suddenly I am breathless with shock because it is Brian's writing; the next instant I feel fury and panic flooding over me. How dare he write to me here? Has he gone mad? Anyone could have seen this letter. Gyp might have seen it first. My heart is pounding and I am weak with apprehension.

It is a very short letter. Brian wants us to meet in London. He says that he's got to make an important decision and that I am the only person who can advise him about it. He suggests that we meet for lunch soon—one day next week if possible. I am to let him know the day and he will be at the Tour Fondue in Soho at one o'clock.

I feel the blood rushing to my face and my whole body is shaking with fury. How dare he? The outrageous suggestion that he only has to ask and I will be there. The impertinence of writing to me here in Gyp's house. I am impotent in my rage.

And then, quite suddenly, my emotion is spent. As Gyp would say, I've had it. My God, I've had it. The sham hollowness of my existence since I left the army; my life with Gyp and my suppression of Brian; the frustration of being a civilian and a housewife again. It occurs to me that I am no longer an individual; my personality is smothered beneath the artificiality of an outward manner. I am not an actress and my performances are third rate. Brian's letter has torn down the safety curtain.

Dear God—of course I shall see Brian again. How, I don't know at this moment, but I shall arrange to do so. I don't know what he wants, but his letter no longer angers me. I re-read it and it is suddenly a most sensible communication. It is not emotional and it is sincere. Underlying it there is an urgency I cannot disregard. I owe that to Brian. There are some debts which will always remain on the debit side. I cannot repay Brian for safeguarding my morale and physical well-being during the latter years of the war. But I can stop being hysterical about him, and therefore I shall meet him in London. It is a perfectly natural and sane thing to do.

But Gyp must not know. Why do I feel that when Gyp is the most understanding person I have ever met? I would like to tell Gyp about Brian, but now I have left it too late. It is better to say nothing at this distance. No, Gyp must not know.

Gyp comes into the room and, without realizing it, I have Brian's letter in my pocket. Gyp is in good form. I can see it in the way he has brushed his hair. It is very grey at the sides, but it is still crisp and much more virile than the smarmy heads of the very young. This evening, the short army cut which he still maintains is shining alert above his wide, tanned brow. Gyp is feeling well.

"Gin or whisky basis?" he asks, moving towards the cupboard where the drinks are kept. We are in the happy, first week of the month, the period when we still have our quota of both.

"Gin, please." While he mixes and whistles to himself, I wonder what he really thinks about me. It is terribly important to know what your husband thinks about you. In the days when you are first in love and married, the familiar questions on personal reactions are answerable because of physical desire. Afterwards they become either routine or—as I now feel with Gyp—embedded in unbreakable reserve.

Gyp brings over the drinks. We raise glasses and sip. Gyp says:

"What's the matter with your hair?"

"My hair? Nothing, why?"

"Just the enveloping drapery." He takes the letters from the mantelpiece.

I realize then that I have not removed my head-dress which consists of an old scarf of Gyp's. I do so and comb my hair out before the mirror above the mantelpiece. It is a nice mirror, Adam's period; when Gyp and I first bought it we used to fantasy about the people who lived on the other side of it—the people who had a room furnished like ours and who drew their chairs up close to the fire so that you couldn't see them or hear what they were saying. It was fun in those days when one could speculate without fear. Today I am glad Gyp has forgotten about the people on the other side of the mirror. I stare at my reflection and feel a little hypnotised.

Gyp has strewn his letters on the sofa beside him; now he looks up and says:

"I'll have to go to London for two or three days next week for a medical get-together. What about coming with me?"

I am too startled to answer. In books, coincidences of this kind are quite unreal. I feel unreal myself. Gyp mistakes my silence for indecision; he continues: "Not if you don't want to. It was just an idea."

"But I'd love to, Gyp. Where shall we stay?" I wonder if I have spoken too quickly.

"Michael Cross said he'd always put us up in his flat. Unless you'd prefer to stay at a hotel. We could ring up a few tonight, but it's short notice."

"No; I'd rather be at the flat. Michael's a dear. It would be fun." My heart is singing and I feel warm with the relief of a problem solved. Now I can do what Brian has asked, and Gyp need never know. It would have been very difficult going to London without Gyp.

I am filled suddenly with love for my husband.

Gyp pours us another drink and grins at me.

"One day I think I shall probably propose to you, darling."

"Don't be silly, Gyp." I feel embarrassed.

"Well, you look so nice and expectant at times; it seems a pity to disappoint you. Just at this moment, for instance, you look like every young girl one has ever taken out to dinner and kissed in a taxi."

"I hardly know whether that's a compliment or an insult, Gyp. I've reached the great age when it might be either."

"It was meant to be nice," Gyp says seriously and, for that, I could kiss him.

Jenny taps at the door and tells us that supper is ready. She has a cold in her nose and I suggest to Gyp that it is about time medical charity started at home, and what about some of those innoculations he forced me to have at the beginning of the winter? Gyp snaps back at me:

"Until Jenny Wren comes and tells me she can't bear sniffing any longer, just as any other villager would do, I'm damned if I'm going to pander to her."

"Why not?"

"Because she's so full of old wives' tales and naval customs that if I asserted my influence she'd immediately accuse me of practising vivisection on her—or worse. Can you imagine the scandal in the village?"

I can, but I think Gyp is exaggerating.

"Well, if your innoculations are really any good, you and I needn't worry about catching Jenny's colds, need we?" I ask sweetly.

Gyp looks at me and says:

"You're horribly factual, aren't you?"

I am glad we have mussel soup because it is one of his favourites. I got the mussels in a jam jar from Mary Cross who was up in London today. She says that the woman in her market who sells them is quite the rudest woman she knows, but the mussels are first class. Mary says the woman has every right to be rude because of the queues, and her son being killed at El Alamein, and being blitzed out three times, and having a murder committed on her doorstep on V.J. night. The police even searched her cellar for the weapon. Mary says the mussels are a miracle.

They are, and Gyp makes appreciative husband noises about them.

"Jenny Wren can cook," he says as we gluttonize over the weekly meat ration—two small grilled fillets of steak. My pleasure is a little overshadowed at the thought of unending fish meals to come—that is if I manage to please Mr. Stokes the fishmonger. If not, it'll be starvation corner on the remainder of our points. I don't think I'm a very good housekeeper; I feel, somehow, that I oughtn't to use up our rations on anything quite so good and small as these steaks. On the other hand, I don't believe Gyp even begins to understand how complicated it still is to cater in this country. He says:

"How were the Watsons?"

"I hate Mr. Watson," I reply and notice that Jenny has not cleaned out the dining room as I intended. Tomorrow I'll do it myself. Luckily I like housework. There is something remarkably soothing in sweeping and polishing. I believe I should have been much happier and learned a great deal more about the important things of life if I had remained an orderly in the A.T.S. as I was when I first joined up.

"The old man is a bit of a bind," Gyp says, "but then Laura is too, bless her heart."

I feel I must stand up for Laura who knows so much about my life that Gyp doesn't.

"Laura has an integrity and loyalty that possibly you and I can't understand," I say priggishly.

"What d'you mean?" he asks sharply.

"Just that Laura has principles and definite ideas on what's black or white, and although her father is a crashing old bore and quite unworthy of the devotion she expends on him, she is nevertheless entirely sincere in her feelings of duty and service towards him. I'm not saying she isn't crazy to be like that, but it doesn't alter the fact that she does it in a completely altruistic way. That's why she's a better person than most of us. She's capable and decent and she could be a success in quite a number of other channels. She ought to have stayed on in the army."

"Stayed on in the army? Good God, why?"

"It would have been a career for her. She wanted to stay when she heard about the 'regular' A.T.S. She's a responsible sort of person and, as I've just implied, she's got a sort of itch to serve. It's too bad that it should be wasted on anything quite as selfish as Mr. Watson. Why, he wouldn't even let her take on a part time job at Little Copse."

"But no one," says Gyp slowly, "no ordinary civilian, that is, ought to have wanted to stay on. It's unnatural."

"Is it?" I wonder at his seriousness.

"But of course it is. I saw the chaps who went all out for deferment when the release scheme started. With very few exceptions, I'd say they were all psychologically maladjusted, sort of mentally arrested—" he stops suddenly and I am conscious again of being married to a man whom I hardly know. It seems to me that he has done and seen so much that I know nothing about. Perhaps he feels the same about me. Shall we ever be able to build up the security of completely shared interests again?

"But, Gyp, we've got to have a strong army, navy and air force, even though the war is over," I say gently.

"Of course." He is dissecting an orange in the way I remember so well: quartering the skin and peeling it neatly off until the fruit emerges, free of its white fluff, with the peel lying, like a golden water lily, intact on his plate. "I'm not talking about the regulars," he goes on, "or the chaps who joined up with the intention of making it their career. But the great multitude of civilians who volunteered or were conscripted—they're the people who want to get out when the fighting's over. Those who don't are the failures, the poor mutts who can't take life in their stride. They can't progress, they've lost the ability to adapt themselves to circumstances and so they try to defer their release; they'll now exist on the past, eternally remembering the good old days of war. Of course they're abnormal. They're frightened of living."

"Or maybe service life has sapped their initiative. After all, it's very comforting always being able to pass the baby, up or down." I like talking like this with Gyp. I like to see him frowning at what I say and taking it in as if I were Michael Cross or some other ex-service friend who has been through the same experiences as he has.

"You've got something there, Helen. That's the worst aspect of service life from an individual's point of view. There always was a bloke to complain to, and whose job it was to see that your complaint was dealt with. You got to depend on an organization, and even when obviously sane and efficient improvements got strangled with red tape or were still-born in a pigeon hole, the machinery still churned out a basic security and a fool-proof justice."

"So what's unnatural about wanting to remain in it?"

"Lots of things. Oh, lots of things!" He smiles across at me and I realize that I am very glad that Gyp was not one of those people who wanted to remain on in the army.

"Let's go up," I say, "Jenny will want to clear."

Upstairs, over coffee, he says, curiously:

"You wouldn't have wanted to stay on, Helen, would you? Even without a returning husband who would have created hell if he hadn't found you back at home?"

"No, I wouldn't," I reply slowly, and I wonder if he realizes that I could have left the A.T.S. on the 18th of June, 1945, as a married woman, but that I stayed on longer than Laura Watson who came out under age and service group ten. Laura, who wanted to stay on, came out because of her father, and I, who wanted to leave, stayed on because of Brian. It was easier to be with Brian as a service woman than as Dr. Townsend's wife in Kirton.

Gyp's arguments are all very well in principle, but they fall down when it comes to an individual case. There are people like

Laura and myself who come out or stay on for emotional reasons; and then there are those who are financially affected or who, like some of the women I know, can't bear to part with the power of a few badges of rank on their shoulders—even honorary ones, like Recruiting Officers. False values, no doubt, but very important for those to whom only a war gives opportunities.

Gyp has lit an enormous cigar. He is very much the master in his own house tonight. To be with him gives me a feeling of safety. He blows unconscious smoke rings and the ash grows in an even circle, blue grey and compact.

"I'm sorry, I decried your friend Laura," he says suddenly.

"But you didn't, Gyp. At least, not much. She is a bore, of course." And I can hear a cock crowing outside the window of a Dumfries hotel.

"What you said about her itch for service is right, and it's a good thing. But you don't have to stay on in the army to serve. You may get the urge there, and I think a lot of people did. Uncomfortable and browned off, they were nevertheless very much part of an act performed for the benefit of a cause and not necessarily to the benefit of an individual. And a number of chaps getting back to civvy street are carrying on where they left off in the army; you'll find them helping with youth clubs, going in for local government, being active in their unions and turning up in all sorts of unexpected situations with a self-conscious grin and a grouse about something. They didn't have to stay on in the army to serve."

I am listening to Gyp but, as usual, my thoughts about him are chaotic. He speaks so unemphatically about things which are important and he is still very much the soldier. When we were first married he was very much the doctor. I wonder sometimes if any other officer in the R.A.M.C. was as absorbed by service life as Gyp. But then Gyp is like that, he never does things half-heartedly. Besides, he spent his war with men who were actually fighting; he was never M.O. in a home establishment or some depot miles behind the lines. My war was a long distance from his, in every sense.

"Tired?" he asks.

"No. Why?"

"Just silent, then."

"Yes. What's on the wireless?"

He turns it on and it is the Brains Trust; we groan in unison; he switches over to the Light Programme and we are assailed by the sound of bagpipes. As he turns off he says:

"If this goes on much longer, I'm damned if I'll pay them ten bob a year."

This makes us both laugh because we have never yet paid a radio licence. It's one of the things we keep meaning to do and never get around to. He leans back in his chair with a smile.

"Thank God I haven't got to bother to listen."

No, but I have—to him. The thought races through my mind and I feel guilty. But I want to think. What does Brian want to see me about and why couldn't he have put it in his letter, once he'd been foolhardy enough to write to me here? I wish Gyp would read a book or something. I brought two new ones from the library today but he has only picked them up, read the blurb on the jackets and flung them aside again. Is our life to be endless evenings of bad radio and indifferent novels? With Gyp and I growing older and dimmer and more rheumaticky in our arm chairs, and the carpet between us spreading its worn pattern until we are separated by a limitless expanse of faded memories.

I do not think that Gyp will ever allow that to happen. He will get up from his chair whilst he still has the power of his limbs and he will walk out. It is I, with my weak fantasies of what our life should be like and my inability either to recapture the past or build a new future, who will be left, crippled in my arm chair.

It occurs to me suddenly how different Gyp and I are. He is fundamentally honest and I am not. Months ago, when he first came home, he told me, in that unemphatic voice of his, that he had not been faithful to me. 'You might as well know about it,' he said, 'because I'd rather you knew everything about me. Physically—at the time—it meant a hell of a thing; afterwards, damn all. Just one of those happenings on local leave you know.'

It would have been so simple to have said then: 'I know, the same thing happened to me.' I would have said, it if I had felt the tiniest twinge of jealousy about Gyp. But I didn't. What Gyp had done meant nothing to me at that moment and so I kept silent. Now, when I could tell Gyp about Brian, it is too late, and I have got to go on living my lie. If today I were to tell him that I had lived with Brian but that he meant nothing to me now, Gyp would not believe me. I have left it too long and the right moment will never be recaptured. In one of the papers today there was an article on wives telling their returned husbands the truth. I scoffed at it as trash, but all the time I knew it was my problem too. But I shall not tell Gyp. There'll be a different solution for us—something else must save us from the drifting armchairs and the spreading carpet.

"I've been thinking," Gyp says quietly, "that it might be a good idea if we packed up here, Helen."

"Packed up? What d'you mean, Gyp?" My errant thoughts crumble before this unexpected impact with the present and I am suddenly drawn close to Gyp with an urgency that I thought could no longer exist.

"Well, the trip to London next week is part of it. Maybe I've got a bit of that urge to serve too. I've been wondering whether it mightn't be a good idea to do some research. I'm seeing a chap about it next week. Tropical diseases, you know. I've had the practical experience; I think I could do something in that line."

"But Gyp, what about your work here?" I am frightened because everything that I know and have built up is shimmering uncertainly before me. It has the fantastic shape of a dream and at any moment I may wake up and find it is gone.

"Any G.P. could take this over," Gyp says shortly.

"But they couldn't, Gyp. Not in the way you do it. Look at the mess Dr. Rawlins made of this practice while you were in the army. Hundreds of people depend on you here, and then there are all your committees and things and the Rural District Council." It doesn't sound very convincing as I say it, and I wonder if Gyp senses the desperation I am feeling.

"There's something in your argument, but I'm afraid it's only because I'm probably a better hack doctor than research wallah. But I'll have a stab at the latter if you'd like me to."

"Me? Why should I want you to?" How can I make Gyp understand that this house and everything in it and our life here as doctor and doctor's wife must continue if we are ever to make anything of our marriage now.

"I wake up sometimes at night," he says, "and think to myself that as far as this house and practice goes, you've had it."

"But, Gyp, I haven't. I . . . I love it." Even if it is only the shell of what existed before, there is security in a shell and time will replenish the vacuum created by war and separation. I can't say this to Gyp because I have never explained the vacuum to him.

"But you're bored—you must be bored. What is there for you in Kirton, Helen?"

"Lots of things, Gyp dear. This house and Jenny Wren and catering and the Watsons and Mary Cross and the Gurney family; being tactful to your patients and—I nearly forgot—the Women's Institute. Not to mention my husband."

He smiles at this and my panic subsides.

"What a come down for a senior officer of His Majesty's Forces!" he laughs.

"Is it?"

"Well; isn't it? After all, you were once on the staff at the War House, weren't you?" His voice is teasing again.

"For the briefest of spells, thank goodness."

"Why?"

"Because I got the sack for not being sufficiently a yes-woman. Oh, you mean why was I glad it was brief? Because I couldn't take it, darling—the almost religious hysteria of an all-feminine War Office directorate. We lost our sense of proportion and spoke of 'Higher Authority' in hushed voices. Our hair grew shorter and our noses longer until we were almost indistinguishable from ant-eaters, terrifying and insatiable and hoping, with all the intensity of our little minds, that the worst would turn out to be the worst. Frightened of our own shadows, but even more scared of the opinion of MEN! You see, most of us hadn't got a man then. That was probably half our trouble."

Gyp says slowly:

"You don't often talk about it, do you?"

"No. It's a long way away somehow."

"I don't understand that. Mine's awfully close still. Come on, let's go to bed."

We do the things to a room which one does before leaving it. Gyp turns out the lights and says:

"I like hearing about your side of it, you know."

"I'll try to remember some more for you."

"Will you?" He stands by the door, hesitating.

"What's the matter, Gyp?"

"Nothing. I just wish you were happier, that's all."

"Darling, I'm all right. I wouldn't say that if I wasn't. Come on, let's go up."

He puts his arm through mine.

"The room looks nice in the firelight, doesn't it?"

"That's what I've been trying to tell you all the evening, Gyp." I laugh nervously and hope he won't ask me why I'm laughing.

* * * *

Lily Cobb laughed nervously.

"Don't do it, Fred."

The tall young man held her at arm's length, searching in the dim light of the spring evening for something in her face which might give him an idea of her thoughts.

"What's the matter, Lil?" His speech was slow and broad.

"Someone might see us. Someone might be passing this way."

He tightened his hands round her arms, almost as if he would shake her.

"And what if they did, Lil? We've as much right to be here as anyone else, haven't we?" He spoke roughly, almost bitterly.

She stared back into his face. He was russet coloured, like Charlie had been, but he was longer and narrower.

There were hollows in his cheeks and his eyes were set wide and deep beneath thick brows.

"You wouldn't understand, Fred," she said, slowly.

He relaxed his grip at her words and fumbled disconsolately in his pocket for a cigarette. She leaned back against the gate and now that Fred was no longer touching her she longed to feel his arms about her. Did he love her? He said so, but that didn't mean a thing—or did it? There'd been plenty of other chaps from Little Copse who'd asked her out to the pictures. Mostly they'd wanted one thing. In the end she'd given up accepting invitations. Until she met Fred. He was different. In any case, she hadn't met him in the bar. He was a friend of Dick's who'd brought him in to supper one night a couple of months ago—a hungry young giant still scarred with the marks of a Jap prison camp.

Fred had found his cigarettes. He offered her one from a torn packet. The light from a match flared between them, casting deep shadows round their eyes. He let it burn itself out and flung it away as the blackened wood scorched his fingers.

"Lil," he said slowly, "Lil, you wouldn't bitch a fellow, would you?"

"Ssh!" she whispered. "Someone's coming." She had heard the steps whilst he was speaking. She pressed herself against the gate with her back to the road. "Fred, turn round, like me. No, not so close. Lean over the gate like I am and just smoke. Don't say anything."

He obeyed the panic of her voice, and the footsteps grew closer. A small bundle of a woman passed down the road and vanished round the bend. Fred drew close to Lil again.

"You're shivering," he said.

"That was Mrs. Metcalf," she answered, "tomorrow all the village will know you and I were here tonight—up to no good," she added bitterly.

This time he did shake her. Then he drew her gently against himself. She smelt the faint aroma of sawdust and kitchen soap which always surrounded him. She let herself relax and felt his embrace tighten.

"Listen, Lil, I want you." His voice was rough and warm. "But I want you for keeps, see? I want you—and Tommy," he added gently.

Suddenly the tears were scalding her eyes and she couldn't speak. He did love her. He meant what he said. She lifted her face to look at him and his mouth was against her cheek, tasting the salt of tears.

"What are you crying for, girl?" he asked softly.

"I'm so happy," she whispered. He kissed her again and this time she responded with all the urgency of her taut, young body.

Presently they drew apart, breathless in the still, soft night. "You love me, Lil." The words were a jubilant statement.

"I love you, Fred."

He was holding her small, square hand in his, playing with her fingers, and she noticed that he had an untidy plaster dressing on one of his thumbs. She thought 'They're always chipping bits off themselves at Little Copse,' and she wondered, anxiously, if the cut was quite clean.

He said:

"I nearly got you a ring, over in Dimstone, this afternoon, and then I wasn't sure, you see."

"Sure of what?"

"That you'd take it. Now I'm sure, I'll get it next Wednesday."

"And you're sure too?" she asked.

"Sure I'm sure!" They laughed and he held her close to him again.

"I'd like us to get married soon," he said. "I'll be through with Little Copse next month, so we might do it then."

Next month. It seemed tremendously near somehow. Would they get married here or in Yorkshire where Fred's home was? Dad and Mum would like her to be married from the Cock and Pheasant, she thought. So far as she was concerned she didn't mind where it happened. There'd be a lot of chatter and stares in the village—but it would learn them. She shook her head defiantly.

"What you thinking about, Lil?" Fred asked. She said:

"Will your family like Tommy, Fred?"

"There's only my old man left at home now," he said slowly, "he's a good one with kids. He won't mind my marrying a widow when he sees Tommy."

Lil felt the lump in her throat again. No one but Fred could have put it that way. Maybe having been through what happened to him as a prisoner of war made him sensitive like. She couldn't remember ever having known a young man to be tactful to a girl. Not even Charlie. But then Charlie was always on Ops., nervy as a bullock waiting in the slaughter-house. Fred was nervy too, but he'd got it more under control.

She said:

"Fred, I'd like you to tell Dad."

"What, ask his permission?" he sounded peeved.

"No, Fred. Just tell him soon. He'd like it, so would Mum. Even if they didn't it wouldn't make any difference to us. But they've been good to me and they'd like it. I nearly left here before last Christmas. Then I couldn't somehow, because of everything they'd done."

"Left here? What for?"

So he was jealous. Charlie had been jealous too. As if she cared. She couldn't ever love more than one person at a time and now she'd got Fred.

"Work," she replied. "Let's go and see Dad now."

"All right."

But they stayed where they were, young and in love. Presently Lily said:

"We'll look in on Else and Dick on the way back. I'd like them to know. Else doesn't get about any more, her baby's coming this month."

Dick Cobb's cottage was narrow and low. There was no light upstairs and only firelight gleamed through the lace curtains of the ground floor window.

"Funny, they don't seem to be home," Lily said, and then added: "They must be, the door's ajar."

Inside the narrow passage, they heard the sound of a woman crying. Lily said:

"Wait here, Fred."

He felt constricted in the darkness, as if the walls would encompass him for ever. Prison. This was another prison. He sensed the sweat on his face and between his shoulder blades. He began to tremble uncontrollably. The sound of sobbing and voices came to him from a long way off. He must get out of here. He must breathe again. But he couldn't leave—Lil was here too. The walls felt wet against the palms of his hands.

Inside the room, Lily searched for matches and the gas mantle.

"Else, Else, what's happened?"

"Go away. Go away."

"It's me, Else. It's Lil." She'd found the matches and the gas spluttered shrilly through the room.

"Oh, go away, Lil." The misshapen figure was crouched on the sofa, but her sobs were less loud.

"Where's Dick? You're ill, Else. Where's Dick?"

"He's gone."

"Gone?"

"Walked out on me after tea."

Suddenly Elsie's face contracted and she gave an involuntary cry; she leaned back and then forward until her head touched her knees. Lil clenched her hands in sympathy.

"It's my pains," Elsie whimpered, "they started just after he left."

Lily felt utterly helpless, inadequate in the face of Elsie's pain and trouble.

"I'll get Mum. Wait, Else; Fred's outside; I'll tell him to fetch Mum."

"I don't want no one. Go away, go away. I want to die." Elsie wept loudly again.

Lily went outside the door. In the darkness she found Fred, lax against the wall.

"Fred, fetch Mum. Tell her Elsie's pains have started. Tell Dick to come too if he's there. Hurry, Fred, please." He seemed difficult to move but she thrust him to the door. He gulped in the cool fresh air outside. "Go on, Fred, go. Else is in trouble," she urged.

"O.K.," he mumbled; then, more firmly, "You staying here, Lil?"

"Until Mum comes. I'll be with you later. Hurry, please." She gave him a little push.

Elsie seemed calmer when she got back. Lil wondered what she ought to do—-kettles, hot water, sheets. . . .

Elsie said:

"We had an awful row, Lil."

"Don't worry, Else. Mum's coming; it'll be all right."

"He's chucked up his job at Little Copse. I told him what I thought of him then. Why should he pack it up just when the baby's coming. Why should he do that—tell me?"

"It's part of his wounds, Else; he can't help it."

"He said he'd join up again if he could. He said the army got you places Civvy Street never could."

"Well, he can't join up again; he's pensioned off," Lily said soothingly.

"But why should he want to? That's the trouble, Lil. I wouldn't want to go back like him. Goodness knows I earned enough on munitions during the war, but once I'd got Dick and then Stevie, I wanted a steady life. Not a lot of chopping and changing."

"I know; but then Dick was wounded."

"So were a lot of others; no—I know the trouble, it's the army. They shouldn't ever have made him a captain. It's made everything topsy turvy. He can't settle now—wounds or no wounds."

Lily's mind buzzed with arguments, but she couldn't contradict Elsie. Not when she had her pains and all. She ought to do something about Elsie, but what? She longed suddenly for the satisfying pattern of the R.A.F. where you just reported to the sergeant. Whatever happened after that, you were clear.

Maggie Cobb bustled in. Lily had never been gladder to see her mother. Elsie was gripped with pain again. Maggie said:

"Put the kettles on, Lil, and then go and tell Mrs. Mitchell. After that go by Dr. Townsend's. Tell him you've called Mrs. Mitchell. And then go home and help your dad. We're busy."

Orders, orders—the blessed peace of carrying them out. Lily reached the midwife's cottage.

"Mrs. Mitchell, Elsie Cobb's started her pains. My mum's there and I'm going on to tell Dr. Townsend. Good night, Mrs. Mitchell."

And then the Townsends' house. Jenny Cookson opened the door.

"Is Dr. Townsend there, Jenny?"

"Hello, Lil. No, he's out on a visit."

"Can I see Mrs. Townsend?"

Jenny wasn't pleased, but she got the doctor's wife.

"Mrs. Townsend, my sister-in-law, Elsie Cobb, has started her pains. I've let Mrs. Mitchell know and my mum's there. Will you tell the doctor."

Somewhere in the background Jenny Cookson's ears were stretched.

"But of course, Lily. He won't be long. He's just gone up to the Manor to see Mrs. Zarek's little boy. I'll tell him as soon as he gets back—or phone him if he's away long. It's her second child so she shouldn't have too bad a time, should she? How's your Tommy?"

"He's fine, thank you." And then, suddenly:

"I'm getting married next month, Mrs. Townsend."

"Oh, Lily, how lovely. Who is it? I'd like to congratulate him."

It was no longer the doctor's wife, but a friend talking to her. It occurred to Lily that Mrs. Townsend was beautiful. Funny, she hadn't seen it before. A wistful and misty beauty like a close-up of Greer Garson. She said:

"To Fred Barrett. He was taken prisoner at Singapore. We shall live in Yorkshire—Tommy too, of course."

"I'm so glad, Lily. But your parents will miss you—we shall all miss you at the Cock and Pheasant; Mr. Barrett's a very lucky man."

Lily liked hearing Fred called Mr. Barrett, it sounded sort of safe.

"Thank you, Mrs. Townsend. I must go now, Dad's on his own."

Hurrying through the darkness, she had time to think about Fred again. It seemed ages since they'd stood by the gate in Pilferer's Lane.

She felt warm and excited because he would be at home when she got there.

She slipped in by the side door and combed her hair through before going into the bars. John Cobb flashed a questioning glance at her as she came in and she nodded a reassuring reply. He was busy on the public bar side. Madge, who was the new help, seemed to be coping with the saloon bar. It wasn't too crowded.

She saw Fred sitting at one end of the counter drinking a mild. She went across and said:

"Isn't Dick here?"

"No, your dad hasn't seen him this evening. Why, what's up?"

"Nothing, I hope. He and Elsie had a bit of a bust-up this afternoon and he went off. Her pains started after that. Poor Else."

"D'you want me to go and look for him, Lil?"

"Yes. . . . No, not yet. Let's wait for a bit, he might turn up."

"Silly mucker. But he can't help it. You know that, Lil?" He looked uncomfortable. He was fond of Dick Cobb, but he was in love with Lily.

"I know, Fred, and so do Mum and Dad. It's just Elsie who can't understand. Maybe she will when she's had the baby. Fred, have you spoken to Dad?"

"About us? No, not yet."

She felt a shiver of disappointment. It was terribly important that Fred should tell her father; She didn't know why, but the fact that he hadn't, brought back the familiar sensations of insecurity. She served a couple of whiskies to a man and a girl whom she hadn't seen in the pub before and then wandered back to Fred's corner.

"Don't look like that, Lil," he said. "Your dad hasn't even noticed me yet. He's been up to his ears with the orders."

She said:

"I must talk to him about Dick. I'll be back in a moment, Fred."

John Cobb had been watching his daughter as he methodically drew beer from the engines and banged at the cash register. She was clear eyed and flushed and he had seen her talking to Fred Barrett.

She came across to him now and he noticed that even her walk seemed different, buoyant and positive, in a way he remembered it before the war. She said:

"Mum's staying with Else, and I've told Mrs. Mitchell and Dr. Townsend. But Dick's gone off. Else and he had words 'cos he's chucked up his job at Little Copse, and he went off about five o'clock."

"Silly young b. . ., what's he playing at?" John Cobb was upset. He hadn't reckoned for that sort of trouble.

"He can't help it, Dad."

"Can't help it? He's got to help it. I won't have a son of mine treating Else like that when she's having her kid. It's time someone told him where he got off. There's been too much of this 'he can't help it' going the rounds of this house. Chucking his job up at a time like this. What's he think he's going to do next?"

Lily was surprised at his reaction; Dad was ever so calm about things as a rule; why had he got his rag out all of a sudden? She said:

"Well, we'd better find him first, hadn't we, Dad?"

"Find him? I'll find him all right and when I do he's going to come into this house and learn the trade. Else will be a grand governor's missus when Mum and I are gone. Lil, go and see what old Tom's grumbling about. I've told him there's no more bottled beer."

Lily went to pacify Tom Cowley and her heart was light and surprised. She'd always known she and Dad didn't have to say much to understand one another, but she'd never seen him the way he was tonight. As if he already knew about her and Fred, when he talked about Else and Dick. With her and Tommy gone, there'd be room for Dick and his family here if they gave over Grandma's room too. Maybe that's how things would plan out. If only someone could find Dick tonight.

She went back to her father.

"Dad, Fred over there says he'll go and look for Dick, but he'd like to have a word with you first." She felt nervous as she spoke.

John Cobb said:

"What's he think I am? A gentleman of leisure? Can't he see the bar's full? Oh, all right, Lil, but mind you keep your eyes skinned. Just because I'm about to produce another grandchild doesn't mean the business can go to pot." He was smiling and somehow the ends of his moustache looked spry like they did on Sundays. Someone was tapping on the counter with a coin. She went over to deal with the orders.

Fred Barrett said to John Cobb:

"Lil and I are going to get married." He said it defiantly.

"I'm very fond of my daughter, young fellow. Maybe there's more to it than what you say," John replied slowly. Fred met his glance and suddenly he no longer felt aggressive.

"I've got a job waiting for me in Halifax. Furnishing business. We can make a home with my old man till we find a place of our own," he said.

John Cobb looked round his house; it was quieter and both the bars were under control. He said:

"What's yours?"

"Mild, thank you."

He drew the drinks slowly, wondering all the time what Maggie was going to say about this. Fred Barrett was a good enough chap but being a prisoner all those years didn't make for steadiness. Then he thought of Lil's eyes when she'd come home tonight.

"Cheers," he said and raised his glass.

"We'd be living outside the town," Fred said awkwardly, and took a gulp of his beer, "that'll be all right for Tommy. There's nothing like a bit of Yorkshire air for kids."

"There's nothing wrong with London, come to that. I was born and bred there." John Cobb said gruffly, suddenly self-conscious about this young man with his red hair and blue eyes. He looked good. You couldn't tell about some people, but Fred Barrett shone like Maggie's brasses over the kitchen mantel. John went on, "Still, country air's always good for kids. Well, son, it's all right with me so long as you make it all right with the missus. She's busy tonight."

"I'll be moving along then. Lil wants me to have a look for Dick." Fred rose from the bar and stretched his hand out to John Cobb. "Dick's being a silly mucker, but he'll be all right when he knows about Elsie. Silly mucker, he is."

John Cobb agreed.

"I'll tell Lil you're going," he said, "she'll want to see you out."

Lil hurried from the bars to the coolness of the night. Fred held her tightly.

"I'll find him, Lil. Don't worry. I know the haunts and he's sure to be with the lads. Your dad was all right. Lil, we're going to be married next month. Lil, I love you—honest I do, like mad."

It seemed as if she couldn't let him leave her on this night when so much was happening.

* * * *

"Every bloody thing's got to happen at the same time," Angela Worthing muttered and thrust her breakfast cup of tea aside.

Two letters by this morning's post. The first from the B.B.C. She'd got the job of Talks Assistant. It didn't sound much but she'd put in for it because, mentally, it was right up her street. It hadn't been too difficult either—an interview, getting on the short list and then another interview. The confirmation now nestled against the teapot. That meant giving notice to the Little Copse Training Centre and moving back to the London flat.

The second letter raised different problems. It was from Jim Cardew. She picked it up and re-read part of the last paragraph.

". . . I'm sorry I haven't written to you sooner about all this, but I've been pretty busy lately and Molly has been ill. She needs a bit of South of France sun, but unfortunately the damn Frogs still don't seem to cater for us there. Personally I've nothing against your Peter Gurney, but he simply wasn't up to the sort of job I'd intended. We parted on the best of terms and I feel sure his particular qualifications lie in a more creative channel. He seemed to be of the same opinion when we said good-bye last month. Let me know if there's anything else I can do. I still think this Government's going to stick its head in a noose and we shall then be able to get back to normal again. Molly says . . ."

Angela stubbed her cigarette out viciously. There were times when she would willingly have knitted to the rhythm of falling Cardew heads. But, at this moment, she'd got other things to do.

She rang up the office to tell them she had to go to town on urgent business and might not be back this week. She also mentioned her resignation from the Training Centre. They knew she was mad anyhow. Any woman who worked for her living because she wanted to, and not because she'd got to—and then bothered about getting a better job—must be mad.

It was a slow train, stopping at every lamp-post like old Mr. Watson's dog. But it gave her time to think. She'd spent two week-ends ago in the flat with Peter and he'd not said a word about losing his job. It had been a good week-end and there'd been no repetition of the Brian-Serena night. Why hadn't he told her then, and what the hell was he living on now?

When she got to the flat it was untidy, but no more so than she remembered it since Peter's arrival. He was sitting in the kitchen in his dressing gown and eating sardines out of a tin.

"Darling, why didn't you tell me you were coming? Have a sardine. There's some bread in the bin."

He looked awful, but then he always did before he shaved. The puffiness under his eyes had a mottled look.

"Got a day off from the office?" she asked.

"Oh, that. I've chucked in the job. Too much Gestapo work attached to it. Always snooping on other people. Not my cup of tea. I wish you'd have a sardine, Angie; you must be starving."

"Thanks, I would like one." She watched him fumbling with a knife and fork. "What are you doing now, Peter?"

"Playing bridge. Not doing too badly either—touch wood. At the Nelson Club. Best players in London there, and they admit women. My God, they're hot stuff. At bridge I mean. But I'm lucky, I've cleared two fifty pounds up to the present."

"What stakes do you play for?"

"Pound a hundred—sometimes two. I used to play a lot before the war and somehow I know their game. When we're partners we win and when they're against me they don't. Anyhow it's keeping me off the drink."

""Why?" She helped herself to margarine and made a sand-wich of the sardines. She was suddenly hungry.

"I can't take more than two or three whiskies if I'm going to concentrate. I need those to steady me, but more gets me mixed up. So I don't take 'em. Bit of a strain, one way and another."

"I suppose it is." She noticed that his hands were shak-ing when he lit a cigarette, but he was more buoyant than she remembered him. In fact, he seemed pleased with himself. She said: "And supposing you'd lost two fifty pounds instead of winning it?"

"But I haven't. I tell you I'm good at the game, Angela. I don't know—I seem to have a thing about it, I just know what to do and when to do it and my partners play well with me and keep their mistakes for when we're opponents."

"I see. So now you're going to settle down to earning a living at bridge."

"Well, no, not exactly." He began to look sheepish and nibbled his thumb nail. "But it's all right as a side line and it's silly to stop when your luck's in."

"Oh, so there is luck in the game, not just skill?"

"Come off it, Angie." He lit another cigarette from the stub he was smoking. She noticed the stained fingers on his left hand.

"I'm not putting on an act," she replied. "I'm just interested, that's all." She powdered her nose and put on her hat.

"Where are you going?" he asked, and there was less confidence in his voice.

"Shopping. I don't suppose you've got a store of provisions in, have you?" She opened the kitchen cupboard and noted a smear of margarine in a saucer, a half emptied bottle of sour milk and some be-whiskered cheese. "Where's your ration book, Peter?"

"In the sitting room, I think. I'll get it." She followed him. The sitting room was full of old newspapers and covered in dust and ash.

"Here it is. But listen, Angie, what about going out on a party tonight. I've got plenty of cash."

"No thanks, Peter. I shall cook a meal here and after that I'm going to scrub the place out. You might tidy it up when you're dressed, it'll make the spring cleaning simpler." She collected a shopping bag from the hall and then stood by the door of the sitting room. Peter had sunk into an arm chair and was glancing at a copy of yesterday's *Evening Standard*.

"I wish you'd told me, when I was last up, that you'd lost the job at Jim Cardew's," she said, slowly.

"I didn't want to worry you. We had a grand week-end, didn't we?" He grinned at her suddenly. "In any case I've got another job I can go to."

"Really? What?"

"Chap I used to know in the Navy. He's something to do with youth clubs, national association of something or the other. He says they like ex-service people to run their boys' clubs and things."

"What sort of salary?"

"Oh, we didn't go into that. But I told him I'd come along and help on the sports side if he liked. It would be fun to get one's hands on a cricket bat again. I might go down a couple of times a week to start with. Voluntary, of course. One can't take money for a thing like that."

"I see." She looked round the room again. "As a matter of fact I've got a new job too."

"Have you—what?" He seemed interested.

"B.B.C. I shall be moving back into this flat on the first of the month. That's why I want to get the place cleaned out. I suppose Mrs. White has given notice again? She used to do it on me in the old days, about twice a year."

"No. As a matter of fact I told her to take a month off; her son's back from Burma."

She thought, 'Why does he bother to lie to me? Of course he hasn't paid Mrs. White and, quite rightly, she's given up the job.' But she said no more as she went towards the front door. Peter called after her:

"Does that mean you want me to clear out by the first?"

"I haven't the faintest idea—yet." She closed the door quietly behind her and then leaned back against it, exhausted. It had needed all her control not to slam it shut.

Outside, London was bubbling with the atmosphere of spring. The lilac bushes in Brunswick Square showed bright green buds against their sooty branches and against the syca-more trees the sky was flat blue like a summer sea except for some lamb's-wool clouds rollicking in a high wind above.

Why had she so nearly lost her temper with Peter? What made him able to get under her skin in this way? And why should she, of all people, feel so responsible for him?

She walked round by Lansdowne Place where, since May 1941, they'd been patching up the blitzed corner. She noticed, with methodical satisfaction, that yet another gleaming yellow brick building was nearing completion. You could date the devas-tation and the rate of repair from the lighter brick walls down to the grey black of the house on the Guilford Street corner.

Yes, spring was certainly here. The ladies of Guilford Street had discarded their utility furs for brighter and shorter jackets. Pale sunshine gleamed on the darkening partings of bleached heads. They are feeling the draught, poor dears, Angela thought, and noted the complete absence of American uniforms from the street scene. That was the big transformation—apart from spring and scaffolding—there were no Americans.

Poor Americans. Angela almost regretted their depar-ture. They'd been good time fellows and the good time girls in London had taken them up in a big way, gum and all. Indi-vidually, Angela had liked them. In herds, they'd been a little overpowering. They'd had too much money and they looked so dreadful in those uniforms—all bottom somehow. She remem-bered someone in a pub who'd once told her that the trouble with American men was that their own women treated them like dirt, which was why they ended by behaving like dirt. It made you think. She thought about Peter.

The blitz scars of Guilford Street were healed with fresh green weeds. In a few months' time they would be carpeted with the yellow of dandelions and speared with the tall bright pink-ness of fireweed. She turned into Lamb's Conduit Street to do her shopping. The tradesmen's sons were beginning to filter back from the services. They were easier to buy from than their fathers and mothers, less fractious and exhausted by five years of rationing and form-filling.

She bought chops on Peter's book and then groceries, preserves, biscuits and kitchen soap. She went off the ration for tinned soup, potted meat, toilet paper and Vim. There was also an egg allocation. She cosseted the egg gently on top of her other purchases. What a tiny amount of everything you got on one ration book. She was used to the communal existence of the Little Copse Training Centre where you handed in your book and somehow ate adequately, if dully, for the rest of the week. You could starve with decency on one ration book. She noticed that Peter hadn't bought his rations last week and felt furious: it was too late now to cash in on the coupons.

She went to the greengrocers across the road and found a queue. There was an orange allocation which accounted for the afternoon crowd. Not that she minded; she rather enjoyed queues when she had time for them. She settled down to shuffle.

The woman in front was talking to her neighbour about a soldier back from Burma.

"Ever such a sad case," she muttered; "his wife's had two illegibles whilst he's been abroad and he didn't know nothing about it."

"Too bad," replied her neighbour; "reminds me of a case in our street, only hers died. But even that didn't learn her and she went off to Manchester with one of them Class 'B' releases—a bricklayer, he was—just one week before her bloke got back from Italy. I never saw a chap so drunk in my life before; they turned him out of three pubs that night, and him with all his ribbons up and the dirt of foreign suns still on him."

The queue moved forward a few feet. This, for some reason, released a cat from between the vegetable crates. It ran haphazardly into the road and seemed to disappear beneath the wheels of a car. There were screams from the women at the end of the queue and an oath from a man passing by. A hoarse voice yelled to the greengrocer:

"Frank, your cat's gone for a burton. Right under the wheels, he went. Saw it happen with me own eyes."

But the cat was walking back across the road, sedately, with nothing more than its dignity hurt.

A voice said:

"Angela Worthing?"

Angela turned and found Mary Cross behind her.

"I thought I recognized your back, my dear. How are you?" Mary Cross noted that this was the first time she'd seen Angela looking her age.

Angela thought: 'Lord, that woman! With all the queues in London, why must we choose the same one?'

"Hello, Mrs. Cross. Are you up for the day?"

"No, I'm staying the week. Our annual staff meeting, you know, and then I'm trying to arrange for Michael's party next month. His book's coming out on the twenty-fifth, so we thought we'd celebrate. You'll be getting an invitation. We still have the flat in Mecklenburgh Square."

"That will be lovely. I've got a place in Brunswick Square and I shall be there then as I'm leaving Little Copse and going to the B.B.C."

"Lucky woman being able to change your job when you want. I seem to be inundated with letters from wretched girls who are either frozen to ministerial desks or directed into uncongenial jobs."

Angela thought: 'What a cat,' but she answered sweetly: "I believe I still have to do something about a Green Card, even at my great age. But I'm hoping it's only a formality."

Mary Cross didn't look like a cat. She looked more like one of the sacks of vegetables in her faded tweed suit and dusty brogues. She exuded earth and tobacco even in a London street. Angela decided that Michael's mother was enjoying her peace. Her eyes sparkled beneath a grotesque felt hat and even in the revealing spring sunshine the creases in her face looked carefree and contented.

The queue gave one of its spasmodic forward movements. Mary Cross said:

"Gyp and Helen Townsend are coming to stay with Michael next week. Michael's so fond of them."

"How nice." There didn't seem anything else to add, but she wasn't going to be silenced by this old woman who seemed so satisfied with life, so she went on: "I expect you're very excited about Michael's book, aren't you? Is it good?"

"My dear child, don't ask me. I'm his mother. I think it's quite excellent." Mary Cross gave one of her loud laughs.

"Let's hope the reviewers have the same maternal instincts," Angela replied and was glad to see she'd irritated Mary Cross.

"It won't be my fault if they don't. Hence the party! But let's not talk about the Cross family anymore. You look tired, Angela; have they been working you too hard at Little Copse?"

The bitch, the queen bitch. Why hadn't she said 'You're looking haggard and your nose needs powdering,' when that's what she meant.

"I am a bit tired, but it's probably only the spring or war reaction or maybe plain liver."

"I know. I get hundreds of tired letters at this time of the year."

"So you're still 'Aunt Jennifer'?" Angela hoped her voice was derisive. She found Mary Cross intolerable at this moment.

"Still Aunt Jennifer? My dear, they've had to give me extra staff. You've no idea of the problems and questions we get asked. On every possible subject—from babies to beehives. Hundreds of them." Mary Cross sounded delighted about it all.

Angela found her sense of humour returning.

"Then you might," she said, laughing, "answer this one for me: what to do with a man who is apparently either incapable or unwilling to settle down to a job of work?"

Mary Cross looked at her seriously for a moment, then she replied:

"If I were you, Angela—I mean, if I were a woman of your ability—I'd have him taught cooking and then marry him."

Dear, old-fashioned viper, Angela thought, good-naturedly.

PART IV

"You've changed a lot, Helen."

"Have I, Brian? I suppose we all have."

He has been silent during lunch, quite unlike the vigorous and voluble creature I remember. And yet I am more conscious of the changes in myself than him.

"I noticed such an odd thing from the top of a bus this morning, Brian."

"What?"

"The trees in Aldwych. They're bursting with green buds, but twisted and caught between the branches there are still some discoloured paper streamers from V.J. day. D'you remember, they flung them out of the top windows until the trees looked like a Swiss Christmas card scene. It seems incredible that any should have lasted through the winter. Like an obstinate hangover."

"Why are you talking so much?"

"Probably because you're so silent." He gives a familiar grin at this and, for a flash, I can see him with past eyes.

I can now admit to myself that I was in a panic when I came to meet him today, a panic of uncertainty. What impression would he make on me? What unknown threads might suddenly draw me close to him again?

I need not have been afraid. I knew as soon as I shook hands with him that I was free.

Dear Brian, he is very sweet and I shall always like him. He looks sleek with his curling dark hair combed close to his head, and wearing that very correct blue suit. There is something almost too commercial about the suit and I am suddenly nostal-

gic for the glamour of a khaki battle-dress and a green beret. I
like to remember people in the clothes that suit them best.

"Would you like a liqueur with your coffee, Helen? They've
got a perfectly drinkable Spanish brandy which has the added
advantage of being Government controlled!" He smiles again
and I forget the blue suit for a moment.

"I'd love one, Brian." I feel lightheaded and I want to celebrate my liberation.

Brian orders and watches the golden liquid being poured
into warmed brandy glasses:

"Make them doubles," he says, "and bring another pot of hot
coffee, will you?"

I am looking round the restaurant. It is small and attrac-
tively arranged. It has no grandeur and no sordidness and I
feel at home here. There are more women than men lunching
today. I am always interested in watching women and I am curious about their lives. There are certain things you can tell at a
glance, and a great deal you can guess at a second glance. But
you're never really sure about them.

There is a girl opposite with a man. She is not very young and
not very beautiful. She wears no wedding ring, but I know she
must have a lot of people in love with her and she certainly has
a lover. You can read it in her hands. She has the most revealing hands I have ever seen. I don't know why. I am reminded
of Angela Worthing, although this girl is blonde. Then there is
a married woman on our right who has lost interest in life. She
is smart and good looking, but her face is dead. The man with
her is obviously her husband and he has been reduced to silent
contemplation of the girl with the hands. In a corner there are
two desperate virgins. It is their own fault because they have
no courage, and I am reminded this time of Laura Watson and
the A.T.S. P.T. officer who, in the early days of the war, used to
address all new recruits on the 'Facts of Life.' I can recall much
of the speech which was an unbelievable blend of sentiment and
obscenity. There was a bit about the 'Little Bell.' The 'Little Bell'

which rang in every girl's head to warn her of the dangers of a too fond kiss or a too long embrace. Laura Watson and the two desperate virgins in the corner had, unfortunately, always heeded the 'Little Bell.' I feel rather giggly at the thought and I wonder if the brandy is going to my head.

Brian says:

"I hear Dick Cobb's gone to work in his father's pub."

"Yes. Lily Cobb married an ex-prisoner of war and has gone to live in Yorkshire with Tommy. Dick's wife had her second baby; he gave up the carpentering job at Little Copse and is now working in the Cock and Pheasant. I think the old couple are pleased. They want to feel that the business will be carried on by one of the family after they've gone. Dick seems to have settled down very well."

"I wonder . . ."

"You mean because of his wounds and war shock?"

"Yes. And other things. It isn't everyone who's been lucky enough to settle down in Civvy Street as serenely as you have, Helen."

"No, I suppose not," I am still fascinated by the girl with the hands, and then I notice the hurt in Brian's eyes. "I'm sorry, Brian. Have I said something wrong?"

"No, my dear. You're just being typically yourself. You were always endowed with an obstinate honesty."

I feel guilty, because of all the things I may possess, I can't find honesty among the qualities, not even the obstinate variety. I am aware that Brian has not yet said anything to confirm the urgency of his letter making this appointment. I have been so filled with my own reactions, so delighted at my self-revelations. On my release certificate from the A.T.S. it said something about being released from actual duty but being liable to recall until the end of the emergency. My emotional emergency is over.

"Are you happy, Helen?" Brian's voice sounds disinterested.

"Yes, Brian, I am." I nearly add, 'thanks to you today,' but he might not understand.

"I came here with the intention of whisking you away with me if you weren't," he replies nonchalantly. I realize then that he is being serious.

"Well, you see, you haven't got to," I say awkwardly.

"Yes, I see that all right. Which makes me all the more sorry I didn't do it months ago."

"Brian, please. . . ." I don't want to hear what he has to say.

"Sorry, Helen, but I'm going to go on talking. Of course I should have taken you away with me when the war ended. Then we would have been together today. You see, I happen to love you. You're one of those things that happen once. I've got you, as the French say, '*dans ma peau.*' I prefer that to the American version, don't you? I made up my mind to let you go your own way last year because I hoped you felt the same about me. I was wrong. On the other hand I could have made you feel that way if we'd been able to stay together. But we weren't. So what? So I asked you to come here today because I'm getting to be a very old man and I've got to know certain things before I settle down to senile decay. I know them now, but I shall always love you, Helen—even through the years of senile decay!" He is smiling at me and I feel embarrassed.

"I'm sorry, Brian. . . ." It sounds inadequate and foolish.

"I suppose I should say that I think Gyp is a lucky man. But I don't. I just think I'm unlucky. I still maintain that you and I found something together which neither of us could or will—have with anyone else. That's why I can't be jealous of Gyp. I only curse myself for not having insisted on you and I going away together last year. I'm not jealous of Gyp because I don't envy anyone a second-best existence. I only blame myself for letting the best slip away from me after I knew it to be the best—for both of us."

I suppose I should feel angry at his impertinence. But I don't. I only wonder at the little boy conceit of a grown man.

"I think, Brian, that you are forgetting one thing when you talk like that."

"What?"

"The war. It was a long war and nobody escaped it. It buffeted our lives like a storm, pitching us out of our homes and into unnatural circumstances. It is not surprising if, emotionally, we rather lost our sense of perspective. I know I did. I knew it as soon as I got over the strangeness of being a civilian again. I expect there are hundreds of thousands of people going through the same reaction, the same process—sometimes painfully—of being imbedded in the security of familiar happenings again. Rather like plants curling their roots into the safety of solid earth when they're potted out in the spring."

"I'm not a potted plant, Helen, and I think your outlook is purely sentimental. Heaven knows, I don't think we have to have a war to spur us on, but it very often works out that way. Even horrible experiences are beneficial when they evoke great things, whether it be courage or love. To want to settle back into an old rut is not necessarily always bad, but it's nearly always sentimental. I hate sentimentality."

"Because you can't discern between that and sentiment."

"Oh God, you don't begin to understand. Have another brandy?"

"No thanks, Brian."

"Then I will." He gives the order to a waiter. The restaurant is nearly empty now. "After that I must go. I've got a date," he speaks abruptly as though he had come to a decision. "As a matter of fact I'm going to get married. No, not this afternoon, don't look so startled."

I am taken aback and I feel rather breathless. It isn't often that you get a man announcing his undying love for you in one sentence and his marriage to another woman in the next.

"I didn't know, Brian . . ."

"Nor does she—yet." He seems to be smiling at something I know nothing about.

"Well, I'm very glad, Brian, for you . . ." It sounds stupid and stilted.

"Thank you, Helen," he says very solemnly and I wonder if he is a little drunk. "You have probably realized that this very natty gent's suiting is not just a rough soldier's disguise, but the outward expression of a worthy citizen who has ambitions to settle down. Like your blasted potted plants." He laughs suddenly. "I thought I'd add that before you could accuse me of it."

I don't know Brian in this mood.

"What's her name?" I ask for something to say.

"Serena." His face looks less harsh. "Serena Hughes. She's a grand kid. I've got a photograph of her somewhere." He brings a wallet from his pocket and grins maliciously across the table. "A horrid rough soldier's habit—carrying photographs around and inflicting them on a bored public. This one among others."

He hands me one with a torn edge and I recognize myself in A.T.S. uniform. It was taken at Dumfries.

I look at it impersonally and register that I looked quite nice in uniform.

"You can keep it if you want," he says.

"No, thank you." I don't want souvenirs of that sort.

"Then I might as well tear it up."

"I should if I were you." But he tucks it back into his wallet. "This is Serena."

It is a snapshot of a child on horseback and, again, I feel a little breathless, because here is beauty that catches me unawares. The clouds, the horse, the trees and the vulnerable girl seem to spring from the same vital force that is life.

"She's lovely, Brian."

"You can't see it properly there. She's got a copper head that is really gold."

"You must be in love with her," I say involuntarily.

"Is one in love with a child? With the moods and mad enthusiasms, the dignity and utter generosity of youth? Of course I am."

"Brian, that's rather a beastly thing to say."

"Don't be a prude, Helen. You, of all people, should know the way I feel."

My memories stir, like moth-eaten ghosts, and I feel very old. Did I ever believe that it was possible to be in love with one person and to love another? That it was wanton and unethical but not madness? The year has turned full cycle.

"Don't look at me like that, Helen."

"How old is she, Brian?"

"Nineteen. Don't say I'm nearly old enough to be her father. I know that. But fathers have been known to be good husbands too."

"I'm not suggesting you won't be."

"Thank you, Helen. Let's go."

Outside, when I have left him, I am eager to see Gyp again, but he will not be back at the flat until six this evening. We are going out to dine with Michael Cross and a girl friend of his. Tomorrow we return to Kirton.

I have forgotten Brian and I have a lot to think about. I want to walk somewhere—Regent's Park is lovely in the spring. I will take a 53 bus there.

I have forgotten Brian, but I am remembering the last six months with Gyp. We have never been quite in step and I think it has probably been my fault. I have been so busy trying to put everything back in its right place, so eager to attain a state of perfection as I imagined it. But life isn't like that. You have to go on all the time, and places and people and circumstances alter. My vision has been narrow and I have no doubt missed a lot of important things whilst I have searched for old keys to doors which no longer exist. Maybe things will be different now that I am free. In any case I want to live, not just ponder and plan and torment myself with fantastic imaginings.

I want to walk in the sunlight, among the daffodils and narcissi in Regent's Park. I have a sudden impulse to go to the Zoo too—but not to the Monkey House.

*　　*　　*　　*

"Nonsense, Laura. Why should I go up to London to hear a lot of people jabbering like monkeys in an over-crowded room when I hear the same people jabbering in the High Street of Kirton every day of my life."

"It was just an idea, father." Laura Watson fingered the invitation card which Mrs. Cross had sent for Michael's party on the twenty-fifth. "There'll be lots of people apart from the Kirton people," she added, hopefully.

"I have no wish to meet strangers at my age, thank you. Have you hidden *The Times* away somewhere, Laura?"

"There it is, underneath your library book."

That was that. Laura sighed, but silently. It never did to let Mr. Watson hear any manifestations of disappointment or irritation. It only made him more obstinate, and she was determined to go to the Cross's party, whether her father accepted or not. She thought, 'I'll accept for myself and I'll get a new dress for it; I've plenty of my demobilization coupons left.' She remembered once when she was a child and had wheedled her father into allowing her to sit up for supper on her birthday. It had taken a whole week before permission was given and Aunt Bessie, who had been staying with them, had remarked to Laura's mother, "That child could circumvent the Almighty."

Mrs. Watson was dead now; Aunt Bessie remained, crippled with arthritis, and Laura's powers of circumvention had diminished with the years. In their place, however, a crust of obstinacy—remarkably similar to her father's—was beginning to harden. It never occurred to Laura that a plain statement of her own intentions would be accepted with acquiescence by Mr. Watson. That was too simple; besides she was too deeply imbued with the tradition of appeasing the old man. It was the same game of give and take, with Laura doing most of the giving, although the balance of power was beginning to shift imperceptibly as Mr. Watson's physical faculties weakened with age.

"Father, I thought I'd ask Geraldine Hall to come down for Whitsun weekend," she said casually.

"Why?"

"She's been ill and the change would do her good. You remember, you liked her the last time she came."

"What, that short-haired creature who was always strumming on the piano? Can't think what you see in her, Laura."

"She was my group commander in Scotland. She was always very nice to me and I like her a lot."

"Group commander! What a lot of nonsense you women got up to during the war. I can't think how the army got along at all with a pack of women dressing themselves up as soldiers, strutting about giving orders and poking their noses into a lot of matters that didn't concern them," he grumbled familiarly.

Laura took no notice. She knew he did it to annoy her. When she had first left the A.T.S. she would flare up at her father's derogatory remarks about women in uniform; on one occasion she had even burst into tears. But gradually she had learned to recognize the malicious glint in his eyes which preceded such remarks as 'to think that I should have sired a female captain, I'm ashamed of myself,' and so now she kept silent.

She began to clear away the tea things.

"Where's Ethel?" Mr. Watson asked.

"It's her afternoon off, father."

"I've never known it not be."

"Only Wednesdays and Sundays."

"Hmm." He folded *The Times* up neatly and tucked it under his arm as he got up. "I shall be in the dining room if you want me; I've got some indexing to do."

"Don't forget your magnifying glass, father."

"I don't need it for indexing, child, I'm not blind yet. It's a pity you don't take more interest in philately," he had reached the door, "then you could be of some assistance to me," he closed it swiftly behind him. The next moment he was back again.

"Laura, I thought your Aunt Bessie was coming for Whitsun. Had you forgotten?"

Laura had not forgotten. She never forgot things like visits and birthdays and anniversaries of weddings and funerals.

"She wasn't certain it would be warm enough for her to travel, father. In any case, Geraldine can have my room and I'll sleep on the bed in the attic," she replied gently.

"Then Ethel will certainly give notice." This time he closed the door with a little slam and Laura heard him shuffling across the hall to the dining-room and his stamps.

She continued to clear and then she washed up and put the tea things carefully away. After that she laid a tray with the cutlery and plates for a cold supper and opened a tin of tomato soup which could be heated later. All the time her thoughts were busy with the dress she'd buy before the cocktail party. Helen Townsend would advise her about it. Should she try Beattie's in Dimstone or would it be better to run up to town for an afternoon and go to Harrods? It would have to be bought immediately in case there were any alterations needed. As a rule she could walk into ready-made stock sizes, but now that she was beginning to put on weight round the hips, what fitted on the shoulders might need adjusting lower down.

There was nothing further to do in the kitchen and so she wandered up to her bedroom. She felt restless and impatient, as though something exciting were going to happen at any moment. Only nothing exciting ever did occur. It would be fun, of course, to go to a cocktail party in London, but there was nothing lasting about that sort of stimulation.

She leaned out of the open window and drew in breaths of cool spring air, but it only seemed to titivate the tingle of suppressed anticipation coursing through her body. Tomorrow she would really get down to doing something about the weeds in the garden. Also she must dig up that bed at the far end where she wanted to sow some annuals. And hoe the front paths. It would be good to get into old clothes and feel the physical benefit of a hard morning's work. Satisfying and soothing in this sort of weather.

Before the war there had always been parties in and around Kirton: Christmas balls, coming-out dances, tennis tournaments and cricket weeks. In the army there'd been concerts and dances and film shows galore. It seemed as if peace had suddenly found people too hard-pressed, too preoccupied to burden themselves with entertainment. Maybe this summer they would start up with tennis and a garden party again at the Manor.

All around her Laura's room lay neat and spotless, with her mother's ivory-backed dressing table set laid out symmetrically and the leather covered sewing box which had been Aunt Bessie's present when Laura joined up as a recruit in the A.T.S. On the writing table was the blotter given to her by her company when she was demobilized—against army regulations, of course, but a pleasing souvenir of a happy, carefree period of her life. And then photographs all around, on the walls and dressing table and chest of drawers. Large, silver-framed ones of her parents; one of Helen Townsend in uniform, wearing a side cap at a becoming angle; Geraldine Hall in a British warm; a shiny, press print of Laura and a bunch of service-women on the steps of the Town Hall at Croydon, taken during a recruiting rally. Lots more, too, but carefully pasted into the bound photograph albums on the bookshelf. Whenever she felt really depressed, Laura would turn to the albums for solace, forgetting for a while the dullness of peace. There was so much that was good to remember.

The front door bell rang and she hurried to answer it before it disturbed her father. It was Daphne Zarek.

"Hello, Laura. Helen asked me to drop these books in on you on my way past."

"Thanks, Daphne. Won't you come in?" Then seeing the doubtful look on Daphne's face, she added: "Father's doing his stamps in the dining-room, so I'm on my own."

Daphne accepted, without grace. She didn't care much for Laura Watson but on the other hand she had nothing else to do.

She looked round the white paintwork and glossy chintzes of the Watson drawing-room.

"What a light room this is, Laura. At home everywhere's like a coal hole unless you keep the lights blazing."

"But the Manor's so lovely, Daphne, with all its panelling."

"You should try living in it. We either have to huddle round the only coal fire for warmth—which means endless family discussions—or else pay the price of privacy which entails freezing and a probable cold in the head. I can't think why father doesn't sell the damn place; it's far too large for us now Peter and Brian have taken themselves off, and in any case we can't afford to live in it. The family's bank balance has to be looked at through a magnifying glass to be seen at all."

"How is Peter?" Laura asked because she was embarrassed at Daphne's reference to the Gurneys' finances. Laura was always uncomfortable when money was mentioned, and would blush dull red if people discussed the price of anything they'd bought.

"Peter? All right as far as we know. We understand he's living in sin with Angela Worthing. Mother takes the dimmest view of the whole proceedings." Daphne laughed suddenly.

"And Brian?" Laura hurried on, disliking the conversation more and more.

"Leading a blameless life, we hope; advertising tooth-pastes or something. He writes occasionally. Peter never does unless he's broke. Mind you, I couldn't agree more with my brothers. I don't believe in children living in the same house as their parents once they're grown up. It's completely stultifying. But then I have no alternative at present. Having been brought up and educated in the arts of leisure only, I am incapable of earning a living for myself or my son. Or am I just plain lazy?" She smiled rather bitterly.

Laura said:

"You're not lazy, Daphne. Look at the way you make all Ian's clothes and look after him entirely yourself."

"Yes, dear, but nobody's going to pay me for doing that, and only my parents are willing to keep me! Too bad, isn't it? Oh well, I suppose things might be worse. At least I don't have to work in a factory."

"Did you hate it so much?"

"I loathed it and the more I got used to it the worse it seemed to be. You see, I don't like my own sex when they're in great numbers. I hate endless stories about other people's boy friends and I don't understand politics or trade unions; my taste in film stars and dance music is apparently quite different from that of my contemporaries; I can't jitterbug and I don't like eating in canteens. I was probably the most unpopular girl in the school!"

"You might have liked it better in one of the services."

"Never. At least my clothes were individual even when they dropped to pieces. And when I'd finished for the day, the night was mine. A few crumbs of freedom."

"I always felt completely free in the A.T.S."

"But then you liked the life, that's the difference. I didn't. As a war worker I was a wash-out. I'll admit I never felt the slightest urge to serve my country or do noble deeds or die winning the George Medal, or any other of the patriotic reactions most people seem to have experienced, even if it was only for a brief moment. I was just angry at having my life interrupted—and frightened, scared pink at the idea of air raids. I hate war," she added vehemently.

"So does everyone," Laura said.

"Oh no, they didn't. Why, you yourself didn't really; nor did Peter, he worshipped those silly ships he was on; and Brian really rather enjoyed being in the army. So did Gyp Townsend. Oh, lots of people enjoyed their war—or at least they were interested in it. I loathed it. It just snatched six years away from me."

"You're not the only one, Daphne," Laura replied dryly.

"No, I know. But that doesn't make it any better. And there is a differentiation in the particular six years snatched. If you're a kid at school or an old person, it can't matter in the same way. But six years in the middle of your twenties is pretty grim. Six years at a time when you're old enough and yet still young enough to enjoy every scrap of life. It amounts to losing your youth. After all, I started this war as a comparative adolescent and I end it practically middle-aged. What a thought!"

Laura thought: 'You are almost the most selfish person I have ever listened to,' and then she remembered that Daphne Zarek had lost more than six years, she'd lost her husband too. They'd only been married a few months before he was killed; Ian was born after his father's death—and all this had happened less than two years ago. You couldn't really judge Daphne by the way she talked. Or could you? It was the same story almost as Mary Cross's in the last war. Laura wondered whether she too had talked this way in 1919. Somehow it didn't sound like Mary Cross.

"What are you thinking about, Laura?"

"Mary Cross."

"Oh, are you going to their party on the twenty-fifth? I see you have the invitation on your mantelpiece."

"Yes, I shall go. Father isn't accepting. Are you going?"

"I expect so. The parents want to go too. God knows why. It'll be the usual hideous scramble to get the last train back here afterwards. Still, I suppose it will give us all something to talk about afterwards. Do you like Michael Cross?"

"I like them both very much. Why?"

"I just wondered. Michael always strikes me as such a pansy sort of man. I expect him to burst into corduroy trousers or side-whiskers or something fantastic at any moment. He's too mothered, I suppose."

"He's very gentle, if that's what you mean."

"Not my cup of tea, but then I don't suppose I'm his! Which is probably just as well. I imagine Mrs. Cross can be pretty viperish to anyone who casts soft eyes at her beloved son."

Laura was rather shocked. Daphne had a strange way of suddenly revealing things to you in a new light. Not that she believed a word Daphne said, but it was disconcerting to have your ideas about people unsettled.

Daphne went on:

"Come down to the Cock and Pheasant with me, Laura. I've got to fetch a bottle of sherry for father. His wine society haven't functioned this month or something. I hate going into a pub on my own," she added, surprisingly.

Laura didn't want to go out, but it seemed unfriendly not to walk down with Daphne.

"I can't stay long, Daphne. It's Ethel's evening off and I've got to get supper for father."

"And I have got to go back in time to tuck Ian up for the night. What a pair we are, Laura; two old ladies tied to their dependants; full of good works and bad memories. Come on."

"You make us sound about a hundred," Laura laughed.

"I feel about two hundred, and old for my age at that. Where are you going?"

"To tell father I'll be back before seven."

"Oh."

Walking through the pale evening light, there was a feeling of frost in the air, spring frost and mist. Daphne said:

"We used to have fun here before the war, didn't we, Laura?"

"I suppose we did," Laura was unwilling to admit to a thought she had so recently had herself. Particularly in front of Daphne.

"Life was gay and exciting," Daphne went on, "people were gay. It's all changed now and it can never come back. I feel like the dregs of another existence, only someone's forgotten to pull the plug on me. Everyone lives seriously now; life is so beastly and earnest. It's worse in a place like Kirton somehow, because of old ghosts. If it weren't for Ian I'd go crazy. I mean that, Laura."

Laura, who loved Kirton, said nothing.

The Cock and Pheasant had only just opened. Farm workers were beginning to straggle into the public bar, and one or two of the tradespeople had already ordered their pints in the saloon. Dick and Elsie Cobb were working the bars between them.

Laura noticed a man and woman drinking sherry in a corner and their faces were strange to her, but Daphne said good evening as she passed them.

"Shall we have a drink first, Laura?" she asked. "I'd rather wait until Mrs. Cobb comes down before tackling father's sherry. Dick and his wife give me the willies."

"Why?"

"I don't know. She always seems to be pregnant and he has that funny look in his eye when he just stares at you and says nothing. Quite terrifying."

Laura felt hot with indignation, but somehow she could never argue with Daphne whose thoughts were frothy and who forgot what she had said the moment she had spoken.

They ordered gins and lime and took them over to a corner table. Daphne said:

"Did you notice those people I said good evening to when we came in?"

"Yes, who are they? I haven't seen them before."

"Mr. and Mrs. Price. They've taken the cottage next to the Cross's. She's a bitch, but he's rather an angel, full of charm and a good sense of humour. She pretends to be ill all the time. I met him in here the other evening and we let our back hair down over a few drinks."

Laura was startled by the expression on Daphne's face. She thought, 'she looks positively lecherous,' and then she wondered how it was that Daphne had met Mr. Price here, when she said she hated going into pubs on her own. Perhaps it was no casual encounter after all. Then she dismissed the subject as being no concern of hers, but she said:

"Was he in the services?"

"Laura, you're impossible. Services, services, army, army. Don't you ever think of anything else? No, as a matter of fact he wasn't. He's got some business in London. May be the Black Market, for all I know! I couldn't care less. Ah, here's Mrs. Cobb. I'll do my stuff about the sherry."

Maggie Cobb and her husband had come out from their back parlour. John was talking to his daughter-in-law, and Maggie looked round the bars. When she saw Laura and Daphne in the corner, she came across to them.

"Good evening, Mrs. Zarek; good evening, Miss Watson. It's been another lovely day, hasn't it? No doubt we shall pay for it over Whitsun. And how is Master Ian, Mrs. Zarek?"

"He's fine, thank you. It's father who's not so good!" Daphne grimaced.

"Sir James? I hope it's nothing serious?" Maggie Cobb's eyes showed quick concern.

Daphne laughed.

"He's not ill, Mrs. Cobb; just thirsty. His wine society have forgotten to put in his quota of sherry this time and we've got people coming to dinner tomorrow night. I suppose you couldn't spare us a bottle from the Cock and Pheasant, could you?"

Maggie's face clouded over. It wasn't so much that Sir James owed for some gin and whisky he'd ordered last Christmas— after all, the Gurneys were gentry and they always paid in the long run—but supplies were still meagre. Still, she supposed John could manage just one bottle for the Manor. She mustn't let Dick hear her asking Dad. Ever so rude he'd been last time they'd mentioned the Gurneys up at the Manor. He still got those turns from his head wound. She leaned forward across the table and spoke in a low voice:

"Well, I think Mr. Cobb might manage one for Sir James. You won't mind if I put it in one of my shopping bags for you? With stocks so low it isn't everyone we can oblige, and people do talk so."

"I don't care if it's disguised in a diaper, Mrs. Cobb. You're an angel. Could we have a couple more gin and limes too, please?"

Laura didn't want another drink, but Mrs. Cobb had moved off to get the order.

"I really ought to be going, Daphne," she said, weakly.

"So ought I. But we'll just have these. Lord, how I hate having to gush to get a bottle of sherry. I suppose I'll have to listen to a lot of talkie-talkie about her grandchildren when she comes back. Won't it be nice when one can just go and buy things again without screwing oneself up to such an emotional pitch?"

"What a perfectly beastly thing to say!" Laura exploded at last.

"Don't be so intense, Laura. You know I never mean a word I say. You wouldn't either, if you were me."

Maggie Cobb had come back with the drinks, and the bottle of sherry was in a green shopping bag. Daphne said:

"I couldn't be more grateful, Mrs. Cobb. Father will be thrilled. Put it down to his account, will you? I'll pay for the gins."

"No, I will, Daphne." Laura brought out her purse.

"Don't be silly. I made you come here tonight. They're on me. Here you are, Mrs. Cobb." She handed the money over and then went on. "I must just go and say a word to the Prices over there, and then we'll go, Laura." She picked up her glass and left them.

Laura felt uncomfortable. Daphne made it sound as though she, Laura, hadn't wanted to come to the Cock and Pheasant—and in front of Mrs. Cobb too. And in any case all this business about the sherry was phoney. It wasn't for Sir James Gurney at all; it was Daphne who wanted it. The fictitious guests at dinner next night—why did she have to lie? It was all so obvious and mean. Laura longed suddenly for fresh air. Maggie Cobb was still standing by the table. There was something clean and clear in the mere fact of her presence. Laura said:

"Won't you have a drink, Mrs. Cobb?"

"Thank you, not at present, Miss Watson. I've only just finished my tea," but she sat down at the table with Laura and her bright eyes took in everyone in the bar, which was now filling up.

"There seem to be a lot of new people in Kirton," Laura commented.

"That's just what I was thinking, Miss Watson. Lots of new faces, and many of the old ones gone. I was sorry when that Miss

Worthing left us; always so cheerful and smiling she was. I hear she's got a job with the B.B.C. in London?"

"Yes, I believe she has."

"Doesn't seem right somehow that a young lady like her should be off after a new job when the war's over and done with. I always said to Mr. Cobb what a good wife she'd make for some nice young gentleman like Mr. Michael Cross or one of the Mr. Gurneys."

Laura wondered whether Mrs. Cobb was just very ingenuous or if, perhaps, she knew all about Peter Gurney and Angela Worthing. The grapevine telegraph system never seemed to fail the village.

"I think she likes working, Mrs. Cobb."

"Or maybe she has to earn her living. The war's done stranger things than that to people," Maggie said briskly.

"Oh, no. Miss Worthing's very well off," Laura replied and wondered why Mrs. Cobb always succeeded in making her gossip.

"Fancy that," Maggie looked genuinely surprised. "Now I wonder why that girl Madge hasn't come down to the bar yet. It's time Dick arid Elsie went off for their teas. We shall be busy later on, being Friday night."

"How are the grandchildren?" Laura asked, feeling hypocritical because of what Daphne had said earlier on.

"They're lovely, thank you, Miss Watson. Stevie's walking a treat now and baby's going to be christened on Sunday week; Rose Elizabeth. She's the very image of Dick when he was a baby."

"Dick's looking better, too. He seems to have put on weight."

"Yes; Dr. Townsend's ever so pleased with him. He still has queer turns though," Maggie lowered her voice confidentially, "Got himself into trouble over at Dimstone again last week."

Laura remembered hearing something about Dick Cobb going off on the night Elsie had her baby and not turning up for two days; she couldn't remember the details, but someone said he'd gone up to London and got himself arrested.

"What sort of trouble, Mrs. Cobb?" she asked awkwardly.

"With the police again. He's that quick tempered when they ask him about his ribbons. I'm tired of telling him they don't mean any harm, but he can't seem to understand." Maggie frowned.

Laura was puzzled. She could see Dick Cobb on the other side of the bar and noticed his disabled ex-serviceman's badge on the lapel of his coat and the line of ribbons pinned across his chest: the M.C., the 1939-'45 Africa Star and Italian Campaign. They were put on crookedly and looked very bright against the navy blue of his jacket.

"Why should the police bother about his ribbons?" she asked.

"Pull him up, they do. It's happened a score of times already. They make him look up at the sky and tell them what medals he's wearing—from right to left. He always tells them, of course, quite politely, but once they're satisfied he starts swearing at them, calls them all the names he can lay his tongue to, and then the trouble starts. That time in London, they shut him up for the night for insulting behaviour. Mind you, Miss Watson, it was partly our fault too because when they rang up here, we was all over at Elsie's after the baby was born and Madge answered the telephone and she didn't know anything about Dick being away from Kirton; so she told the police he was at home. Naturally they held him after that. He was pulled up in Dimstone again last week, when they were looking for a fellow who was pretending to be an ex-officer and wearing a V.C. ribbon. Dick told them if they couldn't recognize a V.C. when they saw one it was time honest folk's rates stopped being squandered on a lot of basket policemen. The Dimstone police don't like being spoken to that way, Miss Watson," Maggie added simply.

Laura began to understand. Of course, Dick Cobb didn't look like an officer; he looked like the lanky country lad he was, blunt featured and rough, honest and working class. Why hadn't she thought about this before? Maybe at this very moment there were other people like Dick Cobb, suffering the insults of the ignorant, being doubted by their neighbours, mocked at perhaps—for doing what? For displaying the symbols of the service they had given to their country, the scrap of coloured ribbon which signified unbelievable courage and, for some, wrecked lives and health. In the army, in uniform, there had been officers of all kinds: voices and accents from all parts of the British Isles, accepted by all because of the jobs they were doing, the service they were rendering. Put them back on Civvy Street, dress them in a demob suit, a farmer's corduroys, a white collar or a 'Sunday best,' and they became divided into social spheres, subject to a class-conscious scrutiny which disbelieved the possibility of an officer's decoration on a navvy's coat. For the first time in her life Laura sensed the burning indignation of injustice. It rose and choked the speech in her throat. Somebody ought to do something about this. If Brian Gurney had been here he would have known what to do, he'd understood Dick Cobb better than anyone else. Michael Cross could have written something about it. Helen—Helen Townsend would have had some suggestion to make; or Gyp, who felt so strongly about ex-service men and women. Only Laura, on her own, felt impotent, incapable of expressing by action or words the vehemence of her thoughts.

"But it's wicked, Mrs. Cobb," she said in a low voice.

"Not wicked," Maggie bridled, "it's just Dick's quick temper. He's the same with his dad, always arguing about something or the other. He just doesn't seem able to control himself like other people."

"But I don't mean that!" Laura was appalled at being misunderstood. "I mean it's all wrong that Dick should be pulled up by the police for wearing the M.C. he won; that they should dare to hold him for telling them off when they're entirely in the wrong." It sounded muddled and not at all what she'd meant to say.

"Oh well," Maggie replied complacently, "you can't blame them really. After all, Dick doesn't look like an officer. It's not his fault; it's like what Elsie says, they shouldn't ever have made him into a captain. Mr. Cobb was a sergeant-major in the last war and that was bad enough when he came home. No, Elsie's right, it's the fault of the army. Mind you, I'm not saying we aren't proud of all Dick did, getting his commission and the M.C. and everything, but it doesn't make for an easy life afterwards. Maybe it would be different if he could remember it all happening. But he can't. That makes him extra touchy about being pulled up."

Laura could find nothing to say and there was silence in the midst of the chatter from the bars. She felt unhappy because she was conscious of not being able to talk to people like Mrs. Cobb about the things that were important in their lives. It seemed there was something lacking in her which left a void where there should have been bubbling confidence and understanding. She continued to sit, twiddling her empty glass and worrying because she was already late in getting home to prepare supper for her father.

Maggie Cobb was unruffled.

"You'll excuse me, Miss Watson, but I must go and get Dick and Elsie off to their teas," and she made her way back behind the counters.

Laura saw that Daphne Zarek was still talking to the Prices. She supposed she ought to tell her she was leaving. Daphne looked up as she passed.

"Oh, Laura, I thought you'd gone ages ago? I'm staying on for a while. You don't mind, do you?"

Laura didn't mind. All she wanted was to be away from the heat of the Cock and Pheasant and back in the familiar, peaceful environment of Vine Cottage.

She slipped out into the street and let the cool night air soothe the turmoil in her mind.

Behind the bar, Maggie Cobb said:

"John, why haven't you sent Dick and Else up for their tea now Madge is down?"

"All in good time, mother; don't you start fussing yourself now." John Cobb patted his wife's shoulder affectionately.

"Maybe you didn't notice we had custom, Mum, apart from those ropey sourpusses you were gossiping with in the corner?" Dick grinned at his mother.

"Now then, Dick, I'll not have you calling our old customers names." The irritation in John Cobb's voice was thinly disguised.

Maggie said soothingly:

"Else, take him off for his tea. Young Stevie was calling for him to say goodnight before I came down, and that must be well over half an hour ago."

Dick raised an eyebrow in the direction of his father and then winked at his mother.

Elsie said:

"Come on, Dick. I'm hungry."

"Oh you managing skirts," he groaned, but he went off good-naturedly enough.

Maggie moved across to the saloon bar, and John went on drawing pints and half-pints for the public customers. He stopped to chat with some of them and presently he drew himself a small mild, but not before he'd looked at the clock: he never drew his first drink until it had gone seven. It didn't do to start in too early when you looked like having a full house, and Friday evenings generally saw the Cock and Pheasant crowded out. All the time he was thinking how much he missed his daughter Lily. Getting a letter today had started it all up again. The same thing happened every time Lil wrote, and she wrote regularly, same as she'd always done in the W.A.A.F. But John missed her more now than he had when she'd been away in the services. Perhaps it was her being married to Fred made the difference. She'd really left home this time.

He remembered the wedding and the way all the village had turned up to stare when the photograph was taken outside the church. And young Tommy had worn his new white suit. Afterwards Lil and Fred had gone off for the week-end leaving Tommy with his grandparents; then they'd all three gone up to Yorkshire, leaving John with an aching void like a drawn tooth.

Lil was happy enough—you could read that in her letters, and Fred Barrett was a smashing good fellow, but it didn't make matters better for John. He was lonely for his daughter and each time he got a letter from her it seemed as if it were only yesterday she'd gone away.

He kept picturing her in the bars, her neat, quick movements and the way their glances would meet across the glasses and beer engines if anything out of the ordinary happened. They'd never had to do much talking, him and Lil; it seemed as if when they looked at one another each knew what the other meant. It was always that way with Lil. With her gone, a part of himself had packed up too.

He wondered sometimes if he was being disloyal to Maggie, and Dick and Elsie, when he thought like this about Lil. It was just that she was something special in his life, something quite apart from his wife and family as a whole. At the thought of his family, he frowned. The place was all cluttered up by Dick and Else and their kids. Funny the way he'd never seemed to notice any over-crowding when Lil and Tommy had been at home. Now there were babies' nappies and bottles of milk and cots and prams all over the place. Maybe when Dick had settled down to the work it would be possible for him and Else to take on a cottage again and live out. But John realized that such a plan would never work. You had to live in a house to learn the trade and to run it successfully; there was a deal more work than people knew of in between opening hours. No, Dick and Else and their family would have to stay on in the Cock and Pheasant if they were to run the place on their own one day. Well, perhaps he and Maggie might retire in time and go and live in one of the cottages in Pilferer's Lane. Smashing places they were if you knew how to fix them up inside. Yes, that was an idea; he and Maggie wouldn't want to go on working the bars for all time. Then his face clouded again as he thought that any plans he made were dependent on Dick settling down to the trade. It was early days to tell yet. After all, he'd stuck Little Copse for over six months and then chucked it up just as they'd all got used to him being in regular work. He mustn't start thinking about cottages until Dick was really settled.

Maggie Cobb came across to her husband.

"What's the matter, Dad? You look tired like."

"It's nothing, Maggie. Just a touch of liver, I think."

"Oh well, so long as it's nothing serious . . ." she went off to take an order from an impatient man tapping the counter with a half crown piece.

John continued to draw beer.

Upstairs, Elsie Cobb helped herself to another piece of cake. Dick said:

"It's funny, Else, I remembered something more today."

"What, dear?"

"Sitting by a roadside with a bunch of fellows and feeling my shirt sticking to me. Blazing sun it was, though it can't have been midsummer 'cos there were a lot of little hills all round covered with grapes, fat green ones with some bluey powder stuff on the leaves and things. We were having a smoke, and a bloke came up on a motor bike, a Don R., and he saluted and handed me a message. Funny, I remembered it as clear as anything when I was downstairs in the bar just now and old Tom Cowley blew a bellyful of smoke across the counter. Lovely day it was, too, all blue sky and sun. Fancy remembering that. It's good, isn't it, Else?"

She noticed that he'd started to rub his hand against his chest, inside his open shirt.

"Ever so good, dear," she said, "specially as it was a nice day. Ready for your second cup of tea, Dick?"

*   *   *   *

"More tea, dear?" Lady Gurney reached across for her husband's cup, "and then I'd like you to explain it all over again to me."

He bit into a thin sandwich, without answering, and then frowned.

"What's in this?" he asked, looking down his nose.

"Meat paste, dear."

"Too salty." He stretched his hand out for his cup.

"It's all we can get locally," his wife replied.

"We used to have jam sandwiches for tea," he remarked.

"We can't now. You know the lot I made last year went wrong—all the fault of that awful recipe of Mrs. Cobb's—and Ian has to have jam or he won't eat a thing; and then the servants. . . . I can't watch everything that goes on in the kitchen," Lady Gurney's face was etched with little creases of worry.

"All right, my dear. I was only saying what we used to have," her husband put in soothingly, but her face remained puckered and anxious.

"Now, James, please be serious for a moment and tell me again what you were saying before tea."

Sir James Gurney stirred his tea intently, then he tasted it; afterwards he put down his cup with quiet deliberation. At this moment Lady Gurney decided that her husband was the most irritating person she knew.

He cleared his throat and said slowly:

"There isn't any more to tell, my dear. It's as I've said, we can't afford to go on living here."

So he does really mean it, Lady Gurney thought; sometimes he just says things for the sake of being perverse, but this time he is serious; he wouldn't repeat himself unless he meant it. She felt herself flushing with apprehension.

"You mean leave the Manor?" she squeaked.

"Yes, Agnes. You see, we've been living above our income for a long time now, dipping into capital. If we continue doing so there'll be nothing left at all in a few years' time." He sounded tired, and he wished his wife wouldn't look so pert and inquisitive. He'd been through all this once before tea, but she didn't appear to have understood what he meant; she'd always been childish about money matters—now she was being positively infantile in her apparent failure to grasp the plain facts he stated.

"But, James, you said only a few weeks ago that the markets were looking up. You said there were plenty of opportunities for making money if one got out of Government-controlled stocks." Like a bird, she kept nodding her head at him as she spoke.

Sir James Gurney fidgeted. Why must she quote his words at him like that? Surprising she remembered them when he thought of her scatter-brained mind about most things.

"It's easy to make money when you've got money," he said gloomily, forgetting that when they had married they were one of the wealthiest young couples in the county. 'Money marries money' the guests had whispered to each other at the wedding and had smiled contentedly at the rightfulness of such proceedings, showering expensive presents and good wishes on young James Gurney and his pretty, doll-like bride. But there had been two wars and a depression since then.

"Surely you could make use of these opportunities," Lady Gurney continued hopefully.

Her husband, who had made use of too many financial opportunities during the past forty years, replied:

"Can't afford to. Too risky. Everything that isn't Government-controlled is risky these days, blast it. That's what your precious Labour Government has done for us!"

"James, you know I canvassed for the new Conservative candidate even though I didn't know him." She flushed with indignation.

"Then I suppose your children put this government in. Someone did," he growled back at her.

"That's most unfair of you. They're your children just as much as mine and you know Daphne couldn't vote because of being Polish by marriage, and the boys were away. I'm quite certain Peter wouldn't vote for Labour."

They glowered at each other across the tea table, neither able to understand why they were squabbling. Then Laura said:

"Don't let's get angry, dear."

"I'm not angry," he answered gruffly and began to fill his pipe from his worn tobacco pouch.

Lady Gurney looked wistfully round her drawing room.

"I hate to think of strangers in this place, James. Prying into all the rooms and cupboards; using all our lovely things and perhaps damaging the furniture and carpets. I suppose we shall be able to lock some things away?"

He looked at her in silence for a second and then his glance dropped and he went on fumbling with his pipe. He felt at that moment like a criminal.

"I don't think you understand, dear," he said gently, "it's not a case of letting the Manor. We'll have to sell."

"Sell? But we can't sell our home, James. What about the children? What about the boys when they want somewhere to come with their friends?" Her voice had scrambled up to the high notes again.

"The boys are men," he said dryly, "and in any case they're never here together. We'll naturally take a place where Daphne and Ian can be with us."

"But where can we live?" Lady Gurney wailed.

"That's something we'll have to discuss, my dear. I don't imagine either of us want to move out of Kirton at our ages. We have our friends here; we don't want to uproot too much."

"Leave Kirton? James, we can't leave Kirton!"

"That's just what I'm saying, my dear. So we'll have to find some small place in the village. I saw O'Rourke in Dimstone yesterday and he told me he would soon have another of those cottages near the Watsons' for sale."

"A cottage?" Lady Gurney sounded incredulous.

"Yes, my dear, if it's going for a reasonable price. O'Rourke will do his best for us; I've told him he can handle the sale of the Manor."

"But we couldn't get into a cottage, James. Where would the servants sleep?"

"Other people manage with a daily woman," he replied quietly.

"Oh, James. Is it as bad as all that?" She felt utterly crushed. To have to live in the village would be bad enough; to be crowded in on either side by neighbours, to lose the space and privacy of the Manor with its gardens and tennis court and wide fields; but to have to put up with a daily woman would be worse. No daily woman knew how to clean silver. This was going to alter the very structure of their lives. Lady Gurney felt too old and tired to start again, to plan and carry out a new routine for living. And then another dreadful thought occurred to her.

"James, the furniture?" In panic her glance swept round the drawing room, noting the gracious proportions of the china cabinet and the grand piano, the bookcases and the writing table; and as she looked it seemed that their gleaming surfaces expanded joyously, exalting in the spacious beauty of the panelled room.

"Yes, we'll have to sell most of it," he was following her glance, "thank goodness prices are still high for genuine antiques; we'll be able to save something that way."

"You talk as if we were ruined, James."

"Not ruined," he replied testily—she made it sound as though he'd been speculating—"but our circumstances are changed. After all, the boys are grown up now and on their own. In any case they've never contributed anything towards the upkeep of the home," he added dryly.

"Contributed? My dear James, we're not working-class even if we do have to go and live in a cottage."

He thought, she's going to take this badly, and he wondered at his own calm acceptance of the situation. Somehow it didn't seem to matter very much whether they lived in the Manor or in a cottage. Life would be much the same, only there'd be fewer responsibilities. Pity Agnes couldn't see it that way too. Perhaps she would in time, when she became interested in the move and making a new place liveable. For himself, he wasn't all that attached to his possessions; he'd never had the pleasure of choosing them in the first place, they'd come from his parents and aunts and uncles. Perhaps he would miss them, but he didn't think so. He only wanted to live simply and not to be perpetually bothered by lack of money. He felt a little excited at the prospect of selling some of the stuff, getting a good price for it. And the Manor, too. O'Rourke had said there were one or two buyers for big houses still left, but that more probably it would be taken for a school or a nursing home or something like that.

As if following his thoughts Lady Gurney said:

"If we're not here, I wonder who will be?" and there was a shrill bitterness in her voice.

"Probably a school or something," he said soothingly, "nobody wants a great place of their own these days."

"A school!" Already she seemed to hear the incessant voices of young people and the clump of shoes racing all over her home, but she felt less bitter at the idea of the Manor becoming an institution rather than someone else's private residence.

"I'm sorry my dear; I'm afraid it's been rather a shock for you." He got up and went round to pat her awkwardly on the shoulder.

"Are we going to have any money left?" she asked anxiously. He felt irritated again; why must she be so intensely curious; but he answered quietly:

"With the money from the Manor and the furniture and the capital we've got left we should be able to live quietly."

"We always have lived quietly." She thought how unkind life was to do this to them now. All they'd gone through during the war to keep up the home for the children was for nothing. Somehow it would have been more bearable if it had happened during the war; to lose your home in peace-time was doubly cruel. She said, wistfully:

"You won't do it again, will you, James?"

"Do what?" he sounded surprised.

"I mean, dear, when we've moved out of the Manor, we won't have to move out of anywhere else. You won't let the money side get worse or anything. I'll do it this time, but I couldn't do it again."

"My dear Agnes," he was annoyed now. "You talk as if I had squandered our money away." He began to pace up and down the room and his voice grew louder. "I suppose you think I've given it away—thrown it away? You've forgotten, no doubt, that we've been through a war, and a depression, and another war? That we've brought up and educated three children at the most expensive schools and universities? That we've paid Peter's debts for years and that we are now keeping Daphne and her child for nothing? You blame me for all this: you think I'm responsible for wars and depressions and Peter's extravagance, for loss of capital and a lot of Red ruffians running this country today. I suppose it's my fault that we . . ."

The door opened suddenly and Ian tumbled into the room followed by Daphne.

"Not in front of the children, James," Lady Gurney hissed automatically, and noticed the effort he made to control himself.

Daphne said:

"Goodee, goodee, there's still some tea."

"I thought you and Ian had gone to tea at the Townsends," Lady Gurney replied, with an eye on her husband's Adam's apple which was wiggling inside his collar as he swallowed his anger.

"We didn't. Ian had tea in the kitchen with May." Daphne picked up a rock cake and began to pick out the currants in it.

"What were you doing, darling?" Lady Gurney noticed the flush on her daughter's cheeks and the unusual brightness of her eyes.

"Walking. Ian, don't bother grand-dad; he doesn't want you to ride on his knee." But Sir James had picked up his grandson and began to play with him, making faces and blowing out his cheeks and giving him lumps of sugar dipped in cold tea.

Lady Gurney said:

"Don't pick the currants out, Daphne. It's a disgusting habit and Ian will copy you. Where were you walking?"

"Oh, just walking." Daphne poured herself a cup of tea and took a couple of sandwiches from the top of the cake tray.

Lady Gurney was worried. Something had happened to Daphne recently. She was secretive and glowing and always going out without saying where she'd been, and then returning with a languorous far-away look about her. Ian was left to May and Cook. She watched the dark-eyed child as he laughed up at his grandfather; there was nothing about him that looked like a Gurney! He was foreign—almost a little Jewish looking—like his father had been. She didn't want to think about Daphne's husband, the stranger with the dark eyes who never seemed to understand the things she and James said to him. It had been a rushed wedding. Too rushed. She closed her mind on the incident. Ian had been a large and healthy baby, even if he looked lean and sallow now. Daphne, her beautiful Daphne, had drifted a long way, into another kind of world, when the war started. War had somehow split all the family up, snatching Brian—who was difficult always—and taking Peter and then Daphne.

Daphne said:

"What's up? You're like the mutes at a funeral."

Lady Gurney looked swiftly at her husband, but he hadn't heard.

"Nothing, Daphne. I don't think Ian ought to have all those lumps of sugar, do you?"

"I think you've been talking about Peter's sin!" her daughter teased, ignoring the red herring.

"Daphne, I wish you would not say things like that."

"Well it's the only topic at every meal, mother."

Lady Gurney looked tearful.

"When Ian's grown up," she said, "I think you'll be less hard."

"Oh, rot." But the glow had gone from Daphne's eyes and her face was set and sullen again.

"It isn't rot, Daphne. Naturally I'm worried about Peter."

"I'm sorry I raised the subject. I was only joking."

"In my place, you'd be worried too. That dreadful woman."

"Angela's all right."

"I don't agree; and I wish you'd never brought her into our family."

Daphne took another rock cake and went on picking currants out of it.

"I never introduced Angela to Peter. She was a friend of Helen Townsend and Michael Cross. In any case I've said I'm sorry to have brought the subject up. Let's drop it."

"It's so easy for you to talk like that. I am Peter's mother." Lady Gurney was pink with agitation. "I didn't mind him taking her flat whilst she was still at Little Copse, but that she should allow him to remain there once she'd gone back to London . . . that I can't forgive."

"Oh, God!"

Sir James Gurney looked up at them.

"I wish you wouldn't swear, Daphne."

"Only at myself, father. I've just blundered. I forgot we were pledged as a family to defend Peter's virginity."

"Not in front of Ian," Lady Gurney pleaded.

Daphne laughed.

"I don't think he's reached the age of indiscretion yet!"

"Daphne, please. . . ." Her mother's voice was shrill.

"All right, all right, but you started this. Just because I happen to joke, you both take me as dead serious."

"This is serious," Sir James Gurney frowned at his daughter.

"Don't I realize it? My dears, of course it's serious. The almighty Peter's reputation is being compromised. His chances of marrying a nice heiress are being spoiled. Angela is a cad. Come on, Ian, time for bed." She picked up her son and carried him shoulder high from the room.

"Don't be cross with her," Sir James said softly. But his wife was crying.

When Daphne came back she brought the afternoon's post with her. Her father glanced at the envelopes and flung most of them aside.

"One for you, Agnes. From Brian."

Lady Gurney opened it eagerly. Her children seldom bothered to write to her; of course Daphne couldn't, she lived in the house, and Peter . . . well Peter was different and he was in difficulties. It was nice of Brian to write. She began to read, with pleasure.

Daphne said:

"What about some sherry, Father?"

"Not a bad idea, my dear." He went to the cocktail cabinet and brought out glasses and the decanter. "Only the dregs, I'm afraid. Can't think how it goes so quickly." He filled two glasses and handed one to Daphne.

"Here's to death!" She smiled at him.

"Your good health, my dear." It was rotten sherry—even the Cock and Pheasant had come down to the third rate. He twisted the stem of his glass, and with one eye closed viewed the tiny particles of sediment floating in the amber liquid.

Lady Gurney gave a little cry of horror.

"James . . . Daphne . . . !"

Her husband and daughter turned to stare at her. She was wildly searching for something in the envelope of Brian's letter and she brought out a small snapshot. Her hands trembled, she was white and drawn.

"What's the matter?" they asked together.

"Brian's married. Oh, this is too much on top of everything else!" She began to cry again.

"Married?" Sir James asked incredulously.

"How clever of him," Daphne said and felt the panic which persistently rose in her at a family crisis subsiding flatly. Who the devil had Brian married? He'd been leching after Helen Townsend; she'd seen that even though Brian had snapped her head off the only time she mentioned it to him. But it was obvious to Daphne. That's why he'd left home so soon after he was demobilized. Now he was married. Life suddenly became interesting and rather amusing.

Lady Gurney was wiping her eyes.

"Why didn't he tell us? Why should he keep it hidden from his family . . . his mother? I don't understand. . . . I don't see why all my children have got to behave in this hole and corner manner."

Daphne suppressed a ribald wisecrack and said instead:

"I take umbrage at that, Mother. Tell us more."

"You're as bad as the boys, Daphne. Always creeping out and never saying where you've been. You and Peter, and now Brian. . . ." She blew her nose, moistly.

"Who has Brian married?" her husband asked patiently.

Lady Gurney who had been hugging letter, envelope and snapshot tightly in the folds of her blouse, relaxed a little.

"A girl called Serena. Serena Hughes." She gulped and unfolded Brian's letter again. "Hughes. We don't know any Hughes, do we, James?"

"I don't think so, dear. May I see the letter?"

She handed it across to him, still tearful. Daphne said:

"Read it aloud, Father."

He skipped the opening sentences and then began:

". . . by the way, Mother, I got married last Thursday. Her name is Serena *née* Hughes, and I think you'll approve. I imagine you must have been very like her yourself when you were her age—that is nineteen—"

"Baby snatching," Daphne interrupted.

"He only says that to appease me," Lady Gurney said sadly.

Sir James went on reading:

". . . Sorry to spring it on you in this way, but although Serena and I have been good friends for a long time, we only made up our minds last week. With my great experience of your enchanting sex, Mother, I suggested orange blossom and bridesmaids, but Serena, who is not only modern, but practical, decided against that sort of a wedding. She said it was too difficult with clothing coupons. Well, after that there didn't seem much object in waiting so we got married that day. You would have been amused at the performance. We'd already wasted a great deal of time over lunch but I found a taxi driver who became co-operative when we explained the circumstances and we drove round London collecting things like wedding rings and special licences. We also bought a hat for Serena because she wasn't wearing one that day. As Dick Cobb would say, it was a smashing hat. And a wicked price, but worth it! The taxi driver whose name was Tom Bowling—believe it or not—acted as witness and we collected a small-sized Yank outside the registry office as the second witness. The rest of the day was spent advising Serena's friends of her change of address and we are now honeymooning in my bed-sitting-room. If you know of a flat to let within hiking distance of Soho Square, let me know. As soon as I can get a week off from the office, I shall bring my bride home. You will like her, I know. We are happy. . . ."

Sir James Gurney handed back the letter without speaking. He pursed his lips until his mouth looked like the cobbled darn in a worn sock. His wife wailed:

"He doesn't say a word about her parents. We don't even know who her people are, James."

Daphne said:

"Is that a photograph, Mother?" She was feeling subtly jealous of her brother. It was so easy to be a man and just go off after lunch and get married. Women were always tied by emotions or responsibility. Except of course very young women like Serena. It was dreadful to be old and tied and dependent on your parents. She longed to be free to follow an impulse as Brian had done. She felt certain it was an impulse; that Helen Townsend business had been the real thing, she was sure.

Lady Gurney glanced at the snapshot and handed it to Daphne. Sir James looked at it over her shoulder. Daphne felt a sudden choking feeling in her throat and the tears were stinging her eyes. Tears of jealousy and frustration because the young girl on horseback was so young, so keenly alive and beautiful. She seemed to be part of something Daphne had almost forgotten and the memory was nearly unbearable. Looking at Serena's photograph, Daphne wanted to feel the roundness of Ian in her arms, the fumbling of his arms around her neck. She forced her mind back to the room and her parents again.

"Well, Brian has certainly picked a beauty," she said, casually.

"Nonsense," Lady Gurney sniffed, "she's not a patch on you at that age, Daphne."

Daphne could have murdered her mother then. Sir James Gurney said:

"That's a thoroughbred, or I'm mistaken."

Daphne tittered:

"It's the girl he's married, not the horse, Father."

Sir James started, as if he'd not meant to speak.

"I know my dear. I was just thinking aloud. The girl's lovely too. Brian will be all right."

"But we know nothing about her, James." Lady Gurney sounded like a bad gramophone record. Daphne felt explosive.

"God, you make me sick. What's it matter if you don't know her? She's Brian's wife, not yours. He's the one who's got her for better or for worse. Personally I think she looks grand, but you've got to damn her before you even see her because you're so beastly possessive. You can't bear to think that anyone else in the world has any private life of their own. Everything's got to be to your pattern or it's wrong. God Almighty, I'd rather be dead than behave that way to Ian." She suddenly ran out of the room, slamming the door behind her.

Sir James Gurney looked across at his wife.

"It's because of Kurt being killed," he said slowly.

"Yes, it's probably that. Poor Daphne." Lady Gurney spoke wearily. "I think I'll go and lie down for a while, James, I've got rather a headache."

*   *   *   *

"You mark my words, Mrs. O'Leary, someone's going to have a thick head tomorrow." Mrs. Thrush, clad in a spotless white apron which hid all but her wrinkled lisle stockings and worn shoes, stood in Mary Cross's kitchen tasting a Manhattan cocktail in a teacup.

When Mary had re-opened the Mecklenburgh Square flat for Michael's return to civilian life, Mrs. Thrush had taken on her old job of 'doing' for them. Today, for Michael Cross's party, she had invited her neighbour, Mrs. O'Leary, to come and give a hand with the preparations and the ladies' coats.

Mrs. O'Leary held a teacup of Dry Martini in a hand which had become ingrained with the dirt of twenty years' cleaning in Government offices.

"I've never seen drink served in a bread bin and a fish kettle before, Mrs. T.," she said disapprovingly.

Mrs. Thrush surveyed the domestic articles in question as they stood, packed round with blocks of ice, in a zinc wash-tub, and she felt very superior to Mrs. O'Leary who, after all, was only a sort of a civil servant. Working as she had for the intellectuals in Bloomsbury all her life, Mrs. Thrush felt she knew more of life than Madge O'Leary could ever hope to learn.

"You'd be surprised, Mrs. O'Leary, at the things I've seen drink served in before now. You wait till we get them white table-cloths swathed round that tub and you won't be able to tell what them drinks are in. And they'll be hidden beneath the table. Never does to let people see just how much you've got or they go and drink it all up at the beginning. I tell you, you have to keep your wits about you at a cocktail party and ration it out fair; and half-way through, you start putting the ice in to weaken things down—nobody notices what they're drinking by then and a lot have probably had more than's good for them."

"What beats me, Mrs. T., is where all the drink came from. All those bottles of whisky and gin and that French-sounding stuff—you wouldn't ever think there'd been a war and was still a shortage." Mrs. O'Leary was a little jealous of Mrs. Thrush's inside knowledge of cocktail parties, so she spoke in deprecating tones.

"Ah, my lady's been collecting it for a long time now, and Mr. Michael seems able to smell it a mile away. Come home with a bottle of Scotch last week and said they were practically giving it away at an off-licence in Fleet Street. I don't think; but he's got a way with him and he and his mum are old customers round here." Mrs. Thrush drained her teacup with relish. "How's yours, Mrs. O'Leary; all right?"

Mrs. O'Leary tilted up her cup and then wiped her mouth on a corner of her apron.

"Bit on the sour side, Mrs. T. Personally I prefer a drop of port type."

Mary Cross came into the kitchen. She was wearing very old tweeds and the ash was about to drop off the end of her cigarette.

"You should have used the glasses, Mrs. Thrush; cocktails in teacups must taste horrible. Let's all try one again in glasses. I like the whisky basis kind." She began to fill three glasses with a soup ladle.

"Not for me, thank you, Mum." Mrs. O'Leary put a large hand over a small glass. Mrs. Cross gave her a shrewd glance.

"I think I've got a wee drop of port left. What about that?" she asked.

"Oh well, I don't mind if I do, thanking you."

Mrs. O'Leary decided that she was going to enjoy working this evening for Mrs. Thrush's lady.

Mrs. Thrush beamed on everyone.

"Well, here's to Mr. Michael's party," she said.

"And may it learn us never to give another," Mary Cross responded. "I'm worn out already. The eats look lovely, Mrs. Thrush—those delicious cheese straws, I've been nibbling at them ever since you put them out."

"Mrs. O'Leary made those," Mrs. Thrush said magnanimously.

"How clever of you, Mrs. O'Leary; mine always go mushy; perhaps you'll let me into the secret one day."

"It's ever so easy, really." Mrs. O'Leary bridled and sipped her port.

Mrs. Thrush was wrapping a white table-cloth round the zinc wash-tub. Mary Cross said:

"Don't go trying to move that on your own, Mrs. Thrush. Wait until Mr. Michael comes in. What time did he say he'd be back?"

"Not later than five, he said, but Mrs. O'Leary and I can manage easily."

"No you won't. I'm not going to have any casualties before the party starts. I've got to have you to preside over the drinks and Mrs. O'Leary to deal with the women's coats. We're going to use my bedroom for the ladies' cloaks and Mr. Michael's for the gents, if they have any."

Mrs. Thrush was convulsed with loud laughter.

"Oh, Mrs. Cross, the things you say!" she gurgled.

Mary, who was unaware of anything but the longing for a hot bath, failed to see the Thrush humour.

"I think I'd better go and clean myself up now, Mrs. Thrush; I feel we're all set for zero hour, thanks to you and Mrs. O'Leary."

When she had gone, Mrs. O'Leary said:

"Ever so like a man in all those clothes, isn't she?"

Mrs. Thrush scoffed.

"Not her. She's as soft-hearted as you make 'em. Took my Alfie and Bertha down to her place in the country all the time the blitz was on. Wanted me to go too, and bring the old man. 'You can bunk down in the dining-room,' she said, but we said, no. Fancy us in the country. Why, it strangles me to go as far as Hampstead Heath."

"You're right, Mrs. T. I went out to Hertfordshire for a couple of weeks with the two youngest and it nearly killed me hearing them screaming for fish and chips and something Christian to eat out of a tin. We came back double quick, I can tell you."

"That's right, Mrs. O'Leary. Come on, let's get the glasses laid out."

Mrs. O'Leary was impressed with the living-room, particularly with the size of it now that the furniture had been tucked back into corners. She approved less of the pictures, which struck her as being arty-farty. Whoever wanted to see a drawing of a lot of cabbages on a table? When she looked again, they didn't look like cabbages and she wondered if the wee drop of port had gone to her head. Mrs. Thrush said:

"Posh, isn't it?"

"So so. Bit awkward to live in. Too empty like."

At five o'clock Michael Cross came in. He had an enormous bunch of tulips which he proceeded to arrange in the vases his mother had left empty.

"Hello, Mrs. Thrush. Drunk again?"

"None of your nonsense, Mr. Michael. Mocking's catching and you're the one who's likely to have a thick head tomorrow, not me."

"I hope we both do, Mrs. T. Damn it, if we can't get stinking at our own party, where can we? Now where's all this famous drink been concealed, in the bath tub?"

"No, Mr. Michael; your Mum's in the bath tub and the drink's in the kitchen. She said wait till you came back before moving it in here."

In the kitchen, he was introduced to Mrs. O'Leary, and between them they moved the drink into the sitting-room.

"Now for a spot of secret drinking, Mrs. T." He began to fill three glasses.

"Not for me, sir." Mrs. O'Leary said primly.

"Oh, come on, keep your strength up, you know."

"No, sir, really, sir; I've had some, and a drop of port."

"Tell you what, then, there's a bottle of Guinness somewhere around. We'll put it in the kitchen and you can refresh yourself during the fray. Now, let's try these poisons." He drank a glass of each cocktail and then grinned at Mrs. Thrush. "Mother certainly knows how to put a kick in them. As far as I'm concerned, Mrs. T., you can sell out on the gin but keep the whisky for me! I'll be seeing you." He went off to wash and change out of the old jacket and flannels he was wearing.

Mrs. O'Leary said:

"Bit of a spiv, isn't he?"

"What, Mr. Michael?"

"That's right. Great big shoulders and that curly hair; wearing a ring and all."

"That's him in uniform." Mrs. Thrush pointed out a photograph above a bookcase. "Air gunner he was, been on all the big raids over Germany. Nearly broke his Mum's heart when he joined up, her having lost her husband in the first war and all. And she's lucky to have got him home safe; he was missing for three months, but she kept her chin up."

From her bedroom, Mary Cross called out to her son:

"I thought I'd wear my black suit, Michael."

A muffled voice came back from the bathroom.

"You'll be the belle of the ball. God, what made us think of giving a party like this." He came into the corridor, still drying his face and neck.

"How could we know everyone would accept, Michael?"

"Even the country bumpkins from Kirton. Still, I'm glad they're coming."

"I don't know half of your friends by sight."

"Never mind, they all know each other. That's the main thing. Don't flap, Mother."

"I'm not flapping, but hurry up and dress, darling, or you'll be late. After all, it is your party."

"My party? I like that, you scheming woman."

At five past six the first guests arrived and after that the bell never seemed to stop ringing. By half past six it was clear that the party was going to be a success, if noise and overcrowding were the measures of a good cocktail party. 'Which apparently they are,' thought Mary Cross, shaking hands with a strange young man wearing a green tie. She saw that he had a drink and then handed him over to an equally blah and unknown young woman. It was wonderful the way you could put people together like a jigsaw puzzle, without any conscious thought.

Michael's publisher had ensconced himself on a sofa and refused to be moved round the room. He'd said he was here for pleasure and not business, but he was keeping a weather eye on a couple of reviewers talking to a blonde in the corner. Mary thought: 'I must do something about him,' and she searched the room for a suitable introduction. Angela Worthing—of course; she wasn't talking to anyone in particular and, at least, she didn't write, so Michael's publisher wouldn't have to put up his defences. Mary swooped and Angela found herself on the sofa talking to a portly gentleman with shrewd eyes.

Mary surveyed the room again. Everything was under control. People had soon learned to circulate up to the bar when they wanted another drink. In a corner, an actor friend of Michael's was holding court. It was interesting to notice the way his glance seemed to cast hypnotic threads on those of the guests he considered worthy of his attention and to watch the way they were drawn into the intimate circle.

And then she saw the Gurneys, hovering uncomfortably by the bar with Peter who had obviously staked a claim on that particular square yard of the floor. She went towards them quickly.

"How nice of you to come all this way," she pecked at Lady Gurney's cheek and noticed the lines drawn like fine smocking on her face, making her look like the very oldest kind of apple.

"Mary, how well you arrange this sort of party," Lady Gurney peeked round the room curiously.

"Awful, isn't it, but Michael and I felt we had to do something to celebrate the book and announce the fact that we were both still in circulation in spite of a war. Agnes, I feel most guilty about you; I saw the announcement of Brian's wedding in *The Times* and I've never written to him or you. That's what being in London does to one. But Michael rang up and asked Brian to bring his wife with him tonight."

"It was a very quiet wedding, Mary; they didn't want a big show." Lady Gurney could not admit to Mary Cross—understanding as she was—that she had not yet met her new daughter-in-law and that she had no idea Brian and Serena would be here tonight. The announcement in *The Times* had been Sir James's idea after a rather abortive exchange of letters between Kirton and London.

Peter said:

"Didn't know Brian would be here. Nice to see him again. Can't I get you a drink, Mrs. Cross?"

"A Manhattan, thank you, Peter, and one for your mother and father. Heavens, I must leave you—there are a lot of strange faces arriving."

Lady Gurney said:

"This must have cost a lot, James. Peter, I don't want another drink and I don't think you should have one yet."

Michael Cross came up to them.

"Now, no family parties. Lady Gurney I want you to meet a great friend of mine, Richard Fleming. He was a Warco with the 14th Army. . . ." Michael skilfully engineered Lady Gurney to the opposite end of the room.

Sir James Gurney, left with his eldest son, felt embarrassed.

"Things going all right, Peter?"

"Not too bad." Peter managed to scoop a filled glass of Martini from under Mrs. Thrush's disapproving glance.

"Haven't seen Angela Worthing. I understand she's here. We miss her at Kirton, you know." Sir James considered he'd used great tact.

"She's on the sofa there, talking to some bastard in a blue suit." Peter's speech was becoming blurred.

By the mantelpiece, Laura Watson perspired like a gentlewoman in her new dress. Helen Townsend had recommended Harrods, but Mr. Watson had a cold, so Laura had only got as far as Beatties in Dimstone. She carried on a pointless conversation with a man with a beard, but her mind was full of the other people in the room. Michael Cross was good-looking as a god in that grey suit.

"Won't you have another drink?" The beard waggled expectantly in the region of her midriff. It seemed that she was doomed to the companionship of short men. He drove through the crowd with their empty glasses like a centre forward making for goal.

Brian and his wife had arrived. Laura cast curious eyes at Serena. She wore an almond-coloured blouse and a black flounced skirt which only the very young and slim could wear. It was perfect with that red hair. Laura felt quite impersonal about Brian's wife. She accepted her beauty as a compliment to Kirton, but at the same time she remembered the special occasions in the mess, when the background had been khaki. How nice women had looked in their uniforms. You could keep your hair above your collar and still look glamorous. In the mess you all spoke the same language, here you had to adjust yourself to unaccustomed speech all the time. The beard reappeared with full glasses.

A reviewer had got pinioned on a divan by a female novelist. Mary Cross found her son and said:

"Michael, can you rescue Mr. Faulkner?"

"I'll find something young and gorgeous to do it."

The female novelist was a little drunk. She leaned over the reviewer and gasped.

"Mr. Faulkner, you remember my last book? You remember what you said about it? I think I'll forgive you, but I'd like to say one thing, just one thing. You recollect the passage about the young man—after the bit about his predilections—well, you pointed out that no young man would have behaved in that way. Let me tell you you're wrong. I know. . . . I was writing from personal experience . . . Mr. Faulkner could do with another drink, couldn't you? But, please, after that I want to tell you about my young man."

Michael intervened:

"I'd like you to meet Miss Jane Fergusson, disguised as a civilian at the moment, but really a major in the A.T.S. on leave from Berlin."

The reviewer revived and rose to greet Jane Fergusson. Michael felt that he had been very unselfish: Jane was his own particular cup of tea at the moment. He swept the female novelist over to Lady Gurney who seemed to be unoccupied.

The party was swinging along. Brian Gurney said to his wife:

"Sorry, Serena, that was a rotten way to introduce you to my parents."

"That's all right, darling. I know a lot more about you than you think I do."

He looked at her and the sight was remarkably satisfying.

"Let's go and talk to Laura Watson." He had caught sight of Helen and Gyp in a corner. Later on he would introduce Serena.

The intense female novelist was saying to Lady Gurney:

"To realize that one has made one human being happy in life is sufficient reward for existing, don't you agree?"

Lady Gurney hadn't the faintest idea, but she was too polite to say so. She was watching her daughter Daphne whose cigarette was being lit by a tall, dark man whom Lady Gurney didn't care for the look of. She wished Daphne's black dress was less skimped, it revealed her shape so much, and she had too much make-up on. It cheapens her, she thought, and was horrified at thinking such things about her own flesh and blood. Her glance searched out Brian and Serena. Too young and too pretty and far too self-confident! Brian should have married someone sensible and nearer his own age—someone like Laura Watson, but, of course, not Laura Watson. Now she could see Peter lolling on the arm of the sofa where Angela Worthing sat. Lady Gurney could have cried with irritation—the way that woman had come up and said good evening as though there were nothing between her and Peter. It was indecent, brazen. Suddenly it occurred to her that this was the first time for nearly a year that she and James and the three children had all been under the same roof, and the bitterness of it being in someone else's house, and not at the Manor, made her feel tearful again.

Michael hovered near the bar.

"How's it going, Mrs. T.?"

"I've put ice in the gin one, Mr. Michael. Ever such a run on it and there's a tall, dark gentleman keeps coming back and back again. I'm only giving him little ones now. Mind you, he's a nice gentleman and he's holding it all right."

"Good for you, Mrs. T. Listen to the noise," he put his hands over his ears, letting the sound beat spasmodically through them, like claps of thunder streaked with the shrill lightning of women's laughter. He thought, suddenly, how senseless this all was, but then he caught sight of his mother, smiling and warm and enjoying herself a great deal, and he forgot the sombre thoughts which had begun to crowd in on him, the restlessness of peace. Everything was all right; he would go and rescue Jane Fergusson from the reviewer.

The occupants of the room seemed to form kaleidoscopic patterns over the floor, clutched into little groups and then breaking away in sharp uneven particles which scattered themselves into corners, only to be drawn abruptly back at the turn of an unseen hand.

Colour and noise and endless talk. . . .

"My dear, don't tell me he went to America because he was a Pacifist. He panicked at the thought of an air raid."

"And now he's back in London—"

"Blown back by the atom bomb—"

"And expecting to be lionized as before—"

Under the chandelier, the woman novelist's voice became alcoholically penetrating.

"But how very interesting. I never realized you had two hundred birds."

"Budgerigars, dear lady. You must come and see them some time."

"But I'd simply love to, Mr. Fellowes."

"The name is Beddoes."

"Of course, how silly of me. I know you so well, Mr. Meadows."

Laura Watson stood alone, thankful to have been lost by the man with the beard. It was so interesting to listen to other people's conversations. A man on her left had started to tell a funny story to his companion. He'd begun it three times, but each time it neared the climax someone else butted in on their *tête-à-tête* and he had to begin all over again. His companion's face began to wear the sort of smile that makes your jaw ache. Laura felt sorry for the man. It was a very old story anyhow; she remembered it going the round of the mess at least three years ago.

The people in front of her were discussing politics and someone behind her was telling an interested group about a dream she'd had in which she was tried as a war criminal for not having been beastly enough to the Germans when they were starving last winter.

An elderly man came up to Laura.

"I say, do you happen to know who the woman in the lace hat is—the one with the reddish hair. We're betting it's the fashion editress on Mary Cross's rag. Are we right?"

"I'm afraid I don't know."

"Oh . . ." the smile left his eyes. "Oh. . . . Well, never mind. Someone will." He drifted off again.

Laura moved up to the group on her right. Not because she wanted to join in their conversation, but because she didn't want someone kind to think she needed to be talked to. It was more fun just to listen and watch.

She could see Gyp Townsend and Helen over by the window, and her glance immediately sorted out Brian Gurney and his wife. Had there really ever been anything between Helen and Brian, and if so did Gyp know? Laura supposed it was what you'd call a triangle—only now, with Serena Gurney added, it was a square. If Helen had loved Brian, it was rather cruel of him to bring his wife to this party where he might have known the Townsends would be; Michael Cross was such a friend of theirs. Had Helen noticed Brian's wife? She was dewy with youth and Helen wasn't. It could be very hurtful if Helen thought about things like getting old. But then, did she? It was so difficult to tell with Helen. You never had any idea of what she really felt. Any more than you really knew whether Brian and Helen had been lovers. There was just the business of having seen them together in a hotel in Dumfries. But perhaps it hadn't been Helen—or even Brian—only two figures in khaki.

Laura looked at the Townsends again. There was something different about them nowadays. They looked so self-contained where they were, as though all the other people in the room didn't exist. What nice clothes Helen wore, pastel shades that somehow were absolutely right for the pallor of her face and hair. Her eyes were her best feature, you could see them quite clearly, even from this distance, huge and grey and very wide set. She had blue shadows beneath them but she looked transparently serene tonight.

Daphne Gurney was still with the tall and dissipated-looking dark man.

"Tell me, which is your wife?" she asked.

"Over there, talking to a chap called Beddoes. He used to be curator of a zoo somewhere."

"Wearing the red hat?"

"That's right. She wrote a best seller once, you know."

"How interesting."

"Is it? I can think of more interesting things." The glance he gave her released a nerve inside Daphne. She felt breathless in the overheated atmosphere and she thought quickly of Donald Price in Kirton. He could do that to her too. Her companion said:

"What about joining me for a spot of food after this? My wife's got a date at the Women's Press Club."

"I'm sorry, but I've got to take my parents home to the country, worse luck. I'll have to be collecting them in a moment."

"Well, have another drink first." His eyes were a little glazed as he approached the bar. Mrs. Thrush took a familiar glance at him and added another lump of ice to the gin cocktail. 'Him again,' she thought, 'however do he hold it?'

The noise seemed to grow as the guests began to depart. It was as if those left were determined to keep the party stretched to the height of sound and gaiety. Late-comers hastened to have their glasses refilled. This was indeed a party.

"Just like a pre-war party," a voice shrilled; "why don't we all give one?"

"First catch your drink."

"A nice old-fashioned cocktail party where friends can be really friendly."

"What a feline remark."

Brian Gurney said to his wife:

"What did you think of Gyp and Helen Townsend, Serena?"

"Oh, very nice, but a bit dim. I shouldn't think they're interested in much beyond themselves, would you?" She couldn't see the numb pain in his heart, because she had no reason to know of such vulnerable places. Instead she smiled back at the hunger in his eyes. He held her by the arm.

"Let's go, Serena. I don't know that I approve of you in a crowd; people look at you too much. I want you to myself, darling."

Angela Worthing shook Peter Gurney by the arm.

"For God's sake, let's go, Peter. You're stinking anyhow." She felt tired and indefinably bored. Bored with the glares Lady Gurney had cast in her direction, bored with Peter because he was tipsy again and bored with Mary Cross's obvious pride in her Michael. Michael was a sweet boy, but so were lots of others. Dear God, what wouldn't she give for a change of faces and a change of environment. Change, change—please let there always be change and movement in life. She wondered what made her feel so defeatist.

The woman novelist had remembered her date at the Women's Press Club. She teetered on high heels, oblivious of everything but the comforting glow of alcohol.

"Good-bye, Mr. Beddoes—no, I mean Meadows—it's been lovely meeting you again and I will certainly come and see your kedgerees one day."

"Budgerigars, dear lady. Good night."

She found the door.

Mrs. O'Leary put her head round the door.

"Mrs. Thrush, Mrs. Thrush," she hissed.

Mrs. Thrush squeezed herself out from behind the bar and went over to the door.

"What's the matter?" She had told Mrs. O'Leary not to poke her head into this room.

"A lady's fallen down."

"Fallen down?"

"Yes, twice. First time I picked her up, but all she said was 'I've left my bag; where's my little bag.' I found it for her on the table but when I turned round, she'd fallen down again. I can't raise her this time."

"I'll get Mr. Michael. Not a word of this to anyone else, Mrs. O'Leary."

"I have my discretion, Mrs. T."

Michael heard the tale in loud whispers from Mrs. Thrush.

"I'll get her husband, Mrs. T."

"Her husband? Who's he?"

"The tall, dark man over there."

"What, him? He's the one keeps coming up for more. Bet he's plastered too." But Michael had gone off to deal with the situation. "Would you believe it?" Mrs. Thrush murmured to herself as she slipped back behind the bar.

Gyp Townsend said:

"Enjoying yourself, Helen?"

"Yes, Gyp. It's interesting in a way. Can you find me some more potato chips?"

"What, more?"

"Yes, darling, I'm insatiable. A real craving for chips. At least it's a cheap appetite."

"I wouldn't mind if it were oysters. Helen, you're the loveliest person in this room."

"Don't be silly, Gyp. What about Mrs. Brian Gurney?"

"Pretty enough, but she'll outgrow it."

"You don't like them?"

"Darling, I'm not interested in them. Sure you're not tired?"

"No, but you are. Let's go."

Michael Cross, watching them, thought suddenly how fond he'd become of Gyp and Helen. Something had been wrong there when Gyp first came home, but the edges were wearing smooth now. They were the lucky ones.

At last the guests were leaving. Mary Cross had whispered to some of her closest friends that it was time the party ended. One by one they were being winkled out. All were loud in praise of the food and drinks. Soon the room was empty except for the friends who were going on to dine with Mary and her son. She said:

"Now I'm going to have a real drink, Mrs. Thrush. Call Mrs. O'Leary and we'll celebrate the end of a perfect party."

Michael said:

"Mother, I've asked Jane Fergusson to join us for dinner. She's powdering her nose at the moment."

"Lovely. We needed another woman in the party." Mary wondered which of the girls at the party was Jane Fergusson. In a moment she would know. And was this anything serious? She took a full glass of Manhattan and turned to the remainder of her guests.

"I get so muddled with Michael's girl friends," she laughed.

Michael put his arms round her and whispered in her ear:

"Maybe you'll get to know this one better," then he grinned at the others. "In any case I'll have to be patient—she goes back to Berlin next week and her age and service group is 54. That's what comes of being reserved for three years at the beginning of a world war."

Jane Fergusson came into the room. Michael moved to her side.

"I was just telling all these soaks about your military career, Jane. I don't think you've really had an opportunity of meeting my mother yet. Mother, this is Jane."

Mary Cross shook hands with a good-looking brunette—rather like Angela Worthing.

* * * *

I am going to have tea with Laura. She and I have less in common as the months go by, and I am always surprised that we still find anything to talk about. Or rather, it is Laura who finds the topics whilst I act as a traditional chorus. It might be said that our pointless conversations reflect the pattern of our lives, but that would not be true; it is only that we assume in front of each other a stereotyped façade which neither has the curiosity to peep behind.

As I walk through Kirton High Street, round the Cock and Pheasant Arms—Elsie Cobb is hanging Steven's smalls on the line in the yard—and turn into Pilferer's Lane where the honeysuckle intrudes over the scythed hawthorn hedges, I am conscious of a deep inner content. It is as if my lethargic body were rooted firmly in this patch of England and I were part of the greenness and blue all around me.

The countryside is sizzling with the sounds of summer and the sun has sucked colour from the hedges. I register that this will no doubt be the last fine spell of the year, and I am not dismayed. I know that I shall be here, walking through the gold of autumn and the brown of winter, filled with the same calm content.

Laura's father is leaving Vine Cottage as I reach the gates. I am sure he is going to have tea with the vicar. Inside his shrivelled body he has the mind of a dictator—and he is triumphant. I dislike being roused by people who are antipathetic to me and so I ignore the gleam in his watery eye and, instead, I smile at him.

He is old and he is ill. That is his trump card. Through sickness he has conquered the tiny flame of independence which only a world war had succeeded in fanning to life in his daughter. Gyp has been attending Mr. Watson for several months now and although Gyp tells me nothing about his patients, I feel that the old man's span of life is nearly completed. Laura does not know this—or if she does, she keeps the knowledge to herself. But Mr. Watson is exultant—his ill-health is a weapon he makes full use of. He is a stupid man because eventually his death will give to Laura the freedom he has always denied her.

He is courteous and creeping—he always has been—as he raises his hat to me.

"Have you heard that we are soon to have new neighbours, Mrs. Townsend? Next week the Gurneys are moving into Old Cottage."

"Yes," I reply dryly. Because I have always disliked Mr. Watson, his little meannesses catch me unawares. Much later on I shall have thought of the perfect answer to his insinuating comments.

"We shall welcome them to Pilferer's Lane. They will be good neighbours."

He says this with malice and I wonder if he realizes how much I despise him.

Laura sees me from the window and I am rescued.

Laura has just finished making new chintz covers for the Watson drawing-room and all around gilt-framed watercolours and china ornaments seem to be busily acknowledging the compliment paid to them. Laura makes me sit in the wingbacked chair facing the window while she goes to bring in tea. I am tired of offering to help, for she has an ineradicable sense of hospitality. I sit and wait and wonder whether I am still the same person who sat here at this time last year—and throughout the fifty odd Fridays since then. Why should Laura be the person to whom I have presented a constant and blank face for all this time? She knows more and less about me than anyone else in Kirton. Perhaps that is the answer.

She comes back with tea and soon we are talking a great deal. Laura is an insatiable talker; nothing is trivial enough for her to spare words over.

"You know, of course, about the Gurneys," she says. "I feel sorry for Lady Gurney. She came and looked over Old Cottage and you could see from her face as she measured each room that she was hammering a nail in the coffin of the grand piano, the canopied four-poster and the billiard table. It's sad, isn't it, Helen?"

"It depends upon whether you like billiard tables and grand pianos," I say shortly, because I am sorry for Lady Gurney and I don't like the gleam Laura has in her eye—it is too reminiscent of the one I saw in Mr. Watson's glance.

"Well, she does," Laura says, gloatingly. "They're moving next week. Daphne and Ian are going to spend a night with us. You've heard about Daphne, of course?"

"What?" I feel a little sick but the nausea passes. "That man called Price who took the cottage next to the Cross's. They say he's in love with Daphne and wants to divorce his wife. Aren't people strange?" I watch her big, capable hands pouring hot water from a silver kettle into the Queen Anne teapot.

"Haven't you discovered that yet?"

She looks at me in a disconcerted manner.

"I didn't mean anything nasty, Helen."

"Don't be stupid, Laura."

She smiles then and goes on:

"Daphne's attractive, don't you think? Not that I like her; I don't. But there's something about all the Gurneys. A sort of charm, I suppose." She looks at me speculatively.

"Why ask me, Laura?" I challenge her and she looks abashed. But the next instant she has given her thoughts away.

"Brian and his wife came down for last week-end; a sort of farewell party at the Manor."

"I know, we had them over for drinks on Saturday."

"Oh." Laura is crestfallen. I am sorry for her because, of course, she does know about Brian and myself, but in my new-found confidence I have sown the seeds of doubt in her mind. I wonder how many times she has speculated on this subject and to whom she may have mentioned it. I am inclined to think she has kept her thoughts to herself, for she has a curious loyalty to those of her friends who were in uniform with her. Poor Laura; living as she does, life must be full of conflicting loyalties.

She helps herself to sugar and says:

"Sir James Gurney has been pottering round Old Cottage garden. I've promised him some hollyhock cuttings. He was quite delighted."

I forbear to point out that Old Cottage garden could well be filled with cuttings and plants from the Manor gardens without their absence being noticed. After all, it will be nicer for the Gurneys if Laura takes an interest in their new garden—however condescendingly.

"They're making the top back bedroom into a spare room— for Peter when he comes home," she goes on.

"Laura, you know everything," I laugh.

"Well, Daphne told me. You know, of course, about Peter."

"I know all about Peter," I reply firmly, but Laura is irrepressible.

"Is it true that Angela Worthing is going to America for the B.B.C.?"

"I haven't the faintest idea, Laura; I haven't seen Angela since Mary Cross's party and that's quite two months ago." I will not be drawn into the tittle-tattle of Kirton by Laura Watson. It is true that Angela has an opportunity of visiting the United States, but she told me that confidentially in a letter. I marvel again at the grape-vine system in the village.

"Helen, you think I'm gossiping." Laura looks hurt.

"My dear, I don't think it, I know it."

Her face is set and unhappy at my words, but I am unmoved. I study her features which are so good and regular; her eyes, large and rather cow-like, are unblinking against palely smooth skin. I notice the lines between her brows and the slight thickening of her jaw. Because her face is static she looks younger than her years, but the scaffolding of age is already there.

"I'm sorry, Helen," she says, "I suppose it's having nothing much to do makes me interested in other people."

I help myself to some home-made plum cake—Laura is an excellent cook—and I wonder how many ex-service women there are like Laura Watson, bored and unoccupied; little minds that glimpsed another life and were then sucked back into the uneventfulness of their drab existences. And is it they or the circumstances who are to blame?

"Haven't you been doing anything interesting yourself lately, Laura?" I ask.

"Oh, me—" suddenly she drops the tea-party manner and her face crumples with worry; "you know Father's very ill, don't you? Gyp has told me that there is no cure."

"I didn't know."

"I thought Gyp would have told you. It's cancer. It'll probably only be a question of months now."

"I'm terribly sorry for you, Laura." I feel beastly now because I have been superior about her village gossip. What else has she to think about but that and her father's health?

"I'd rather not talk about it if you don't mind." There is a kind of dignity about her in her misfortune.

We sit in rigid silence for a moment and then Laura smiles at me.

"You've changed, Helen."

"Have I?"

"Yes, you even look quite different now. Sort of radiant—I can't explain it."

"Oh well, I lead a very easy life, Laura." I feel embarrassed by her curious eyes.

"We've all changed, I suppose," she goes on; "do you remember one evening at the Cock and Pheasant last summer? Gyp wasn't home then, and everyone was sitting around and arguing with Dick Cobb about the rights of ex-service men and women. The three Gurneys were there, and Angela and Michael Cross and you and I. What a lot's happened since then, hasn't it?"

"Wasn't it bound to, Laura? We were all just back in Civvy Street getting ready to start a new life."

"Yes, but such big things have happened, like marriages and births and the Gurneys selling the Manor and Michael Cross writing a book. No one's done quite what one expected them to do, having known them before the war, and during it."

"But what did you expect them to do, Laura?"

"Oh, I don't know. As a matter of fact I could never imagine people like you and Gyp and the Gurney boy out of uniform again. Or myself, for that."

"I sold all mine to a junk shop for ten shillings," I laugh suddenly at the memory.

"Sold all your uniform?" Laura sounds incredulous.

"Yes, why?"

"Oh, I've kept mine. We're supposed to, you know. We're only on the reserve now; we shan't be demobilized until the end of the emergency."

"As far as I'm concerned the emergency ended at the Dispersal Centre," I reply.

"But we could be recalled," she says wistfully.

"Let's hope the occasion never arises. If it does I'm afraid the army's going to find itself short of one senior commander A.T.S."

The garden gate makes a noise and Laura looks up.

"Oh dear, it's Lady Gurney, and the tea must be stone cold. Fill up the pot, will you, Helen? No . . . it's all right, I will. No, you do it while I answer the door."

I do as I am told and the whole scene of last year returns vividly to me. Have I ever moved out of this chair? I see Laura's glance in my direction as she follows Lady Gurney into the room, but I no longer have to compose myself to meet Brian's mother.

"My dears—" Lady Gurney is like an old-fashioned bathing tent in her faded striped dress; "I didn't mean to intrude and I certainly don't expect a cup of tea at this late hour. Oh, well, perhaps. . . . Thank you Laura, dear. How well Helen is looking, isn't she, Laura? But I must tell you my news. You'll never guess. . . . Peter has come home!"

It seems that Lady Gurney has lost all sense of discretion in the joy of having her eldest son home again. Laura and I gape at one another in embarrassment.

"Such a silly boy, he's been, and so glad to be back. He's tired, of course—been working far too hard in London and we're going to try and fatten him up a little. But isn't it lovely to have him home again?"

"In time to help you with the move," Laura says thoughtlessly.

But Lady Gurney is unperturbed.

"That's just what I said to the others, and how lucky we planned to keep the top bedroom for him. It's almost like old times again. I feel years younger."

"I expect a holiday will do him good," I say stupidly.

"Holiday? Oh, my dear, he's not going back. The flat he was in has been sub-let. The person it belonged to has gone away."

I feel an appalling desire to giggle at the anonymity thrust upon Angela Worthing, but Laura's intense interest in everything Lady Gurney has blurted out makes the whole scene suddenly tawdry.

Perhaps I am unduly sensitive—the two of them are deep in friendly gossip. I break in:

"Laura, I must be going."

"So must I," Lady Gurney jumps out of her chair and her gloves fall to the ground. "Oh, thank you, Laura, I'm always losing them, and thank you for a lovely cup of tea and that delicious cake. I'm just going round to see Mrs. Cross. She's promised to house some suitcases for us while we move and I must find out if I can take some over tomorrow. Good-bye, Helen—you really are looking splendid; putting on a little weight at last, and about time too. Isn't she, Laura?"

Four eyes converge upon me and I wish I had made my exit first; but Laura accompanies Lady Gurney to the front door and I am left to my thoughts.

Laura comes back.

"Helen, must you really go?"

"Yes, I must. Gyp's getting back early tonight."

"Oh dear, I wanted to show you the last copy of the *Old Comrade's Gazette*. Did I tell you I'd become branch secretary of the association for this county?"

"No, I didn't know."

"I wish you'd join, Helen. You ought to, you know."

"Perhaps I will sometime." I edge my way out to the front door.

"Oh, do. You can have the magazine for five bob a year, but you can be a life member and get it free for five guineas. We're going to arrange some reunion dinners as soon as rationing and transport improve. In any case, it's a bit too soon now; quite a lot of people are still in the service. But were building up the ex-service side as hard as we can. We must keep some organized link with the past, don't you think?"

"Dear Laura, I never think!" I am on the doorstep now.

"Helen, you say such silly things. But you're looking much better and I believe Lady Gurney's right, you are putting on weight and you're fuller in the face too."

"I shouldn't be surprised. Good night, Laura."

"Good night, Helen; I'll drop you in a membership form for the Old Comrades' Association tomorrow."

It is cool and clear outside and I walk slowly down Pilferer's Lane, round the Cock and Pheasant Arms—they are just opening the doors—and into Kirton High Street.

As I walk I am filled with the pleasure of being alive and I think of Gyp's delight and my own deep content at the child I am bearing.

THE END

FURROWED MIDDLEBROW

Printed in Great Britain
by Amazon